Morgan watched as Christiana's grave smile turned impish for his brother James. "Does that mean you will be in Town long enough for me to learn whether you dance with as much skill as your brother?"

Minx, Morgan thought. *Flirting is as natural to her as seduction is to James.* That could be an incendiary combination.

"Not on this occasion, Miss Lambert. But I will be happy to prove my dancing ability when next I come to Town." James's smile actually reached his eyes. "Surely I will be back to London before the Season ends."

"I will consider it a promise, my lord. You now owe me a dance. Though you do face formidable competition in your brother."

Morgan wondered if she might be overdoing it. It was singularly difficult to view this exchange with any objectivity. But it did seem that her flirtation was conveying just the right element of interest in him.

Then Morgan realized that she was genuinely enjoying his brother. That was much of her charm. Her flirting was only a thin cover for the sincere pleasure she found in almost everyone and everything.

Jealousy welled up in Morgan and froze his smile into something less than benevolent. He did his best to tamp it down. His heart was not involved here, he reminded himself. Only a little pride. . . .

BOOK YOUR PLACE ON OUR WEBSITE AND MAKE THE READING CONNECTION!

We've created a customized website just for our very special readers, where you can get the inside scoop on everything that's going on with Zebra, Pinnacle and Kensington books.

When you come online, you'll have the exciting opportunity to:

- View covers of upcoming books

- Read sample chapters

- Learn about our future publishing schedule (listed by publication month *and author*)

- Find out when your favorite authors will be visiting a city near you

- Search for and order backlist books from our online catalog

- Check out author bios and background information

- Send e-mail to your favorite authors

- Meet the Kensington staff online

- Join us in weekly chats with authors, readers and other guests

- Get writing guidelines

- AND MUCH MORE!

**Visit our website at
http://www.kensingtonbooks.com**

HIS HEART'S DELIGHT

Mary Blayney

ZEBRA BOOKS
Kensington Publishing Corp.
http://www.zebrabooks.com

To my mom, Mary Simpson Saccardi,
for a lifetime of love and
for introducing me to the
Regency world of Georgette Heyer

Prologue

Braemoor, Sussex, 1797

Young Morgan Braedon sat stiffly in the chair near the bed and waited for his sister's ghost to make an appearance. He made himself say "ghost" aloud, for Maddie was dead, and even if his sister did appear to him, she would not be the same as she had been only a sennight ago.

His breath caught in a hitch. He *had* to see Maddie, even her ghost. He must tell her how sorry he was that he had insisted she show him the place where the wood sprites lived. That he had insisted that they sneak out in the fog and damp.

He had not realized how easily Maddie could catch a chill or how easily a chill could become a serious inflammation—or how easily she could die. Tears filled his eyes. It had been a tease, a silly joke that had gone monumentally wrong.

He had spent last night by her grave. It was good Maddie's grave was right next to Mother's. He noticed that the trailing rose his sister Mariel had planted the spring after Mama's death would bloom this year for the first time. How many years would it take before Maddie's grave looked like something more than a scar on the earth? Two years? Five?

Despite the cool April night he had stayed until long

after dark, but no one had come. He'd felt no presence, no relief, no forgiveness.

Morgan stood up and moved toward the mantel, his sigh long and wavering. He felt as though he would be alone forever. Leaning his head against the marble, he closed his eyes and tried to imagine Maddie in heaven. She would not have to wait until dusk to see the sprites she was so sure lived in the home wood. She could play with them in the sunshine. There would be no chill to interrupt her pleasure.

And Mama would be with her.

Please, God, he prayed, *let her be with Mama and let her be happy. Give me all her aches and ills. Give me all the things that make her sad. Give her the doll I broke and the book I stole from her when she would not play a game with me. I am sorry. I am so sorry.*

He let the tears drip down his face. She would not come. He had not believed in her wood sprites when she was alive and now there would be no ghost to console him. It was only fair.

He braced himself and walked toward the door. He surveyed the room once more, determined to leave his grief behind even if it meant leaving his heart there too.

He would go to the billiard room. Everyone else would be there. He would teach Rhys how to hold the cue and even be patient with Mariel's inept play. And then he would challenge James to a match. He would focus all his attention on beating his brother, on winning. If he did that then there would be no room in his brain for anything else.

Morgan shut the door to the small rose and green bedroom and listened for the click of the latch. *Goodbye, Maddie.*

One

Braemoor, Sussex, 1809

Morgan Braedon was not a man easily distracted. The billiard room smelled of old leather, dust, and memories, but one sneeze had been all the notice he had given. The rise and fall of the wind could be heard despite the muffling cover of maroon velvet drapes, but he ignored it. The tight fit of window and sash kept the wind without and the coals of a warming fire curbed the cold. The blaze heated the room too adequately. He'd shed his coat an hour ago.

But a new sound, the ominous click of sleet against glass, succeeded in drawing his attention from the billiard table and his next shot. If the insult of ice on the roads progressed, it might well delay his return to London. It was not a happy thought. Still, the weather had been mild of late. With a little luck the sky would clear by morning. And Morgan Braedon could usually count on Lady Luck.

With the single-minded focus of a successful gamester, he eliminated consideration of the weather and once again gave his full attention to the game at hand.

This match belonged to him. With his back to his opponent, he smiled in anticipation. Despite his twenty-six years, he still drew sweet satisfaction from serving his older brother a dose of humble pie.

Circling the billiard table, Morgan measured the shot to win. He could make a safe move and hope James missed his next chance, but such caution did not mean victory, at least not for him. Morgan took the long odds, whatever the stakes. For reasons known only to the gods, his risk usually garnered the prize.

He gave this play more attention than his last love affair. Eliminating every other thought from his mind, he aimed the cue and shot with confidence. With narrowed eyes, he willed the ball to cooperate. It did, sinking into the leather stocking with a satisfying thwap. Morgan looked up from the table and grinned at the loser.

James raised his brandy in salute. "Been practicing, brother?"

Morgan could not help the laugh that escaped. The pure pleasure of victory drew it from him. And there was no denying he had a use for the extra blunt. He left his cue on the table and reached for his almost empty glass. "I do have my reputation to uphold. I could hardly let it be said that my own brother bests me at the game."

Morgan split the last of the brandy between their two glasses, inhaled the heady fumes as he took a sip, and stretched out on the sofa, closer to the fire. A warm room and fine brandy were one of the few pleasures to be found here these days.

Years ago Braemoor had been different. His mother had brought welcoming smiles and warmth and made it a home. Her death had taken life from the old house as well; now it was no more than a pile of stone and wood perfectly maintained by an obsequious staff.

He would rather be alone in the London town house for weeks than spend three consecutive nights here at Braemoor.

He glanced at his brother and wondered if he felt the same. Until recently James had never spent much time here either, but ever since their father had taken ill he had been in residence. So far he had not complained. As a matter of fact, his brother was looking at him now with a speculative eye that eclipsed Morgan's maudlin thoughts and made him curious in a vaguely uncomfortable way.

"The marquis has a task for you." James sipped his drink and waited.

Surprise gripped Morgan, followed by a flutter of unease. "Father is speaking? I count two months since his apoplexy. I thought words were beyond his power."

James smiled. Morgan swore to himself, knowing this was just the reaction James had anticipated. He hated being predictable. "The marquis manages to make his wishes known."

Morgan summoned the nonchalance that suited his gamester's facade. "I imagine there is more than one bruised footman about."

"He wants you to find a wife."

Morgan straightened and all but choked.

James maintained his casual pose, leaning against the billiard table, no doubt enjoying the discomfiture he had caused.

"He sees things differently now, Morgan. He wants you to ensure the line. He wants a grandson."

"Hell, James, why stop at one? He wants a dozen grandsons. Why should I be the stud?" Anger pushed him on despite the pain his question would cause. "What about you? You're the heir after all."

"The marquis needs me here," James answered with his usual calm. "Besides, you know as well as I that he does not want the Braedon line tainted with my mother's blood. He sees her every time he looks at me."

So, James had bruises too. Not physical ones, to be sure. But as Morgan well knew, bruises to the heart took much longer to heal. "Nonsense, James. You are more Braedon than any of us. You are as tall as any

Braedon, your hair's shades lighter than mine, and that stubborn chin goes all the way back to the Crusades."

"None of that matters. It never has. My eyes are gray. Not one of the rest you have gray eyes. They are direct from my slut of a mother."

"James, Annabelle's elopement is decades old. She died within the year. The story is old to everyone but father. And yet you would be willing to go along with this absurdity? You would sacrifice marriage and your own children because our father demands it?"

"Since when has marriage been a goal worth fighting for?" James laughed, a sound with more bitterness than mirth. "I pick my battles very carefully these days, Morgan. A wife and children mean as little to me as what Cook serves for dinner."

"So he, and you, expect me to search the marriage mart for some foolish twit willing to play brood mare in exchange for money and having her son inherit a title?"

James nodded. "Better you than me."

"And if I refuse? Will he disown me? There certainly is precedent for that in this family."

"If he does not, then I will." James held his gaze, his eyes flat and hard.

"And you truly agree with him on this?" Morgan watched his brother, trying to decide if this was a bluff or if he was serious.

"It is my wish as much as his," James said with a solemn nod.

"To the devil with both of you! My plans do not include marriage this Season."

"Then tomorrow you will be turned out of the town house. Have your man pack your things. The door will be locked to you as soon as my order reaches London."

"The way Father did with Mariel when she married Charles?" Morgan shook his head. "There is no need to repeat history to prove you're Father's son."

James remained silent and Morgan began to feel desperate. Being turned out of the town house was not a problem. The height of the Season was weeks away. He could find rooms elsewhere. It was his property in Wales. The tenants there were depending on him. "Damn, James, this is ridiculous. Can you see Rhys as marquis? That's what will happen if I am disinherited and you refuse to marry."

James nodded. "The estates would go to ruin. All our brother cares for is the night sky and whether the Astronomer Royal will grant him a meeting. I'm willing to take the risk that I will outlive him."

"More than ten years separate the two of you. And Rhys has lived an exemplary life." Morgan saluted his brother with his brandy glass. "Despite our efforts, Rhys lives for his studies."

Without comment, James crossed the room. He was at the door before he spoke again. "Morgan, the Braedons have never yet shirked their responsibilities. This is a chance to prove yourself. Easter is early this year and the Season will be long enough. Go back to London and find a bride and bring her back here before the New Year." James's smile was tinged with pleading as much as humor. "Do at least that much for me. Why else do you think I let you win tonight?"

The door closed firmly behind him before Morgan could respond. Curses, varied, colorful, and obscene, filled the air and stopped as abruptly. Why exercise his considerable ability if no one sat close enough to appreciate it?

He tossed off the last of his brandy and considered throwing the glass across the room. He closed his eyes instead and fought for self-control, then put the glass down very, very carefully. Pouring the rest of James's brandy into it, Morgan began to pace the room, trying to find a way out of this coil.

Was this one time when risking it all might not mean a win? Just last Thursday he'd sent all his holiday winnings to his bailiff in Wales. He needed to improve the property his mother had left him if it was ever to turn a profit and give him the independence he sought. One more winning season like the last one and he would be free of absurd demands like the one James had made tonight.

A summer of good weather and rain, in addition to the money he was sending for improvements, and the land would be as productive as any in the Glamorgan. He'd promised his tenants that the future would be brighter and their loyalty had been encouraging. He would not fail them now.

Wales was where his true responsibility lay. Not in a lonely pile of stone that tainted everyone who lived in it.

Morgan stretched out completely, concluding that the brandy made the sofa marginally comfortable. He put his hands behind his head and began to consider other ways to play the cards that had been dealt him.

Two

"This is perfect!" Christiana Lambert's first London ball vibrated with excitement. She clapped her gloved hands, as if to dispel the excess of delight that turned her carefully practiced, blasé smile into a grin.

Glowing words had worn thin with use during her few days in London. Christiana found everything about Town remarkable, wonderful, and thrilling.

Joanna Lambert smiled weakly. Christiana knew the adjectives her sister would choose shared a closer connection to "intimidating."

She patted Joanna's arm. "That set was lovely, was it not?"

Standing straighter, Joanna nodded and truly smiled this time. "You are right, Christy. The first dance is over and I did not disgrace myself."

They moved together through the crowded room, looking for their mother, but the sheer number of guests made locating anyone difficult.

"I cannot believe we are finally here." Christiana guided her sister toward the doorway into the receiving room, all the while looking around, trying to absorb every detail.

"Oh, Christy, I am so sorry to have lost Grandpapa as we did, but the year of mourning made it possible for us to be here together. Last year you would have had to stay behind, practicing the pianoforte."

In truth Christiana would not have come to London last Season even if she could have danced at every ball. "You would have shone like a gem all on your own, Joanna."

Her sister looked doubtful, but Christiana gave her the look-that-would-brook-no-argument and Joanna settled for a slight shrug. "I am so much happier to have waited and have you with me, Christy. I know it is selfish of me, for I am sure you would rather be home preparing for your wedding and the day when you will be Mrs. Richard Wilton."

"You are confusing me with a saint, Jo!" Christiana could only laugh at the thought. "There will be plenty of time to prepare once Richard and I are formally engaged and the announcement sent to the papers. And I can dream of him anywhere. To be honest though, I do feel painfully guilty caught up in all this excitement when he could be facing the French tomorrow."

Joanna grew serious too. "You must write in the journal you are keeping to share with him. He will seem closer if you do."

"Joanna, I could make tonight's entry very short and lose hardly any sleep. I can sum up this evening in four words: bright, colorful, gay, and exciting."

The light came from hundreds of candles, their flame reflected in the crystals that surrounded them hanging on four of the most magnificent chandeliers Christiana had ever seen. They shone with a brilliance that surpassed anything.

"The colors are wonderful, are they not? The ladies' gowns. Diaphanous!" She turned to her sister. "Is that not the perfect word?"

Joanna nodded and then added something as she gestured to the corner where their mother stood.

Christiana did not hear her words and followed the gesture instead. For the moment the musicians rested, but the voices of the hundreds of guests swelled to fill the void. Outbursts of laughter or cheers from the card room drew everyone's attention, and then the momentary silence was eclipsed by even louder conversation.

Mrs. Lambert stood with several girlhood friends Christiana recognized, now matrons as stately as she. *How can they look so bored when Joanna and I are so very excited?* She hoped she never grew so old that such simple pleasures were beyond her.

Her mother looked to her. "You are promised to Richard's brother for the next set?"

Christiana nodded and Mrs. Lambert, apparently satisfied that her younger daughter was appropriately engaged, took Joanna aside. Christiana hovered close in case her sister needed support. Mama could make a funeral out of a wedding with her endless scolding. And Joanna would lose all the confidence that first dance had given her.

When Mrs. Lambert asked about her partner, Joanna replied with a smile and made to point him out. As she scanned the sea of faces, Joanna gave Christiana a less than ladylike wink.

Why do I worry? Christiana thought. *She has been dealing with Mama for two years longer than I, and made a much better job of it.*

She let the conversation float around her. Anticipation filled the air, and surely tonight she was queen of that emotion. She had months with a wonderful city to explore and shops by the hundreds! It was no burden to accompany Joanna to boost her confidence, to help her secure a match so that her sister's happiness would equal her own. Surrounded by the excitement, she could almost ignore her fear for Richard.

Fear he'd made her promise to forget when he'd urged her to accompany her sister to Town. His own inclination did not include visits to London and he'd insisted that he wanted her to enjoy it now and be content to stay at home once they were wed. She felt a fresh burst of guilt at the realization that it was so much easier than she had anticipated.

A woman spoke to her and Christiana turned her attention back to the group. On closer look, Christiana saw that they were not all matrons; some were the dowagers, grandmothers, and maiden ladies old enough to remember when no one had heard of Napoleon. She moved closer and curtsied as she recognized the Dowager Duchess of Halston.

They had met briefly earlier in the week when they had visited the same milliner.

Months ago she thought she might faint if she met an actual duchess, but how could she be intimidated by a woman in a years-old gown, whose most frequent word was "Eh?"

"Why ain't you dancing?"

Christiana smiled and bent close to her. The old lady's skin was parchment fine and her scent was of roses and something else that was old-fashioned but charming. Christiana spoke above the steady hum of voices. "The musicians have stopped for the moment, Your Grace."

The old woman tapped Christiana's arm with her fan. "In my day they would not stop until we told them to."

"It must have been wonderful."

She nodded with a smile that showed teeth still white and strong. "Why, I recall when the King—before he had all those children, you understand—I recall the King and Queen came to a masquerade that the duke gave—my husband's father that is."

The old duchess spoke on, telling her how the King had eyes for no one but his wife, though several ladies did their best to catch his attention. "Everyone knows his constancy to his wife caused his madness."

Christiana had never heard that outrageous suggestion before. She moved closer and steered the conversation away from the delicate subject of the King's health and asked her about the clothes of the day. It was a subject the old lady warmed to. Of course, one could not compare the somber clothes that men wore today with the elegant satins and brocades of days past.

"I am forever telling my grandson Morgan that men must dress in finery. How else are they to attract ladies?"

The musicians moved toward the small stage, and once again she tapped Christiana's arm with her fan. "You must dance. This is not the time or place to speak with an old woman. Besides, they play so loud that I cannot hear. Call on me tomorrow and we will talk more." She left abruptly with a brief word of farewell.

With a curtsy to the retreating figure, Christiana turned her attention toward the ballroom, wondering if Richard's brother would remember their dance. Peter's excitement about the London Season matched hers, though his interests differed significantly. Christiana knew that if he were settled in the card room there would be no hope he would remember his promise.

If he was so easily distracted by a game of cards, then her original plan to rely on him as escort for the Season was not a good idea. But where else could she find someone who would be willing to be no more than a friend? Someone not interested in courtship. Where could she find a man like that when the whole purpose of the Season was marriage?

She searched the ballroom, looking for Peter, trying to hide her disappointment. He was not coming; she was certain of that. She did, however, have the full attention of at least one gentleman present. He stood with the duchess, who had stepped back into the room, and was watching Christiana as he listened. It was a neutral look, but steady and considering. The kind of

expression a man used while he decides if he wants
to be attracted or not.

Christiana smiled at him. She knew it was unexpected. Most girls her age would turn away, embarrassed at being the object of such direct observation.
*But most girls my age do not know what I know about
men,* she thought. *Most girls my age have not sent
their love to war with a kiss and a prayer.*

Some might call her a flirt, but she was only trying
to help the gentleman decide that yes, indeed, he must
invite her to dance. So she smiled at the nameless
male whose casual gaze did not mask his curiosity.
Perhaps I am flirting, she thought, *but it comes easily
because it means so little.*

As she watched, a smile transformed his cool, de-
tached expression into something lazy and sensual.
Her own smile froze as the suggestiveness of his look
sent a frisson of wariness through her. How could a
smile convey such intimacy?

Had she been too inviting? Perhaps dancing with
him was not a good idea. More unnerved than she
would admit, Christiana turned her back to him, hoping he would understand the rejection as clearly as he
had understood her blatant invitation.

She gave the group nearest her full attention and
berated herself with as much reproach as Mama would
have. This was London after all, not the local assem-
blies.

Who is this chit and where has she been? Morgan
Braedon struggled to recall the name his grandmother
had given him. He'd barely listened when she had insisted he dance with "the young miss over there." His
mind had been on the last turn of cards, and the distress on his opponent's face. Morgan understood that
quickly masked look. The vowels he now held were
worthless.

The fool had been caught up in the game and his quarterly allowance was now spent. By the time the next quarter arrived he would have lost or won it five times over. Someday an opponent would refuse the sympathy Morgan extended. The jackanapes had been in Town long enough to know the rules.

He shrugged away the sense of responsibility, but not soon enough. He missed the name of the vision that invited him with her eyes and her smile. Who would have expected one of Grandmama's interests to be so appealing? Ah, now he did recall that Grandmama had said that she was late to the Season because of mourning for some relative. Whatever the reason, she was a wonderful change from the girls who had cluttered the dance floor so far.

The beauty had met his gaze, and at first she did not shrink away. No, indeed. She had smiled—and what encouragement that smile held. At the moment it promised a dance. He smiled back, anticipating so much more, but then her confidence faltered and she had turned from him.

In spite of that, Morgan still wanted this dance. He moved across the room looking for someone to introduce them.

She stood next to a group of matrons, several of whom he knew, but they were engrossed in conversation, unaware of him. He waited and watched the dance floor fill rapidly. Finally, he turned to his intended partner.

"May we pretend my grandmother introduced us, Miss Lambert?" Where had her name come from? He thanked the gods of love that it had stayed with him even when his mind had been elsewhere. "I am Lord Morgan Braedon and the Dowager Duchess of Halston is my maternal grandmother." He introduced himself with another bow.

He could see his impropriety did not shock so much as disconcert her. Still, decorum won out over the daring creature of that first smile, for she shook her head just as one of the matrons realized his presence. Lady Abernathy turned from her conversation to hurriedly introduce Miss Lambert to him, urging them to the dance floor.

Miss *Christiana* Lambert curtsied sweetly, her uncertain eyes never leaving his. Morgan kept his expression as pleasantly neutral as the situation commanded. She seemed reassured. Whether that came from his bland smile or the older lady's casual approval made no difference. Whatever the reason, Miss Lambert's uncertainty was gone, replaced by a conventional bored expression. Her eyes ruined the pretense. They were lit with a smile that no amount of effort could curb.

With all the formality he could muster, Morgan offered his arm, and once she took it, they moved toward the edge of the floor. He found them a place in a set as the first notes sounded. She did not look around, did not look to see how the rest of the dancers were paired. She closed her eyes for a moment and drew a deep breath.

Oh no, where were the gods now? Was this truly her first ball? She had seemed so much more assured than most.

She leaned a step closer and smiled. "This is my first ball and I want to remember every moment."

Morgan nodded, trying for an understanding smile, and cursed his brother and his ridiculous demand. This was her first dance at her first ball and he was to be her teacher. He could think of a dozen things he would like to teach this beauty, but dancing was not one of them. He wanted to be almost anyplace but here.

How could he have forgotten what he'd so recently learned. The new crop of marriageable misses lost their confidence the moment they took the dance floor for the first time. All at once they realized the difference between a local assembly and dancing in the

Countess of Westbourne's ballroom with dozens of strangers watching. Eventually they would recall what had been so carefully taught. Until then, however, dancing seemed as much a threat to life and limb as Jackson's Boxing Academy. The scent of nerves stretched to the limit was as palpable as any perfume. Finally, the musical introduction was complete, the set fully formed. He turned to Miss Lambert.

When had he become so jaded? His partner was an undeniably beautiful girl, as fresh as the spring air pouring through the open doors. How could he prefer cards to that smile and those eyes?

"My lord?"

Miss Lambert held out her hand and he took it. Now he was the one who had missed the first step. He glanced down in apology, but Miss Lambert did not seem offended. She smiled her understanding and moved into the dance with confidence, even pleasure. She did not count the steps as his partner at Hobson's had. She knew when to take his arm and when to move back.

She loved to dance. That was obvious. What else would she love to do, Morgan wondered.

With each step his partner's restraint eased. The music captivated her and her caution disappeared. He could see an adventurous woman tucked just beneath a surface decorum. With each promenade, his interest was more thoroughly roused. By the time the last move was complete, the scent of her had slid into his memory, woven into a fantasy that would have shocked her.

There was more than one place where a controlled face was an asset. He took her arm and escorted her back to the ladies with an amiable smile that completely masked his daydream.

They had almost reached the group of chaperones when a young man came rushing over.

"Christy, my apologies, my deepest apologies. Did I miss the dance?"

A friend from home, Morgan decided, *and I do wish he would disappear.*

"Yes, Peter, you did." She bit her lip, obviously debating further reprimand and then deciding against it.

"But it is too perfect an evening to take offense. After all, someone did ask me to dance." She turned to Morgan. "My lord, may I introduce Mr. Peter Wilton."

Peter flushed and bowed. Then his face lit with an enthusiasm that made Morgan feel older than his grandmother. "You played that last hand magnificently, my lord. It was a pleasure to watch."

Morgan nodded his thanks, not sure he wanted this boy's obvious admiration. Yes, he could play cards, but he did not do it to find favor with a greenhead like Wilton.

"Come, Peter. This dance is not promised," Christiana interrupted. Clearly his card-playing prowess did not impress her. "You can make your apologies while we dance." She turned and held out her hand. "It was a pleasure, my lord. Thank you."

Prettily said and the smile that lit her eyes gave the words special meaning. Morgan took her hand and bowed over it. He wanted to move the glove aside and kiss her wrist, her palm, but despite the smile, she was a country miss and this was her first ball. Balls littered the Season like bad players filled a card room. With any luck they would find themselves together again.

Morgan watched her walk away. She did not turn back and he had the unsettling thought that she had already forgotten him. As he watched, Christiana said something and Wilton's earnest contrition dissolved into laughter. Morgan smiled, enjoying her self-confidence. Christiana Lambert still thought the world was hers to command. Morgan Braedon hoped this Season would spare her the truth. If the gods were generous, it would live in her memory as one shining moment when all fairy tales come true.

He decided to return to the card room. He had danced with the loveliest girl in the room. James would have to be content with that.

Christiana listened to the introductory notes of music that called them to attention and closed her eyes. She loved this air. The music made her feel as though she could dance with the lightness of a fairy. Even with Peter as her partner.

"Lord Morgan asked you to dance, Christy?" Peter Wilton moved into the first figure, only half attending to the steps.

Christiana pulled him in the right direction and tossed an apologetic smile at the couple he almost collided with. "Pay attention to the figures, Peter, or you will step on Joanna and offend everyone in the room."

He returned the smile, which took the edge off her criticism, and concentrated. Silence followed for a few moments. When they had moved through the entire figure twice, she nodded her approval and answered his question. "Do you think I asked him to dance? Of course he invited me, though I think he was ordered to by his grandmother."

"Nothing romantic about that is there, Christy?"

She took his arm and they began the promenade, which would keep them together for the next few moments. "Exactly. I think I might have been offended if I were looking for anything more than a dancing partner. As it is, a man honoring the whim of his grandmother suits me perfectly."

They danced in silence until the promenade brought them arm in arm once more and Peter picked up the conversation. "Thing is, he's years older than me. Or Richard for that matter."

"He is not so very old, Peter. I would say he has not yet reached his thirtieth year." She had done her best to contain her curiosity, but Peter would persist in talking about him. "Who is he, Peter? From where do you know him?"

Peter looked panicked for a moment. "Can we speak of it later? I seem to have forgotten the next step."

Oh, he does make me laugh. Christiana turned it into a sigh and let her partner concentrate. If curiosity was her besetting sin, patience was a virtue she was attempting to cultivate. Perhaps she could learn more about Lord Morgan later.

Christiana made an effort not to compare Peter's dancing with that of Lord Morgan's. However, as the set progressed, it was clear that the two men did not view dancing in the same way. For Peter it was an exercise, rather like running a race. For Lord Morgan it was part of a courtship ritual that teased and tempted and only rarely allowed the couple to touch. Each touch became a tender gesture that had made her want to cling a moment longer. The whole accompanied by a smile of such singular appeal that it made her efforts at flirting seem cow-handed.

The dance might be one of her favorites and Peter a lifelong friend, still Christiana was vastly relieved when the set ended. And she had already promised him another after supper. She suppressed a groan. Well, he did indeed need the practice. She looked around for Joanna and saw her sister being escorted in another direction, while listening to her partner with rapt attention.

Christiana took Peter's arm and led him from the ballroom. "It is almost time for supper, is it not?"

"Oh, yes! An excellent notion."

Peter's enthusiasm was exactly what she'd expected. He had the usual appetite of a still-growing young man and Christiana knew if she was willing to share him with the lobster patties and sweets she could learn what Peter knew of Lord Morgan.

The doors to the dining room were open. Even though supper had not been announced, a large group had already discovered the buffet.

They moved along the serving table with Peter taking something from every platter: lobster patties, a bit of duck sausage, and some poached fish. Christiana admired the variety of dishes and selected more sparingly.

She hurried Peter through the sweets, anxious to find one of the small tables for two free, so she could speak with him privately. Unable to decide between the cakes and jellies, he grabbed one of each and followed her with a longing backward glance. "Be seated here with me, Peter, and answer my questions."

He swallowed something whole, cleared his throat and asked, "What questions?"

"Lord Morgan. How long have you been acquainted? What is he lord of?"

"Oh, the Marquis of Straeford's son? Not exactly a friend, you know. The thing is, you actually were the first to introduce us. I'm certain that was the first time he has ever heard my name."

Christy reminded herself how often Richard had said Peter was a gifted observer of his fellow man. But Peter also understood things in only the most literal sense. She tried again. "Peter, dear, tell me what you know about him from watching him play."

"A cool one. You could never tell what he holds by looking at his face." He warmed to the subject. "Christy, even when he wins, his expression does not change. One never knows what is going through his mind."

In gambling that might be an admirable trait. It was not, however, a quality one looked for in a potential friend. "He is a gamester then?"

"One of the best. But he only does it for pleasure. He is not one of those who makes his living at the tables." Peter paused. "I do think it must have been all of ten years since the King raised his father from baron to Marquis of Straeford. No need to worry about money there, even if he is not the heir."

"A second son?" Not that it mattered. She was merely curious.

"Yes," Peter said slowly. "Not married." He seemed to be debating further disclosures.

Christy wanted to hear it all. "What else, Peter, you cannot turn prudish on me now."

"I understand from one friend who heard it from a friend of his, that Lord Morgan's been told to find a wife this Season."

Whoever believed that men did not gossip as much as women had never talked with one. Nevertheless, the possibility that he was looking for a match was not what she wanted to hear. "Are you certain?"

"Yeeesss."

His reply was several syllables long and Christy decided he was not certain at all.

"Thing is, his father is ailing, most likely at death's door. That I know, for the Earl of Westbourne himself mentioned it. The marquis wants to be sure his son is leg-shackled before he passes on."

Leg-shackled. It was a phrase Christy detested. She bit back a reproach. "Why should Lord Morgan need to find a wife, if he is not the heir?"

Peter shrugged, then realized where the conversation was heading. "Why do you care, Christy?"

Christy sighed. "I am looking for someone who will remember our dance even when the cards are good."

"Oh. Not Lord Morgan then, Christy. Cards are more important to him than the dance floor. Whoever he courts will have to accept that gaming is in his blood and not expect him to dance attendance on her."

Wonderful, Christy thought with a rare show of

petulance. Cross Lord Morgan off her list of possible escorts. She might be willing to share her true love with the army, the cause was noble enough, the greater good of the country depended on men like Richard. But if she was to find someone who would be willing to dance with her and escort her to supper at balls such as this, then she very much wanted him to recall her presence.

Lord Morgan Braedon was obviously not that man. She had best look elsewhere for her temporary beau.

I am not disappointed, she told herself. And believed it.

Three

"Christiana, what have you done!" Mrs. Lambert burst into the bedroom, waving a newspaper as though it were a much-used handkerchief.

Christiana heard Joanna sigh but she felt a moment of true panic. Was it news from Portugal? On a relieved sigh of her own, she realized that was not at all likely. Even her mother would not hold her responsible for the army and its failings.

Apparently a quiet morning was too much to hope for, even the day after a ball. Life had been anything but peaceful since their arrival. Christiana longed for one uninterrupted hour to drink chocolate with her sister in peace. But tranquillity was not Mama's style. If she could manufacture a crisis, she would. Today's drama was obviously under way.

"Is that the morning paper, Mama? Joanna and I have not seen it. We have not been below stairs yet." She pulled off her cap and ran her hand through her loosely braided hair to make the point. "Sally has just brought our chocolate and we were debating the best way to spend such a beautiful day." The paper could be read later if Mama could be distracted from this morning's irritation.

"Christy is anxious to find a ribbon the exact color of her new gown." Joanna spoke around an unladylike yawn. "And I would very much like to have Peter escort us to the exhibit I learned of last night. Would you care to join—"

"You will most likely spend the day refuting this idiotic gossip." Mrs. Lambert handed the paper to her daughter. "How could you, Christiana!" The last was given in the vexed tone that marked most of Mrs. Lambert's conversation with her youngest daughter.

With a puzzled look at Joanna, Christiana took the paper from her mother's shaking fingers and the two of them read the few lines they were directed to:

Lord M—— B——, danced but once last night and that was with the lovely Miss L——. Could it be he has already found the match his esteemed parent hopes for?

Christiana bit the inside of her lip and tried not to smile. "Mama, it is nothing more than gossip."

Her mother tapped her foot and waited.

Joanna tried. "Mama, Christy can not control who Lord Morgan invites to dance!"

"That does nothing to relieve my irritation." Mrs. Lambert turned to Christiana. "It is true we are only recently arrived and wish to be noticed. But not in this way. This is Joanna's Season. And a year late as it is, she has no time to waste. *She* is the one society should be noticing. You, my girl, have made your choice, as you have so pointedly told everyone who will listen."

"Mama, that is not true. I have honored yours and Father's wish that I tell no one of my understanding with Richard."

"It is not an understanding until we permit it!" With a sharp indrawn breath Mrs. Lambert turned to Joanna. "Get up, get dressed, and come to the green salon. There will be callers today."

She turned to her other daughter. "Christiana, I will not tolerate behavior that will jeopardize our vouchers for Almack's. You will spend your day reading improving works. I will tell Lord Morgan, should he call, that you are not well."

Both her children nodded and she swept from the room, closing the door sharply behind her.

"Oh, Joanna, London has not changed Mama one whit, has it?" Christiana sighed. "I was hoping that the shopping and society might distract her from my shortcomings."

"And now you will be trapped in your room all day." Joanna scrambled from the bed and headed for the dressing room. "There will be no shopping together and you will not be allowed to see the art exhibit."

"It is almost a relief."

Joanna stopped at the dressing room door and looked back at her sister in some confusion.

"You see, for a moment I was certain there was news from Portugal and that Richard was in danger."

"Oh dear." Joanna came back and gave her sister a comforting hug. "He is safe. He has only been there for a few weeks. And it is too soon for the fighting to begin. It will be weeks before there are any battles."

"Very well. I will allow you to convince me that Richard is safe for today and perhaps even for tomorrow."

Joanna went back to the dressing room and Christiana sat in the slipper chair near the fire.

"There are worse things than spending my day indoors, Jo. I can write in my journal. There is so much more to remember than what I wrote last night."

Joanna emerged with three dresses, which she draped over a chair. "I could barely stay awake long enough to undress and you stayed up to write in your journal?"

"I only wrote a few lines." But fatigue had not been the problem. The music and the dancing had left her wide awake and too restless to settle down and find mere words that would do the evening justice. Christiana hopped from the bed and picked up a white lawn gown washed through with the palest pink and trimmed with roses about the hem and sleeves. "Here, wear this one." She shook the wrinkles out and placed it carefully on the bed after she smoothed the covers. "It is above all your favorite gown and your rose-colored pelisse will complement it perfectly."

"Christy, it will never take you all day to describe the ball."

"I suspect that I will have time to dress, finish my entry, and read the rest of today's gossip before Mama recalls that the dowager duchess invited me to call."

Joanna shook her head. "How is it that you find your way out of every punishment Mama hands out?"

Christiana grinned. "A lifetime of practice."

"The gossip column is hardly improving literature, Christy. What if she asks what you have been reading?" Joanna untied her nightcap and began brushing her hair. Christiana took the brush from Joanna's hand and began arranging her sister's curls, sprinkling in the lilac-scented powder that was her sister's favorite.

"Joanna, the only problem with having a sister who has never broken a rule in her life is that you worry about the most nonsensical things." The scented powder made her sister's hair easier to manage and Christiana curled it around her face carefully so as not to pull it too hard. "I remember the last sermon she pressed on me and will quote it freely if she asks for proof."

Satisfied with her efforts as a hairdresser, Christiana put the brush down and stood back admiring her sister's blond loveliness. Joanna was quiet and reserved; that was the only reason people did not notice her at first. It was unfortunate that Christiana herself possessed neither of those virtues.

The truth was she had inherited her mother's flamboyant personality, without her inclination to dramatic complaint, she hoped. Joanna was much more like their father. Of her two parents Christiana would infinitely prefer a day on horseback with Papa to a day shopping with Mama. And she did adore shopping.

By the time Joanna tied on her pink kid slippers, Christiana had convinced her that she would not be wasting the day in her room. Joanna hurried down to the green salon as the first knock on the door sounded.

Christiana ran through the connecting door and into her own bedroom, which faced the front of the house. Drawing the damask drapes, she peeked through the sheer material that blocked eyes but not light from her room. The street was full of carriages, moving as quickly as the congestion would allow. Several were drawn in front of their town house. One matron and her daughter hurried up the steps.

She sighed. Despite Mama's criticism she had kept her commitment to Richard a closely held secret. Why had she ever promised Papa that until she returned from London there would be no formal engagement?

Why did he find it so hard to credit that a lifetime of friendship had grown into something more? There were moments when she wondered if Papa entirely approved of Richard. That was foolish! Of course he approved. The Wiltons and Lamberts had been neighbors for generations and friends almost as long. When Richard had asked to speak to him, Papa had not seemed surprised. He'd maintained it was inevitable that someday proximity and friendship between the Wiltons and Lamberts would lead to a closer attachment.

Christiana did not like the idea that their connection was "inevitable" or "expected." She longed for the day when they married and she could join Richard. She had even decided that if, heaven forbid, the war persisted she would join him in Europe. She would follow the drum. She would not be the first to show her devotion that way.

In the meantime she needed to find someone as unconcerned with courtship as she was. Then Mama could not berate her for stealing attention from Joanna. She thought again of Lord Morgan. He would have been perfect. He danced beautifully and could flirt with such skill that all other thoughts fled her brain. One glance across the Westbournes' ballroom had convinced her of that.

But if he were, as Peter said, seriously searching for a bride then he would not do at all. If his lone dance with her had any significance, then he needed to know that she was not available, but how could she tell him if she had promised not to tell anyone? She sighed again as though one long breath would dispel her quandary.

Taking a last look at the street below, Christiana could see a gentleman of more mature years climb the front steps, a small nosegay in hand. She leaned a little closer to the window and he must have caught the movement, for he looked in her direction.

With a little squeal Christiana stepped back into the room. *Oh, please do not let him see me gaping like a peagoose.* It was the flowers, not the bearer that had caught her attention: a cluster of colorful blossoms, casually arranged, and they reminded her of the time she and Richard had gathered a similar bouquet.

She drew her wrapper around her, sat at the writing table, and considered what she had written last night. Letters between them might not be permitted yet, but she could pretend. So her journal was written in letter format all of them addressed "Dearest Richard."

Do you recall the wildflowers we picked that spring only a few months ago? We sought a flower in every color and I treasure that bouquet to this day. I must tell you that the glory of those flowers is nothing compared to the color that was only part of the thrill of my first London ball.

* * *

Mrs. Lambert would have been gratified to know
that Morgan Braedon read the bit of gossip with as
much annoyance as she had. She would have been less
pleased by the soft-spoken but thorough expression of
disgust that caused Morgan's valet to raise his eyebrows. Roberts stepped closer, bending as if to pick
up a discarded neckcloth.

He was a loyal servant, but endlessly curious. Morgan was certain that Roberts knew as many of the
latest *on-dits* as he did. Now he watched from the
corner of his eye as Roberts looked over his shoulder
and tried to see exactly what had caused the display
of words Morgan reserved for only the greatest vexation.

"Here, Roberts, you may read it without damaging
your spine." Morgan thrust the paper under his valet's
nose and held it out to him until the manservant took
it. "You will have no trouble deciding which lines have
ruined my morning."

He watched Roberts carefully set aside the crushed
lengths of fabric before he ran his eyes down the columns of small type. Middle-aged eyes squinted at the
print and then he pursed his lips. He said nothing.

"Roberts, I hired a valet who could read so that you
could do something besides tie a cravat. Now you can
tell me how to set this problem to rights."

Roberts folded the paper and placed it near the door.
"The services I perform, milord, have nothing to do
with dancing or beautiful young ladies."

Morgan leaned back in the chair and closed his
eyes, calling on whatever god inspired stupid bache-
lors and inveterate gamblers. He turned to look at his
valet. "I could call on 'Miss L' today and extend my
personal apologies for making her the subject of gossip."

"It would seem to me, milord, that calling on, ahem,

Miss L, would only draw more attention to her. Of course if that is your intention . . ."

He let his voice trail off and the phrase became a question. Morgan gave him a mischievous grin. "Curious, are you, Roberts?"

He bowed. "Only to the extent that it will enable me to serve you better, milord."

"No plans, matrimonial or otherwise, Roberts. I had an enchanting dance with a lovely lady and returned to the card room. The play was challenging and rewarding and I never gave the ballroom another thought."

"As you say, milord." Roberts nodded and began gathering shaving items.

The man was an insufferable snob. Morgan picked up two of the discarded neckcloths before Roberts could reach them, just to irritate him. Roberts had dressed and shaved him since he'd come to Town. He had seen him ill, drunk, and close to ruin. Despite that familiarity, his valet maintained a formality that was as admirable as it was irritating.

Morgan held out the discarded neckcloths and Roberts took them with obvious reproof and moved toward the door. "Is there anything else, milord?"

Advice, damn you, I want advice. Truth to tell, he would rather have Roberts's advice than ask almost any of his friends. There was thirty years difference in their ages and Roberts had, after all, spent his life observing society.

The man was right. If Morgan called on Miss Lambert it would only add fuel to the idea that he was courting her. No, the solution was to make an appearance at Almack's, preferably on a night when Miss Lambert was otherwise engaged. If he danced with every eligible chit in the room then surely that would put the gossip to rest.

Almack's. He groaned. He had managed to avoid

the weekly assembly so far. Now it would be a penance more than worthy of his thoughtlessness.

He thought he had found the perfect solution to James's command that he find a wife. He could dance his way through a dozen balls and convey the essence of courtship with none of the heart. He could pretend to find a wife. It had worked beautifully until his overconfidence had undone him.

It was such a good plan. There must be a way to revive it. Once he had sufficient funds he could establish his own Town residence and see to it that the property in Wales had the subsidy it needed until the harvest. In a year or two the land would produce enough to support a wife and family. It would be a time of his choosing and not because of a command from an arrogant brother willing to step into the shoes of their autocratic father.

Those few lines of gossip taught him a valuable lesson: *Pretending* to find a wife would be more of a challenge than a real courtship. Unless he exercised unusual discretion, he could stumble over his pretense and find himself engaged. Last night had been a simple error on his part: He'd let the cards distract him. And that mistake had become today's *on-dit,* interpreted in such a way as to embarrass everyone involved.

"Everyone" included his grandmother. For all practical purposes she had been the one to introduce them. Miss Lambert had caught her eye and, without a ducal granddaughter, cousin, or niece making a debut this year, it was entirely possible his grandmama would make Miss Lambert her protégée. Heaven help them both if that happened.

He groaned again. What he really must do was pay a call on his grandmother and convince her that Miss Lambert was not a candidate for the coveted position of Braedon wife.

Of course that meant that the delectable Miss Lambert could not be considered for any other part in his life. He acknowledged some disappointment. She was lovely, lively, and had not seemed at all averse to a flirtation. Just as well it was not to be, he rationalized. Girls in their first Season were not in his usual style. They were too easily hurt and rarely understood the finer points of dalliance. But Christiana Lambert had been a rare one. He'd been tempted to make an exception with her. The feeling that wedged itself right under his heart must be hunger, Morgan decided. He'd delayed breakfast too long.

Roberts cleared his throat and Morgan realized that the man was still waiting to be dismissed. He waved a hand at his valet and the man moved to leave, then turned back. "I believe your brother arrived last night and will be waiting below. Perhaps he can advise you."

As unwanted as the news was, Morgan hid his surprise. "James is here?"

"No, milord. I am speaking of your younger brother, Lord Rhys."

A reprieve only, he thought. Eventually James would arrive. There was at least one good thing about having Rhys in residence, Morgan thought. He never read the gossip columns.

The breakfast room was bright, the curtains pulled open to encourage the rare burst of London sunshine.

Rhys looked up from an empty plate. "Happy to see me?"

"Most days." Morgan made the concession, but was more honest with himself. *I need your honesty, your enthusiasm. Yes, I'm devilish glad you're here.*

Then he spied his brother's empty plate. He could smell bacon and ham, but saw little more than dirty dishes on the sideboard. "Did you leave me any food at all, you pig?"

Rhys grinned at the welcome. Morgan reached for a muffin as his brother grabbed the last piece of toast and slathered it with strawberry preserve.

Before he could ask, Rhys announced his reason for the rare Town visit. "Morgan, I have an appointment with the Astronomer Royal." Rhys made it sound as though he had an audience with the King.

Morgan nodded and bit back a grin as Rhys prattled on about comets. His brother had been fascinated with the night sky since childhood. It did not appear he was going to grow out of it.

Morgan stood up and tossed his napkin on the table. "Your meeting is tomorrow?"

When Rhys nodded, Morgan welcomed an inspiration. "I'm off to visit our grandmother. Come with me. With you along she is much less likely to try to convince me of the joys of the married state."

Rhys shook his head without even a hint of regret.

"If you called with a day-old beard she might be less inclined to treat you like a lad." Morgan leaned closer and took on an exaggerated air of supplication.

Rhys rubbed his beard. "No, she will guess I traveled by moonlight and rant at me while she calls for a razor. No, Morgan, I am going to wait. I will call on her when I am ready. . . ."

"To be treated like her favorite?" Morgan suggested, as he straightened and turned for the door.

Rhys threw a napkin at his brother and was reaching for a piece of muffin. Morgan escaped before their conversation descended into a food-throwing contest that would validate Grandmama's assumption that her youngest grandson was more boy than man.

By the time he raised the knocker at the town house and was shown into her too-warm salon, Morgan knew the day was not going to move along on his terms. He had taken the long way round to her door and stopped at White's to check the betting books. There was a new entry. His name was now firmly linked with Miss Lambert.

He'd been fully prepared for a tongue-lashing from his grandmother, but her words surprised him. "Really, Morgan, I stopped putting any credence in the gossip columns long ago." She pulled her shawl closer around her and looked at him. "Move away from the fire, boy. You block the heat."

He sat on a chair next to hers and let himself be soothed by the lavender and rose scent that had been his mother's as well. Did she know about the betting book?

"One of the great pleasures of old age is watching others make the same mistakes I did. There is reassurance in the truth that stupidity is a function of all youth."

So there would be a lecture after all.

"Still, my boy, I can not count your stupidity the most unfortunate thing. How long would it have taken you to pay me a call if this gossip had not compelled you to apologize?"

"Grandmama"—his voice was filled with reproach—"you know that you are the first person I call on when I am in Town. I know how you rely on me for all your news." The last was said with his usual cynical smile for it was a joke and they both knew it. His grandmother had as wide a network of friends as the Queen did.

"So you say, but I did not know you were in Town until I saw you at Westbourne's." She rapped his knuckles with her fan. It was a gesture of affection.

"I only returned in the late afternoon from Braemoor. I had some business there."

She leaned still closer, obviously distracted from her more immediate concerns. "Eh? Did you say business? I thought you were at Roland's house party?"

He flicked dust from his sleeve. How did she know about Roland's? Did she have a spy on her payroll? "Roland's was a bore and I left early."

"And went to Braemoor?"

He heard the surprise in her voice and almost wished they would return to the lecture she had begun.

"Yes, I stopped in Sussex. It was hardly out of the way."

"And how did you find your father?"

"Much the same. He will allow only James to see him plus a couple of servants and, I suppose, the doctor. James tells me he is not improving." He tried to keep emotion from his voice, amazed that the imminent death of a parent who had never approved of him could make him feel so melancholy.

"We can be thankful then that he is not reading the papers. You know how he loathes gossip."

Back to the lecture again. "On my way to Town I stopped at Cashton to visit with Mariel and Charles."

His grandmother raised her brows. "Eh? You say you visited your sister and her husband?"

"Yes, I did." He knew that tidbit would distract her.

"Despite your father's express orders not to acknowledge them?"

"Yes." He bit back a smile and kept his face as solemn as he could. Surprising his grandmama was a rare event.

"Your mother's death was the worst thing that ever happened to the Braedon family."

Morgan nodded even though he could not see the connection to his sister's situation. His mother had been the light in all their lives.

"When your father buried her, he must have put all his common sense in the ground with her. How he could have given Mariel the ultimatum he did." She shook her head. "Yes, she looks the picture of my daughter, but she was also born with a full dose of Braedon rebellion, as her life has proved."

He could swear there were tears in her eyes. Or was it a trick of the light?

After a bare moment of silence, she rapped his knuckles again. "Tell me how they go on! Mariel, Charles, and my great granddaughter. Are they comfortable?"

"Oh yes, they seem to be thriving, quite settled into the life of a country parish." As comfortable as love and like minds could make one. "Being disinherited does not seem to have affected their happiness one jot."

She sat back a moment, satisfied. "Just so."

She said no more, but Morgan had heard the words often enough. *There are definite benefits to a happy marriage.* It was one of Grandmama's favorite sayings. He was not convinced the benefits outweighed the sacrifices.

"Do Charles and Mariel see the Harbisons?"

"Yes, Mariel is teaching the girls the harp and pianoforte so she is at the manor quite regularly."

"And it gives Mariel an opportunity to play herself." She nodded her approval. "Good, for I know how much pleasure it gives her." Glancing away from him, his grandmother made a show of examining the tea tray.

"One of the Harbison girls is ready for the Season, is she not, with the two others champing at the bit." She said nothing more for a moment and then chuckled at some private joke. "The oldest. Is she pretty?"

"Elaine? Blond hair and very blue eyes. A kind of porcelain . . ." Morgan stood up and walked back to the fireplace. "Not matchmaking are you, Grandmama?"

"Eh? Matchmaking? Certainly not." She paused a moment then added with a small smile, "Still, Morgan, Elaine Harbison would be someone to dance with besides Miss Lambert." She laughed at her own joke and missed the scratch on the door.

When she did hear she called, "Enter."

The butler shouted the names of her guests, "Mrs. Lambert and Miss Christiana Lambert."

Four

Now here was a stroke of purely rotten luck. Best not go near the tables today. He glanced at his grandmother. Her lack of surprise was all the hint he needed. She'd known this was going to happen. He swore to himself with real annoyance. This was carrying meddling too far. It was hardly the first time that Morgan wished for a god that would bless him with the ability to disappear.

Mrs. Lambert sailed into the room and made an elegant curtsy to the duchess. Christiana followed, paused for the briefest of moments when she saw him, and then smiled. It was a conspirator's smile, meant only for the two of them to share. In a thousand other circumstances, he would have found it easy to return, but in the present situation it would almost surely make things worse.

He bowed slightly and held back an answering smile. It was not easily done. He swore he could smell the floral scent she wore. It had lingered on his glove long after last night's dance. And when faced with Miss Lambert's laughing green eyes, it was almost impossible not to give in to the urge to share the joke with her. Oh, those eyes spoke to him as surely as her lips did.

The last thing you need right now is to appear even slightly interested. He kept his expression neutral.

Her smile changed. No, not her smile. It was her eyes that changed. The smile had been as firmly in her eyes as it had been on her lips, but with his reserved response it faded, replaced by confusion and a glimmer of embarrassment.

Mrs. Lambert called her daughter forward to make her curtsy and Morgan stepped back a little farther into the shadows. It would be the height of bad manners to make an escape. No matter, he was sorely tempted.

"Morgan, come be introduced!"

Morgan moved forward to obey the summons, wondering if he was the only one who understood the mischief she was brewing. Before he turned to the Lamberts, he took her hand and kissed it. "I live to entertain you, Grandmama."

He'd spoken for her ears alone and she responded with her usual "Eh?" but he could tell by the twitch of her lips she understood him.

With a plea to the gods for inspiration he turned to Christiana Lambert's mother.

Mrs. Lambert did not appear overly surprised at his identity. She accepted his bow with a curtsy of her own and then turned to her daughter. "I have no need to introduce Christiana, do I?"

Her tone was a blend of arch and vexed. There were worse combinations, he decided. Christiana returned his bow with a curtsy as formal as required. Her smile was gone and the chill he had expected from her mother flowed from the daughter instead.

Disdain did not become her. Her lips were made for laughter. Her eyes could barely register the hauteur that made her lithe body tense. They both made to speak, but Mrs. Lambert spoke over their greetings. "What a rogue you are, my lord, to make my daughter the subject of such singular attention."

Arch had given way to coy. He knew where this game was headed. She would voice her displeasure but displeasure only. There was no disapproval. Morgan suspected his suit would be welcome. He glanced at his grandmother, who was watching with a raised eyebrow and a small smile. No help from that quarter. Devil take it.

He took Mrs. Lambert's hand. "My apologies to you and your daughter, ma'am." He thought about telling her the truth. That he had been lost in the card game, but she might construe that as an insult to her daughter.

The larger truth, that he had no wish for a wife, was equally unacceptable. The game he was playing with James would be pointless if it became common knowledge. And he would wager his newest coat that discretion was not among Mrs. Lambert's virtues.

She rescued him again. "La, my lord, if you find Christiana so appealing then you must call on us and meet my other daughter. Joanna is a year older and even Christiana would agree, by far the loveliest young woman to make her come-out this Season."

Christiana stood behind her mother, almost directly in his line of vision. As her mother continued her ingratiating monologue, he could almost swear he saw sympathy in Miss Lambert's eyes. Then she shrugged lightly and turned toward his grandmother, leaving him trapped in a one-sided conversation with her mama. *Please, Grandmama, do not you try to help me smooth this over. Let this conversation with Mrs. Lambert be considered punishment enough.*

Let him suffer, Christiana thought. He was responsible for the ruin of her day. She'd been subjected to Mama's harangue for the last endless hour and had heard quite enough.

Her mother was brilliant, really. She had not seemed at all surprised to see Lord Morgan here. Who had told her of his connection with the duchess?

True, even from home, Mama had followed the Season these last few years, but her attention was centered solely on courtships and engagements. According to Peter, this was the first year that Lord Morgan had shown a similar inclination.

The duchess was watching the cat and mouse game with obvious glee, but pointed to the seat beside her. "Sit here." With her back to her grandson, she gave Christiana her full attention.

"We will let him make his explanations. I have no doubt that he can charm his way into her good graces."

Christiana did not doubt it either, but merely nodded. It would not do at all to show any concern.

"You have an older sister?"

The duchess's tone showed nothing more than polite interest and Christiana hoped that was all it was. As much as she would like to distract the duchess from consideration of her as a possible match for her grandson, Joanna and Lord Morgan would not suit at all. "Yes, I do have an older sister. I would not like today's gossip to harm her chances this Season."

"Not to worry. It will be forgotten in a day. As we speak some other young man is doing something equally half-witted that will fill tomorrow's columns."

Christiana hoped it was true.

"In my day, the gossip was so much more entertaining, but I imagine that was because I was a part of it. Every smile meant something then." She held out her hand. "And no lady was without her fan. If we could not speak our thoughts out loud then our fan could speak for us."

It was hard to envision the woman before her as an ingenue with all the same fears and worries she had. But then there was little possibility that the duchess's worries were anything like hers. "Did you make the duke's acquaintance during your first Season?"

"It was an arranged marriage." She spoke matter-of-factly and then leaned closer to Christiana. "Only no one ever told me." The duchess looked at Christiana intently. "There is nothing more rewarding than a happy marriage."

Christiana nodded. Her own dreams were rooted in that belief.

The old lady tapped Christiana's hand with her fan. "Never lie to me, girl. I can not abide liars."

Christiana was startled at the abrupt change of subject. "I beg your pardon, ma'am?" When had she lied to the duchess? She had agreed marriage was rewarding and she did, indeed, believe that. Perhaps Mama had said something. She glanced toward her mother and the duchess laughed. "She ain't the lying sort, not your mama. She lives to make the world spin her way and that's as truthful as you can be. For that is what we all wish, is it not?"

Christiana considered the question. "I suppose so."

"Of course it is," the duchess insisted. "And the bigger our world becomes the more difficult it is to manage. Now that's something your mama does not realize."

Christiana tried to restrain her smile. It was so true, but she did not want to be disloyal.

"She thinks with a little nudge here or a small hint there she could manage the world and everyone in it, including that villain Napoleon."

The dowager let out a breathy laugh and Christiana let her own smile show. The image of her mother managing England's greatest enemy was a picture made for the cartoonists of the day.

"But Napoleon will not be welcome in our drawing rooms any time soon, so my grandson Morgan will have to do."

They both looked at her mother as she continued to prattle on to a politely attentive Morgan. At the moment he was bearing the full brunt of her managing ways with seeming equanimity. Christiana would have been embarrassed by her mother's behavior if the duchess had not made it sound like the most natural thing in the world.

"Now this grandson"—she gestured to Morgan—"he never lies either. Just plays his cards too close to his chest, that one. He almost never lets on what is going round in his brain." She looked fondly at him and Christiana liked the obvious affection.

" 'Tis time he starts looking for a wife. The foolish boy thinks he will be as lucky in love as he has been in cards and that may be true, but no one is so lucky that the first person he dances with can claim his heart and he hers."

Was she being warned? The duchess needed to know that no warning was necessary or else she would be perilously close to the liar she had been warned not to be. "Your Grace, if you believe so strongly in honesty then there is something I must tell you."

Christiana spoke impulsively and then recalled her promise to her father. But everything she had heard of the duchess convinced her that confiding in her would not be a mistake. She would not have the ear of so many if she were rash in her gossip. "May I confide in you, ma'am?"

The duchess hesitated, glanced at her nephew, and then back.

The hesitation convinced Christiana all the more.

She watched her grandson as she spoke. "Morgan would not suit you at all, my dear," she whispered from behind her fan lest he hear.

Christiana responded with her rippling laugh and spoke her previous thought aloud. "Oh, I know. I agree with you completely." She leaned closer to the old lady. "I have no idea what possessed him to behave as he did last night, but it can hardly be that he was so taken with me that he could not countenance dancing with another. It was a lovely dance, ma'am, but no dance can be that powerful."

She bit her lip as she spoke the words, not entirely sure she was speaking the truth. It had been a wonderful experience. Despite the roomful of people she had seen no one but him. His eyes held hers, his hand touched hers and hinted, hinted at something she could feel even though she could not put it into words. It was a shame Richard did not like dancing.

"Yes, my girl, I can see that you are rethinking that silly statement. A dance is as powerful as a skilled lover can make it. And Morgan is just that, Christiana. He would as soon seduce you as dance with you."

Christiana could feel the color rising in her cheeks.

"Stop the blush, gel. You waste it on me."

Christiana took a moment to compose herself and once again looked at her mother and found that Lord Morgan was staring at her and not her mother. He'd maneuvered Mama so that it would appear he was giving her his full consideration, but with the slightest movement of his eyes, Christiana had all his attention. He was smiling slightly. Her mother would think it was at what she was saying. Christiana knew it was her blush that amused him. Of course that made her blush anew.

She turned in her chair slightly so that he could not so easily see her face and spoke to the duchess in earnest appeal. "Please, ma'am, let me explain."

The woman nodded slowly and Christiana rushed on, explaining her attachment to Richard, his commitment to military service, and her promise to her parents. "So you see, if you feel that Lord Morgan should find a suitable *parti,* I am not the one. You are right we would not suit, but even before that practical consideration, my heart is already given.

"The Season is well underway for we were late to Town. I would hate to distract him from a more appropriate match. I am in a very awkward situation as I have promised not to make my attachment known."

The duchess nodded thoughtfully and then tapped

Christiana's arm with her fan. "I will be your ambassador, my dear. I will be as discreet as your papa would wish." She sighed and her shoulders drooped. In that one gesture she turned frail and disappointed. "Morgan would not suit you at all, I know that is true, still I was rather hoping for a mild flirtation. It would be a first step in the proper direction. You could be the making of him."

Christiana did not understand. She looked toward Lord Morgan. He had been in Town for years and years and she was but newly arrived. "How could I teach him anything, ma'am?"

"You could have reminded him what it is to be young and happy. He lost his youth and happiness far too soon, far too soon. And has tried to make up for it in all the wrong places."

He lost his happiness far too soon. Christiana tore her eyes from him and looked at the duchess, who was watching her with an intensity that was at odds with her solemn face. She leaned closer to hear another tale, when Mrs. Lambert approached them and destroyed the mood for confidences.

Christiana was uncomfortably aware that they had overstayed their twenty-minute call. She was sure it would take her mother another ten minutes to say farewell.

"I am so grateful, Your Grace," Mrs. Lambert began in farewell.

The duchess smiled and nodded with all the charm of a hostess used to guests who made an endurance contest of her hospitality. The embarrassment that Christiana had suppressed before took firm root in her mind, coloring her cheeks and testing her patience.

Mrs. Lambert spoke on one long incredible breath. "We are to Mr. Philips's gallery this afternoon. But first we must hurry home to collect my daughter Joanna and another friend who are to accompany us."

She finally paused long enough for the duchess to

interrupt her mama's farewell. The old lady did it with such finality, Christiana wondered if she dared copy it. There was nothing left but to curtsy and leave.

Blissful silence. Morgan stood facing his grandmother and absorbed the absolute lack of sound. It was a gift from the gods.

When the silence had stretched to a full minute, the duchess invited comment by simply raising her eyebrows.

Morgan spoke very quietly. "I am telling you, Grandmama, that *if* I had ever been more than mildly tempted to form an attachment with Miss Christiana Lambert, that conversation with her mother put an end to it. Conversation? It was a monologue."

Her lips twitched but she did not encourage the subject. "The daughter reminds me of Maddie and your mother."

And so it was with his grandmother, no subject off limits. "Where are your spectacles, Grandmama? Her hair is dark, not blond. For Miss Lambert everything is anticipation and delight. Maddie observed life. Miss Lambert embraces it."

"Not the looks, no, Morgan. That inclination to trust, to see things as magic. Your mother was the same."

Grandmother might welcome the reminder, but he did not. He lived with the fact that Maddie had never known her first Season, had never walked in Hyde Park.

"Do not dwell on it, Grandmama, it does no good."

She rapped his hand. "I am not being morbid. Some days I am more a part of their world than this one. They are not gone so much as waiting." She recalled herself to the present before Morgan could grow seriously worried about her state of mind. "You should not have singled the girl out the way you did, boy."

"Yes, it was stupid, but I assure you, not intentional." He bent closer. "And surely even you will agree that a morning of Mrs. Lambert is punishment enough, especially when her delightful daughter was in the same room and I was allowed nothing more than the briefest of hellos."

"Leave the gel alone, Morgan."

Morgan hid his irritation behind his gamester's mask and waited for more. He would have thought his grandmother would be thrilled at his courtship of an eligible chit.

"Christiana is too young, too impressionable, and much too taken with your dancing style."

Is this what the two of them had been talking about while Mrs. Lambert prattled on? It was hard to believe that Christiana had felt comfortable gossiping with his grandmother. "And how is it that you became her confidante so quickly?"

"She sees some parallels in our situations."

Morgan laughed out loud at that absurdity. "Pardon me, Grandmama? You are an aging widow and she is an eighteen-year-old virgin. Where are there parallels?"

She snapped at him. "We both think you are impertinent."

He took her hand and kissed it. "I am sorry, ma'am. I would not hurt you for all the world."

"And we both know you are much too charming to be safe."

"Did she say that?" He was surprised at how much he wanted to know.

"She had no need to. No woman would deny it. Even her tiresome mother was bewitched."

He bowed and held his tongue.

"However, even an appealing rogue like you, Morgan, can not expect to find a match so quickly. She tells me she has a beau from home and is not seeking a match."

He shook his head. "Is there a girl in England who does not have a beau from home, Grandmama?"

"He is on the Peninsula and she intends to be loyal to him." She paused a moment and then added, "An innocent flirtation is not your usual style, my boy."

It had been years since she had lectured him on propriety, or was it that she was turning protective of her newest protégée? Morgan held on to his good humor by reminding himself that she lived through her grandchildren now. He should be grateful that she was not trying to bring them together. He took her hand and held it with both of his. "I can see that you are sorely disappointed that your newest friend does not need your help in finding a husband."

She pulled her hand from his and let her irritation show. "Your cynicism is not one of your more attractive traits, Morgan."

He straightened, ready to give up his efforts to restore her good humor. "Grandmama, dearest, I am near twenty-seven years old and have been in Town long enough to know what is acceptable and what is not."

She looked away from him. "Once, just once I would like to see you knocked to your knees. It was the making of your father. It could do you nothing but good."

He recognized the story coming: how his mother caught and tamed his father. It would be a fairy tale if his mother had lived longer and if his father had not reverted to his old ways.

Grandmama might be forever saying that a happy marriage made life a joy, but she never added what was obvious to him: that the end of a happy marriage made the rest of one's life an empty misery. Morgan knew a way to distract her and apologized to his youngest brother for offering him up as a sacrifice.

"You were asking about Father before. Rhys arrived in Town today. He may have news of him."

"Eh? You say Rhys is in Town?"

"He arrived this morning."

"Riding at night again. The boy will catch his death of a chill."

Morgan nodded. "He will call as soon as he has rested. He promised." Morgan lied glibly, but in fact it was the truth. He was going to insist Rhys call before the day was over. There was always the hope that she would be less inclined to meddle in his life with her favorite close at hand. She could worry Rhys to death and leave him in peace.

Morgan lost over a hundred guineas at faro before the solution struck him. He tossed a coin to the dealer and left, not certain he had the time he needed to put his plan into action. Thanks to the loquacious Mrs. Lambert, he knew exactly where to look for them and reached the exhibition rooms within a half hour of its close. He made his way through the several rooms, greeting friends, pausing for conversation, and curbing his impatience until finally he found his quarry.

Christiana Lambert stood in front of a large allegorical picture featuring Daniel in the lions' den. She was not alone. He did indeed recognize Peter Wilton. There was another young girl with him. The sister, the one Mama had wanted him to meet. And thank the god of mercy, Mama was not part of the party. If she had been he would have left and waited for another day. But this situation was ideal. His luck had turned.

Morgan ducked back into the next room they would approach, pleased that the only other party examining the paintings was unknown to him.

As the group made their way to the door, leaving the room empty, Morgan took a moment to examine the paintings himself. More religious allegory. Not to his taste. Who wanted such a strong reminder that the life one led was too full of pleasure to merit entrance into heaven through the martyrs' gate?

". . . But it seems to me that they could convey the same sentiment without so much dark and brooding feeling." Christiana's voice carried through to him.

Her sister's voice was much quieter, but it still reached him. "Exactly how would sunlight and smiles make one feel the pain of the martyrs?"

Christiana laughed. "I would prefer to imagine it all on my own. When I see it in color like this and larger than life, I feel nothing more inspiring than guilt. It becomes quite clear that any effort to improve myself is bound to fail when compared to these saintly people."

"I think Mama wished you to be inspired, not discouraged."

"You will notice she is not here, hoping for insight." Christiana sounded more relieved than aggrieved.

Joanna giggled. "She said she had all the excitement her nerves could tolerate."

Morgan suspected he was directly connected to the excitement that had so exhausted Mrs. Lambert. He sauntered over to the small group, careful to give Peter his full attention. "Mr. Wilton! Miss Lambert! Well met!"

"My lord!" Peter seemed stunned at the recognition, and delighted. *The boy does do wonders for the ego.* Morgan chanced a quick look at Christiana. She was smiling. Good.

Wilton knew his manners. He turned to the ladies. "You know Miss Christiana Lambert of course. My lord, this is Miss Joanna Lambert, Miss Christiana's sister. Joanna, may I present Lord Morgan, he is the son of the Marquis of Straeford."

The introductions made, Morgan accepted young Wilton's invitation to join the group. He discussed the pictures they had already seen, even though he had not viewed one of them. It was easy to earn Miss

Christiana Lambert's approval, having heard her one comment. "It would seem to me so much more inspirational to show the joys of heaven rather than the cruelty of one man to another."

Christiana stopped abruptly and the other three turned to her. "Exactly so, my lord."

They paused before a particularly poor painting of the crucifixion and then moved on as one. Christiana shook her head. "And to think the artist—"

When she stopped, Morgan picked up the thought "—to think the artist spent hours painting in hopes of conveying some worthy thought—"

At this pause, Joanna waited a moment and then added, "—and failed miserably."

Three paintings later they were laughing heartily and in complete agreement with the gentleman who inherited these paintings and was now willing to sell them.

"Philips tells me that his uncle bought them at the urging of his second wife, who was extremely devout." Wilton stopped there but Morgan was certain that they were of the same mind. *What a burden that marriage must have been.*

Christiana whispered something to her sister, who shook her head and turned to their escorts, trying not to laugh. "Mama thinks that I will have a steadying effect on Christy, but you must know already that the opposite is true."

The elder Miss Lambert was indeed lovely when she smiled, but therein lay the difference between the sisters. Joanna Lambert's expression was solemn in repose, while her younger sister's held the promise that laughter was a heartbeat away and she was about to share it with you.

Joanna drew out his fraternal, even protective, feelings. Christiana made him smile and roused not one brotherly thought. Exactly how committed was she to her distant lover?

Morgan walked over to where Wilton stood, trying to regain his composure. "Wilton, I was wondering if you might join me for dinner tonight. My brother Rhys has come to Town and I thought he might enjoy meeting some others his age. I thought afterward we could stop in at the Quarter Moon."

Surely Wilton would not refuse a chance to visit the private gaming club. It was a generous offer, made even more generous by Morgan's determination that none of his guests would come to ruin at his invitation. That meant a night more inclined to caring for children than deep play.

Wilton's acceptance bordered on incoherence. Morgan nodded, thanking the god of wisdom that he had never been this young. When he spoke again, it was for Peter's ears alone. "Now let me have a moment of conversation with Miss Lambert."

Peter looked hesitant.

"God bless us, Wilton. I just want a word or two with her, nothing more, I promise."

Wilton blushed and Morgan turned toward the ladies.

It took a moment or two, but Peter managed it so that he and Joanna were several depictions of hell ahead, leaving him and Christiana staring at a painting of a monk in chains.

Christiana turned to Morgan, her back to the painting. "I cannot bear it."

She looked surprised at her own admission and shook her head, the hint of laughter eclipsed by a look of horror. "Zuburan is a very good artist, is he not? It is such a simple painting, but still so moving. This man is willing to die because he knows what he is doing is right."

She kept her back to the picture and the smile crept back into her eyes. "But you see, if the artist means to shock me into a life of good works he does not succeed. For all I can see is a man who is giving up his life without ever fully living it. It is a waste."

"One could say that this monk knew more of God and service to Him than most do if they live to be seventy."

"Do you think it impossible to serve God and enjoy life too?" She blushed when he took her arm and they moved on to the next painting.

Oh, Lord. Oh, heaven. He was lost. This woman could undo him with a smile. He was about to condemn himself to a Season of pure torture. He could hardly wait.

Five

Service to God had not occupied a single one of his waking moments as far as Morgan could recall. He had, however, heard enough of his brother-in-law's sermons to improvise. "I think the secret to serving God is to understand what His mission in life is for us." He felt like a hypocrite, thinking of her lips one moment and then prosing on like a man of God the next.

"That sounds like something your grandmother would say."

"She might well have."

The porter was making the rounds, announcing the closing time, some fifteen minutes away. He could hear the others in the next room. But all he could see was Christiana Lambert's eager eyes full of question and curiosity.

There was an inherent vulnerability in such an open manner. He wanted to provide the answers and satisfy the curiosity, but he also wanted to shield her from insult and slay every dragon that threatened her door.

Morgan shook off the melodrama. That was not what this proposition was about. It was the means to a very practical end.

They were alone in the room. He had her complete attention. Morgan took her hand and bowed over it.

"Miss Lambert, I am sorry if our dance last night caused you any embarrassment."

If his gallantry had succeeded, she would not be blushing.

"Oh no, my lord, the dance was wonderful. It did not cause me one moment of embarrassment."

Ah, so that was why she was blushing. How flattering.

"It is only Mama who was concerned about the gossip in the paper. And after all, my lord, how many people actually read that?"

Only everyone in London, he thought, but was not about to admit it. "With the Season fully under way I think we can count on something far more intriguing catching their attention tomorrow."

She nodded, her expression hopeful, close to confident. "Only this afternoon someone was telling me that Lord Ramsdon has bet his favorite horse in some ridiculous wager. Surely that will draw more attention than who you are dancing with."

Satisfied that each had convinced the other, he pushed on to the greater challenge of the day. "Grandmama tells me you have a beau from home."

She looked around the room. Was she afraid that it would become the next *on-dit?* "My grandmother shared the secret with me and I understand that it is not something you wish widely known."

On a sigh of relief Christiana nodded. "His name is Richard Wilton and I hold him in great esteem. But I have agreed to honor Papa's request that I remain unattached until the end of the Season."

"I suppose your father does not fully appreciate that this will make things somewhat difficult for you." He hoped his sympathy might strike a chord.

"Yes, my lord, that describes it perfectly." She brought her hands together and spoke with the intensity of strong feeling. "It is so unfair to anyone seeking a match to pay their addresses to me. It is not that

I think I will have all London at my feet, you understand, but it seems to me the height of selfishness to receive attention you have no intent of returning. I do hope you understand."

"Of course I do, but so that you will understand me, please be assured that neither do I have any plans for making a match this Season."

"But, my lord"—she looked surprised. Then she pressed her lips together and spoke with her eyes. He tried to decipher their message. Was it embarrassment at her awareness of the gossip or possibly confusion at the obvious contradiction?

"You have heard that my father wishes me to find a bride?" Even if it was not what she had been about to blurt out, it was best to get rid of all the losing cards right away.

She nodded slowly and spoke with apology. "There is gossip everywhere, my lord."

"A fact of Town life that we may use to our advantage." But here he was running ahead of himself. He took a mental step back. "Between the two of us and the two of us alone, my father does wish me to make a match. My brother insists that it is his dearest wish." *Please let her be more discreet than her mother,* Morgan prayed to any god that would listen. "And also between the two of us alone, be assured I have no intention of making one."

She angled her head, her eyes narrowing a bit. "My lord, I am confused now."

"In truth, my dear Miss Lambert, that is hardly surprising, since I have said one thing and then its opposite. As you have made clear, in your family one does not disobey parental decrees. Let me assure you it does not happen often in my family either."

Now there was an understatement. "My father may wish me to marry, but I am not ready to wed. I do have property in Wales but it needs more work before I can support a family."

She nodded again. "I know how difficult it is to go against one's father's wishes."

He wondered if she really did. In all her country-bred life had she ever encountered anyone as autocratic as the Marquis of Straeford? He doubted it. If she had, that vulnerability that was both appealing and appalling would be gone as his was, beaten out of him years ago.

She obeyed her father out of loving respect. He obeyed his out of a primal need for self-preservation. Now that preservation, and concern for dozens of tenants, demanded another approach. This was the right thing to do. If only he could get her to agree.

The beginning of a smile pulled at her mouth, though it had not reached her eyes, but it was all the encouragement he needed.

"I would like to satisfy my father that I am at least making an effort to find a match." That statement left him feeling positively virtuous. It was the stark, sun-blinding truth.

Christiana's incipient smile disappeared.

He kept on, feeling as though he were playing a losing hand, but was unwilling to throw in the cards. "My father is ill, very ill and not likely to live out the year. I have no desire to wed yet, but do wish to make him happy. I am hoping I can convince you to help me give my father peace of mind. With your own heart engaged elsewhere there will be no danger of misunderstanding." The whole damned thing sounded as tentative as a marriage proposal. He hoped he did better with one when the time came.

"You want me to help you deceive your father?" Then the enormity of it struck her. "To try and trick the *ton?*" She was obviously not inclined to help, whether from a dislike of deception or fear of failure. He could not say which.

"True, it is a deception, but one for the best."

She looked skeptical and that made him laugh.

"That sort of logic will not work at all, will it, Miss Lambert? Of course, this little deception is what I think is best for me, but I must come up with a better argument if I am to convince you."

When she said nothing, he continued, taking her silence for curiosity if not compliance. "It would not be fair for me to court someone like your sister, who honestly hopes to make a match. And it will become wearing for you to discourage would-be suitors. All the more so when you have promised not to speak of your attachment."

Her censure eased and she nodded.

"Once the legions of young men who appreciate your grace on the dance floor realize we appear to have developed a *tendre* for one another, they will move on to other eligible young ladies, leaving us free to entertain each other and enjoy the Season with un-encumbered hearts." He tried for a teasing tone, and was satisfied when he drew a smile from her.

"Put that way, my lord, it is almost exactly what I had hoped for." Delight lit her eyes. "At first I thought Peter could serve as my escort, but he is too involved in his own pursuits." She frowned though the smile still lit her eyes. "But will it not be the same with you? Peter tells me that you prefer the card room to the dance floor."

"That was before I met you, Miss Lambert." He bowed to her.

She clapped her hands and laughed aloud. "You are such a flirt!"

He hoped that was a compliment.

"It is one thing Richard is not. His flowery phrases are heavier than Mrs. Purdy's fruitcake. If I had your grandmother's fan I would shrink behind it and blush."

She would do no such thing. She loved every minute of it. He kept his mind on the compliment and not the mention of Richard Wilton.

Her excitement faded a little. "But what will they

say when I leave London at the end of the Season and nothing comes of our"—she hesitated over the word— "our 'friendship.' "

He tried to conceal the surge of relief at her question. This one he could handle. "The *ton* will say what many have said before: that I lost your hand to a better man. There is no discomfiture in that."

Christiana looked around the room. "Wait until Joanna hears. She was certain my plan to find an escort was a cork-brained scheme. Wait until she hears that it was your idea!"

He could feel his smile die. Were cardplayers the only ones who were able to control their emotions? "I think it best not to tell anyone."

"I must tell my sister. We have no secrets from each other." A small sigh expelled half of her excitement and dimmed her smile. "I do see that the fewer people who know of this the better. Mama will think I am flighty." She shrugged that off. "If I am lucky Papa will not hear of it. Joanna and I are the only ones who write to him and I doubt he ever reads the gossip pages." She paused and he could see her enthusiasm wane still more. "Your grandmother will think less of me if we do not tell her."

He shook his head, fighting hard to resist her pleading smile. "She will be thrilled at the prospect of me being 'knocked to my knees.' I think that is the way she phrased it."

"I will not be a part of a deception that will hurt her." On this she spoke with conviction.

He took her hand, wondering if he would ever find out if her shoulder was as fine and soft. "My dear Miss Lambert, in her view it is not my grandmother's feelings that are at risk."

Christiana understood then and looked shocked. "She thinks that I might break your heart?"

He leaned closer to her. "She lives for the day it

happens. Ridiculous, is it not? The world knows that Braedon hearts are made of stone."

She stepped back from his intimacy. "I know no such thing." Regret replaced delight. "No, sir. I can see that this is not a wise idea."

Now he was the one confused. Did she actually mean she was afraid she might hurt him? Should he be touched or annoyed at the very idea? Or could it be propriety had reared its useless head? Just like last night when she had invited him to her side with a smile, and then had second thoughts. He thought he had won her cooperation and now he seemed to have lost it only a moment later.

Morgan's hopes for the Season crumbled before him. He took her arm and escorted her to the entry hall just as the porter came into the room to announce the imminent closing of the gallery.

Peter Wilton and her sister watched them from the door. They were the last of the patrons. He refused to hurry. "Do not reject this idea out of hand. If you must, ask your sister's advice. We both know she has only concern for you at heart. Tell her, but beyond that, remember, my dear Miss Lambert, tell no one else. If we decide to play this trick on society and it becomes common knowledge, I will not be heartbroken. It will be worse. I will be embarrassed."

Christiana laughed, exactly as he hoped she would. "I understand, my lord. I understand completely. Your standing in society will not suffer at my hands, not ever. I have managed to keep my attachment to Richard a secret as my father asked. I am worthy of your trust."

They joined the others and made their farewells.

As he escorted the group from the building to their carriages, he let the banter float around him as he considered their last words. He had no doubt Christiana Lambert was worthy of his trust. The only thing that worried him still was how widely known her attachment to Richard Wilton was.

Though little more than a farce, this game he hoped to play was not with dice, but with society and his family. He did not want to destroy her reputation or his own.

He needed to know how things stood between the lovely Miss Christiana and her Richard. She insisted that their romance was a secret, but he had only her word for that. If her attachment to Wilton was more than that—an understanding, or worse, an engagement in the eyes of all back home—then word would reach Sussex and Braemoor as easily as it reached London. Society would take umbrage and James would call him a cheat.

He hoped to find out tonight at dinner. What young Wilton knew would be the deciding factor on his part. As for Christiana, he knew she would not proceed without her sister's support.

He bowed to the party as their carriage moved away and looked to his own, wondering if he would have to hire a new cook when Pratt learned that he was preparing dinner for four on five hours' notice.

The dinner went better than Morgan had hoped. Pratt was neither French nor temperamental and had a family to support, so the food was ready on time with little complaint. If it was not as elaborate as some he'd enjoyed at this table, the quantity of dishes more than compensated for its simplicity.

More to the point, with the aid of some excellent wine and a few probing questions, Peter Wilton seemed willing, even eager, to tell Morgan of his family and his older brother's hopes, both military and matrimonial.

"Richard's been army mad since he was old enough to understand what 1066 meant. We played with soldiers for hours on end." The covers had been removed and the four sat with glasses of port and an evening of amiable play ahead of them.

Rhys and an Oxford mate, William Gaffney, were discussing some esoteric astronomical discovery with the intensity only two inebriated intellects could command. Morgan gave Peter his undivided attention.

He sipped his port, wondering how much of Wilton's childhood he would hear about before Christiana entered the picture.

"When my mother was ill with her last confinement, all three of us, even our oldest brother Henry, spent much of our time at Lambert Hill. Christiana's brother was as keen on battles as Richard and we would combine our soldiers for some dashed fine fights."

"Miss Lambert has a brother?"

"Yes." Wilton nodded. "George. He is in Jamaica visiting an uncle."

"If you three and George were anything like me and my brothers, more than once those battles escalated into fistfights and bloody noses. Did the Miss Lamberts nurse the wounds?"

"Christiana and Joanna were always underfoot. So we put them to work, constructing the Alps from papermâché when we reenacted Hannibal's invasion and then made up battles of our own. But Richard tired of those games years ago.

"Father knew General Moore and after Corunna he finally consented to purchase a commission for Richard in his old regiment. Now he is off on what Father calls 'Napoleon's version of the Grand Tour.' "

"Hardly the pleasure trip the Grand Tour was supposed to have been," Morgan drawled and recalled the awful stories of the Corunna retreat. "Your father is Sir Howard Wilton?"

Peter nodded. "A second son who inherited when my uncle died from an inflammation of the lungs. Father was set on a military career himself. He loved the army but had only six months' service before he had to sell out."

Which explains why he was willing to let his second son go off and risk his life.

Morgan had dismissed the footmen with the covers and offered to pour Peter another glass of port. Wilton smiled, but covered his glass with his hand. "If I am to play tonight I must refuse." His youth was apparent when he added, "I learned that from watching you, sir. You always have a glass at your elbow but you rarely do more than sip at it."

The boy was observant. He would give him that. On the other hand, Wilton should have stopped three glasses ago if he truly did wish to keep a clear head.

"I expect that your brother—Richard is it?—will find plenty of opportunity to test his skill at cards in the army."

Peter laughed. "Not to be disloyal, sir, but my brother has no skill at cards at all, though he thinks he does. He told Christiana he would not play but, sir, I know there are battles, but there must be equally as many long encampments. What else is there to do?"

"Miss Lambert does not approve of gaming?"

"Oh no, it is not that, my lord. It is my suspicion that she wants him to save every bit of his pay."

"Are they engaged then?" Morgan sipped his port and cleared his throat.

"Oh no, my lord! Not with Christiana's Season and Richard in harm's way as he is. It is only my assumption that they will one day find their way to the altar. I mean she has been forever around our home and we hers. They get along well enough, and a union between a Lambert female and a Wilton male would suit my father perfectly. It will put an end to a squabble over some property that both families have claimed for four generations."

Morgan controlled his smile. It was about settlements and not sentiment after all. "The land would be part of the marriage settlement?"

Peter waved his hand. "Some nonsensical arrangement made years ago that the land would go to the first Wilton-Lambert union, with the land to go to the male half of the marriage regardless of which family it was. Of course, there is no doubt that the property belongs to us. It is only that Lambert land borders it on three sides."

Wilton's words were spoken with a righteous indignation that he must have inherited direct from his father.

Morgan frowned. "Does Miss Lambert know this?" He could not believe that she would agree to it if it were expressed quite that way.

"I think not, sir. It would not suit her romantic nature at all."

Exactly. But why did the phrase he had just thought sound so belittling when given voice by Wilton? He considered it a moment as he watched Rhys and Gaffney still talking with earnest intensity. To Wilton, Christiana's "romantic nature" was a shortcoming and for Morgan it was an intrinsic part of her charm.

He could almost convince himself that she needed to be rescued from the machinations of her land-hungry neighbor. But that was not what this was about. It was a ruse to satisfy James, to win for himself the time he needed to earn his own fortune so he could declare his independence.

It was hardly a sacrifice to escort a lovely lady to such entertainments as they would both enjoy. If, in the process, she learned there was more to romance than a provincial land-hungry beau, then she would learn what dozens before her had. It sounded less noble put that way, he decided, and just a little more cruel. But then the truth often was.

* * *

"Christy, the truth is cruel." Joanna sat on the edge of her sister's bed and tried to make herself understood. "He is a gamester. That means games are his specialty. I do not trust him."

Christiana was sorry that she had brought up the subject. Why had she, when the evening had already proved trial enough? Because she had not expected Joanna to disagree with her, that was why. And now the little ache behind her eyes threatened to blossom into a full-blown headache. She would change the subject.

"Was that musicale not a colossal bore? Two women singing in German for two hours." She shuddered. "I do wish Mama had not turned down those other invitations so precipitously."

Joanna sighed, sat on the bed, and began to pull pins from her hair. "She was so certain that we would be invited to the Richlands' ball." Joanna smiled at her sister and sat upright, imitating their mother. "My mother was the daughter of an earl."

Christiana smiled with relief. "That may be, but apparently Mama has been gone from Town too long. I suppose it will take time to reestablish herself. At least that was the excuse she gave me."

Joanna's answering smile disappeared. Her sister stood up from the bed and took her hands. "I do not trust him, Christy."

"Yes, he likes to gamble, Joanna. But that is no sin, at least not in a man I have no intention of marrying. Peter tells me he has a reputation for scrupulous honesty and fair play. And no one, not one person, has suggested that he is a womanizer. I do trust him."

Joanna let go of her sister's hands and stepped back. "But how can you know? You have danced with him once, chanced upon him at his grandmother's, and met him at Mr. Philips's gallery. And there is another curious thing. What was he doing there, alone? No one goes to that sort of thing alone."

She shrugged away Joanna's curiosity. "Perhaps he was there to make a purchase and chanced to see us as he was leaving?"

"Sister dearest, you can be so stubborn. Why do you trust him? Give me one good reason and I will relent."

"His grandmother loves him."

Joanna flopped back on the bed in an unusual gesture of exaggerated disgust. "Christy! All grandmothers dote on their grandchildren, especially the rogues who know exactly how to deceive them."

"But that's exactly it. She is not deceived by him. She hates dishonesty, Jo. She told me so herself. It has something to do with her marriage to the duke. But no matter what the reason, she can see right through a lie."

"And how do you know that?" Joanna sat up and began to gather the pins lying on the bedcover and then stopped. "Did you lie to her?"

"No, of course not."

"So you are willing to spend the entire Season in company with this one man, whom you barely know, and not even so much as flirt with another?"

"But is it not the perfect solution?"

"Only if you are absolutely certain that Richard is your heart's delight."

"My heart's delight? You are reading too many novels, Joanna! And everyone thinks that I am the romantic in this family!" Christiana turned toward the window. Did Joanna really think that the perfect lover existed outside of the pages of the Minerva Press? "Richard and I have known each other from the cradle, Jo. The military life he wants will suit me perfectly." She crushed the totally unexpected glimmer of uncertainty with something akin to panic and turned back to Joanna. "Why is it impossible to accept that I wish to be loyal to Richard, especially now that he is away and lonely?"

Joanna avoided an argument, as Christiana knew she would. "If you think that this plan you have devised with Lord Morgan will work, then I will support you. I do feel that you should seek wiser counsel than mine, though."

"Lord Morgan did say that the fewer who knew the better it would be."

"Then I must count myself lucky to be one of the chosen few who know the truth."

"Joanna, please, I can not abide it when you are upset with me."

The chill disappeared, replaced with urgent entreaty. "But, Christy, the whole purpose of this Season is to see if you have made the right choice, to prove to yourself that your affections are truly engaged and that Richard is the best choice for your life's partner."

At least she had avoided using "heart's delight" again. "I know that is what Papa and I agreed, but I have made the right choice. I already know that."

Joanna threw up her hands in surrender. "You are exactly like Mama, you know."

It was the ultimate insult. Joanna knew that. Christiana rubbed her temple, trying to erase both the headache and the irritation. "I am like Mama? Pray, Joanna, what does that mean?"

"She thinks everything should go on as she ordains it. Even if it means fitting a square peg in a round hole."

Christiana whirled away from her sister's bed and threw the next words over her shoulder. "I am committed to Richard in every way, Jo. We have spent the night together!"

"No, Christy!" Joanna's shock was palpable. She forgot to breathe for a moment and then gasped. "When?" It sounded as though it was the only word she could manage.

"The night before he left. We met in the summer house and stayed together the whole night. He escorted me home just before first light and then walked back home and rode off to the war."

There was a long silence. Christiana did not dare look at her sister. She knew she would see hurt, disbelief, maybe even disgust.

When Joanna did speak, her words were so softly spoken that Christiana had to strain to hear them. "Then you are truly committed and there is nothing else to say. You must do whatever you think best to resolve the situation."

"I am sorry, Joanna. I have one of those awful headaches and am not thinking properly." She did turn and look at her sister then, and Joanna's expression was one of disappointment.

"I suppose you would never have told me, if you were thinking clearly." With that she left her sister's room. Christiana could not think of three other occasions when they had parted for the night without good wishes.

As she undressed and prepared for bed, Christiana realized something else: Joanna had been wrong. It was not the truth that was cruel. Lying was infinitely more painful. And she had lied to a sister who was one of the dearest people in her entire world.

Why had she told Joanna that she and Richard had spent the night together? To end the argument? To convince Joanna in any way she could that her ruse with Lord Morgan made sense?

Sally helped her comb out her hair and then disappeared with her dress. Christiana let the tears that she had been holding back trickle down her cheeks.

Yes, she had lied, but she wished desperately that her lie had been a truth. She had wanted that night with Richard more than she had ever wanted anything. All the bouquets in the world, every hand-holding walk in the park, every kiss good night would not have meant as much as being held in his arms for one long night. It would have been undeniable proof of his commitment and his love. One thing to carry her through the months of worry for him. A tangible promise of their future together.

Richard had refused. Indeed, he had been as shocked as Joanna at the mere suggestion. "What would your father think of me?" he'd demanded. When she had insisted he would never know, Richard had still refused. It was not the way a proper young lady behaved. A gentleman would never take advantage of a young lady's weakness in that way. He went on and on until she was almost convinced that he was right.

He did not understand, she had argued, that this was never about weakness or propriety. It was about passion.

And then Richard had said something that had frightened her. "We share a mutual respect and know each other as well as most brothers and sisters. That is a much better basis for marriage than passion."

Christiana did not care what other people's marriages were based on. She wanted passion in hers. She had dreamed of marriage since she was twelve. She knew what happened in the marriage bed and was willing to share that with Richard. Surely passion was the only thing that made such intimacy anything but sordid.

She had tried to convince him with more delicately phrased words, but he had been adamant. He had ended the discussion with three words: "We will wait." He'd spoken with a cool smile and calm resolution, and then followed it with one final unarguable statement. "It is the sensible thing to do."

She did not care a pin for sensible then, and even now longed for some memory that was more romantic than prosaic. Christiana turned on her side and prayed for sleep, afraid guilt would keep her awake. She wished she had not lied to her sister. With a sigh she realized that she would have to tell Joanna the truth

in the morning. There had never been any dishonesty
between them and she knew it was wrong.

Her conscience eased, Christiana eventually drifted
into a fitful sleep, her last waking thought the realization that Lord Morgan had exhibited more gallantry
to her than Richard ever had. But that was all London
charm, she dreamed. Exactly what her father had
wanted her to experience.

Six

"I swear, Morgan, if Dante were writing *The Divine Comedy* today, it is certain that he would have included Almack's on one of his levels of hell." Rhys was nervous and the slow progress of the carriages on the rain-soaked streets only added to it.

Morgan decided to humor his brother. "Surely you overstate the case. You would not actually call the Assembly Rooms the abode of Satan, would you?"

Rhys relaxed against the squabs and considered the question. "No, that would be an insult to Dante, for that was at the very bottom of the chasm. But there are nine circles between that and limbo. Plenty of room for all kinds of sin there."

Morgan tried to recall if he had ever actually read the *Divine Comedy*. "Then tell me, what level of hell was reserved for mediocre music and ambitious mamas?"

"Circle Eight is for hypocrites and panderers," Rhys suggested.

"Too cruel, brother. These mothers do only what they think is best for their daughters. And one can hardly call them hypocrites when they are quite open about their hopes for an advantageous match."

"Then we will call them avaricious and place them on Circle Four."

"May the gods save me from the judgment of

youth." Morgan was only half joking. Rhys did see everything as black and white.

Rhys shrugged and then smiled. "Let me see, I wonder where he put gamesters."

Morgan held up his hand. "Spare me. Let it be a surprise." They had reached St. James Street and he could see Almack's entrance ablaze with lamps. He counted seven coaches ahead of theirs, each stopping only long enough to discharge passengers.

"Exactly why did we choose to arrive at the moment the doors opened?" Rhys asked, as though only now realizing how unusual that was.

"I thought it would add a soupçon of humility to the game. If the gods of vanity are with me, the patronesses will see my early arrival as a gesture of respect." Morgan had given each play of this game careful thought.

"And tease the rest of the *ton* with the prospect that you may indeed be seeking a bride?"

His brother was not a member of White's. Did the information come from gossip or family?

The two welcomed the umbrella the porter held and were urged inside by a sudden gust of wind. They could go no more than a few steps into the lobby.

The hall was crammed with people, voices raised in excited greeting. Young ladies dressed in pastels and adorned with pearls were making their way to the withdrawing rooms to repair the damage of wind and wet. Groups of young men, dressed in self-conscious grandeur, clustered in small groups as though they needed the strength of numbers to storm the fortress of propriety that was Almack's. Morgan nudged Rhys to the side, away from the entry, and they waited beyond a pillar for the passage to the receiving room to clear.

Rhys leaned close. "Gaffney says that every single thing about this place is mediocre."

"Except the snobbery of its patronesses," Morgan whispered back.

A lovely young woman nodded slightly at Rhys as she passed and Morgan watched his brother's next criticism die on his lips. Rhys's eyes followed the beauty, one with black hair and the flashing dark eyes foreign to English girls. Rhys watched her, but he spoke to Morgan. "May not be such a waste after all. Do you know who that is?"

"How good to know that your intellectual studies have not damaged your eyesight. She's a beauty, Rhys, but I'm willing to wager her English is minimal."

"I've always wanted to learn Spanish." Rhys gave her a slight bow as she passed from view. "Or do you think it would be Portuguese?"

"Whatever it is, Rhys, she will be guarded more fiercely than any of the English chits here. Do be careful."

Rhys only laughed.

The entry hall emptied quickly. Morgan nudged Rhys toward the patronesses. The next play of the hand was as predictable as the watered lemonade. "Go make your bow."

When Rhys looked at him, Morgan nodded. "I'm right behind you." *And yes, brother, I am using you as a shield.*

The patronesses were delighted to see them both and Morgan decided that he and Mrs. Lambert had been the only two people embarrassed by the lines in the morning paper, lines that were now the better part of a sennight old.

He bowed last to Countess Lieven, who promised him an evening perfectly suited to his "more recent inclinations." The arch smile that accompanied her words told him that more than one matron would be watching him.

In which case his first move would be to the card room. To arrive early was one thing, but to seek a dance partner immediately, when he had not graced these rooms in any number of years, would indicate a desperation that would only increase the gossips' notice.

Rhys walked with him. "Countess Lieven rapped my knuckles when I told her that my reason for coming to Town was academic and not social. She wanted to know who gave you a voucher. I *think* she was jesting."

"Grandmama asked for me." He had no idea what sort of magic Grandmama held, but Sally Jersey never said no to her.

When Rhys saw where they were headed, he stopped short. "No cards for me." He scanned the room. "I am going to find an introduction to that Spanish girl and ask her to dance."

He watched his brother cut across the floor, aiming directly for the dark-eyed beauty who had caught his attention. Morgan surveyed the room as the musicians invited the first dancers. No, definitely not the first dance. He buried himself in the card room for an hour until boredom with the small stakes permitted drove him to the dance floor.

This was the least he could do for Miss Lambert. The simple expedient of dancing with a variety of eligible young ladies would repair any harm to her Season. His good intentions were the only consolation for an evening that stretched out before him with no promise of real enjoyment.

Three sets and three carefully chosen partners later he was, at last, rewarded with a partner who could dance. If his first partner's eyes had reminded him of Christiana Lambert and his second partner's hair had been similar, then Miss Perry's vivacity was a copy of Miss Lambert's, but without any appreciation of the music that had brought them together.

Miss Perry did not sigh with pleasure when the first notes sounded, as Miss Lambert had, but chattered on about her hopes for the Season. Miss Perry accepted his hand graciously but certainly not with Miss Lambert's surprised glance of awareness. She moved with confidence, if not Miss Lambert's grace, and talked through the whole about the advantages of city shopping and the best milliners. By the time the set was over Morgan hoped he never saw—better yet, never *heard*—Miss Perry again.

No wonder he had not been to Almack's in years. But if he left this early he would undo any goodwill he had created. He would remain until shortly after the doors closed at eleven. Then he would pull Rhys from the arms of whatever young lovely had caught him and the two of them would find a suitable reward for this show of penance.

He heard a laugh he was sure he recognized and turned sharply, but it was a very tiny blonde, not the girl he had hoped to see. Admit it, he told himself, he had been gambling on Miss Lambert's appearance tonight. Apparently they had made other plans. The best he could hope for was that news of his venture to Almack's would reach James and add credibility to his supposed search for a bride. One more dance, he decided, then on to the Quarter Moon and some serious play.

As he was escorting his last partner back to her mama, he saw the Lambert party enter the room. They made their curtsies to the patronesses and he could see that Sally Jersey and Mrs. Lambert must, indeed, have been previously acquainted.

He watched the Lamberts as they found friends and exchanged pleasantries. His carefully orchestrated play would be ruined if he invited Christiana to dance the moment she entered the room.

When he found his attention drawn to her for the fifth time in less than two minutes, Morgan turned abruptly and left the dance floor.

With calculation designed to deter the scrutiny of

any observer, Morgan retreated to the card room once again, determined to stay there for two more dances.

He merely watched the play, though, and kept the dance floor in sight. He saw Joanna engaged with Lord Monksford while Christiana strolled by on the arm of a dashing member of the Horse Guards, one arm in a sling that would make dancing difficult.

With deliberate effort he turned his attention elsewhere, watching Monksford and Miss Lambert, wondering if they were enjoying the dance as much as it appeared they were.

Monksford was a stalwart, upstanding citizen, a widower with two daughters and apparently on the lookout for a wife. Let the gossipmongers print that, but they never would, for it was nothing out of the ordinary. There were dozens of men in this very room who were pursuing the same end. The couple passed the door once again, still smiling at each other.

"Do you think he would seriously consider Miss Lambert as his baroness?"

From anyone but Rhys the question would have drawn a snub. Instead he shrugged. How had Rhys identified Miss Joanna Lambert? When he remained silent, Rhys decided to answer for him.

"Monksford and Miss Lambert. It would be a perfect match from his perspective. She has an excellent pedigree and is young enough to give him the heir he needs. But she could do better. He is too old to find much pleasure in many more London Seasons and has two ready-made daughters who would demand his money and her time." Rhys drew the logical conclusion. "Monksford could not do better, Miss Lambert certainly could."

Morgan turned and looked directly at his brother with some amazement. "If this is your idea of conversation, I would suggest you join that group over there." He nodded toward the far side of the room where a group of women stood, nodding approval as their young charges danced.

Rhys glanced at the group and scowled. "I do sound like Grandmama! Do you suppose it's contagious?"

Morgan grinned. "I think it must be. Avoid the orgeat. I suspect that is where the potion is dispensed."

Rhys's hand went to his throat in a mock gesture of alarm and the two laughed aloud. They stepped back into the card room as more than one head turned in their direction.

"Go practice your whist, Rhys. This group plays at exactly your level." His brother laughed at the insult and headed for the card room and Morgan decided he had waited long enough. He would ask Miss Christiana to dance.

He walked toward the alcove where her mother stood, but he was too late. Lord Monksford was escorting Christiana to the floor and the music was about to begin.

It was Miss Joanna Lambert who was not engaged. Even better. He thanked the gods for intervening and approached her mama, who enthusiastically approved. Miss Lambert did not seem quite as eager. Had Christiana not been able to win her sister round to their way of thinking?

He took Miss Lambert's arm, determined to do his best.

They bowed to each other as the dance began.

Bare greetings and polite smiles were the sum total of their conversation through the first half of the dance. Everyone else in the set seemed at ease; the ladies had gained confidence, the young men had forgotten their consequence. They were enjoying the dance despite the poor quality of the music. But Miss Lambert was aloof from the general good humor. After the first few movements he was certain that his presence was the reason. She had enjoyed her dance with Lord Monksford.

His own discomfort grew as he realized that her coolness grew from more than disapproval of the plot that he and her sister had hatched. Joanna Lambert quite obviously did not like him.

It came to him as they finished their figure and moved to the bottom of the set. There might be some qualities of his sister Maddie in Christiana, but there were even more in Joanna. He saw it in her manner, in her quiet watchful way. It was in her eyes, in their purely honest expression. And the disappointment in anyone who did not treat her with the same courtesy.

She looked at him, surprised, when he missed a step. He took her arm and resumed the figure. "The truth is, Miss Lambert, you are making me nervous."

Joanna truly smiled and the smallest of laughs escaped. "And you are absurd, my lord."

"No, I am being completely honest." He knew if there was any hope of garnering her support then honesty was his only chance. He prayed to the god of would-be lovers that the prize was worth the risk.

The musicians brought the dance to a close with a rather ragged ending, each one choosing his own stop. Morgan took Miss Lambert's arm and began to escort her, very slowly, back to her party.

"I do believe that you think that your sister and I are tempting fate with the scheme we have devised."

Joanna looked at him. "The plan is a stupid one, my lord. You are too old and too experienced to find any merit in Christy's silly idea."

That was an honest response. Direct to the point of insult. Old? He would have preferred "mature" but perhaps "old" had been a deliberate choice. At least she was voicing her concerns instead of ignoring him completely.

"Miss Lambert, it is exactly my experience that makes me see the advantage in this. Both your sister and I are laboring under parental demands that do not suit us. We have found in each other a solution that will preserve family harmony and allow us to live the lives we have planned. Where is the fault in that?"

Joanna made an impatient sound. "I am not going to attempt to explain it to you, my lord. Your differences with your family are not my concern." Her look was a direct challenge. "I have always believed that Christiana trusts far too easily."

"I realize it. I truly do." He wanted to look away from those serious eyes. But he made himself hold her regard. He had opted for honesty, but never quite realized it would force him this far. "My sister Maddie once told me that sprites lived in the home wood and she told me it was a secret. I told our brothers and she cried when they took their toy guns there and went hunting for them. I learned then that once trust is lost it is not easily regained."

When he looked back at Joanna, he saw such surprise on her face that he stopped speaking. Did she think he had no sensibility? "I saw that same openness in Christiana that first night at Westbourne's ball and at every meeting since."

She was blushing and he spoke before she could stumble over an apology.

"And that trust is so important to me, Miss Lambert, that I promise you I will not abuse it. I will treasure it for the gift it is. I have learned from my childhood experience, you see."

Joanna stopped their slow progress and turned to look at him with an arrested expression. The blush was gone. She regarded him with such intensity that it seemed she was trying to read his mind. He waited with irritation. He had told the truth, more truth than he had ever told anyone, and this girl was still unsure of him.

"Very well, my lord. I am convinced."

The smile she was trying hard to restrain took some of the asperity from her matter-of-fact tone. The relief he felt was out of all proportion to her approbation. He tried to match her manner.

"Thank you, Miss Lambert. Your concern for your sister is everything that is admirable. We will rely on your good sense to keep us from making a mull of this charade."

"I have no skill as a conspirator, my lord." She took the arm he offered and they completed their long detour to her mama's side. "But I do promise you that I will hold your secret."

"That, *mademoiselle,* is all I ask. And I hope I will never again give you cause to doubt my sincerity." He bowed over her hand and left her. He desperately wanted something to drink, something stronger than whatever was available here. Even speaking with all the honesty he was capable of, he had earned only the most guarded acceptance. He hoped he would not ever have to plead for more.

Christiana tried to catch up with her sister and Lord Morgan as soon as the dance ended, but Lord Monksford seemed inclined to chat with the group who had been part of their set.

Joanna was still upset with her, despite Christiana's morning confession. The closeness they shared had been damaged by her lie and Christiana knew that Joanna was not yet entirely sure which story was the truth.

Lord Monksford took Christiana's arm and held it with a firmer than necessary grip. Christiana twisted her head round for one more look at Joanna and Lord Morgan, desperately wondering what they were speaking of with such serious faces.

"My dear Miss Lambert, if you continue to watch them so assiduously, you will attract exactly the sort of gossip that your mother wishes you to avoid."

Lord Monksford spoke in a conspiratorial whisper

that did not entirely rob his words of paternal reproach. "You need not worry. Your sister has enough maturity not to be taken in by Braedon's sort of charm."

Christiana stiffened. "His sort of charm, my lord?" She made it a question, and tried to control her irritation. *I hate your supercilious smile, you arrogant paper scull!*

Monksford was not wise enough to leave the subject alone. "My apologies, Miss Lambert. My concern for your sister has made me less than gracious to Lord Morgan. The Braedons have more charm than any one family needs. I would wish that they will always use it wisely."

Meaning Lord Morgan did not? It was a weak apology and Christiana decided that no matter how rich he was, Lord John Monksford was too severe to suit Joanna at all.

When Lord Morgan finally sought her out for a dance, it was Monksford's admonition as much as the touted Braedon charm that caused her to respond with radiant enthusiasm.

"Miss Lambert, if you continue to smile at me that way I will not be able to see clearly to follow the steps."

She made a face at him. "You say it charmingly, but still I hear censure. 'Tis only that I have been waiting all evening to have a word with you."

The dance floor was not the place for their conversation. He did not need to raise his eyebrows in warning. With a small sigh, she gave her attention to the music. By the time the dance was over and they bowed the conclusion, she was in charity with the world and everyone in it, even Lord Monksford.

Lord Morgan took her arm. "Our dance and this walk about the room are my reward for the time I have spent with each of my partners this evening. I thought to have a word with you without attracting attention. To do that I have had endless conversation with endless partners and their mamas so that this tête-à-tête would not appear singular. You may congratulate me on my foresight, my dear Sprite."

She laughed instead, charmed by the nickname, wondering what he meant by it. "Oh, I am certain it was a trial to dance with Miss Perry." She knew her sarcasm was at least saucy and at the worst an impertinence. "And Miss Halersham is, by all accounts, the prettiest girl here." It was so lovely to have someone she could gossip with and not feel as though she were being malicious.

Morgan squeezed her arm. "That is all a matter of opinion. But I swear by the gods of chance that not one of them dances like you do."

It was even lovelier to have someone who knew how to give a compliment. "That might be the truth, my lord, but only if you were always my partner."

"You seem in amazingly good spirits considering your sister's reluctance to approve our plan."

That brought their progress to a halt and erased her smile. "Did she say she opposed it?"

He shook his head. "But the last time I received such minimal approval was when my sister told me it would be all right for me to jump into a stream and try to catch a fish with my bare hands."

"Yes, Joanna was the same with me"—Christiana nodded slowly—"but she did agree even if it was half-hearted. The truth is we had words, an argument."

Lord Morgan took her arm again, urging her toward the chaperones, even though Mama did not seem the slightest bit interested in their whereabouts.

"I am sorry if I was the cause of difficulty with your sister. It is the last thing I would wish."

Christiana studied him, trying to gauge if his regret was sincere. The smile was genuine, but there was a reserve behind it that made her wonder how much of the true man she had yet to meet. She trusted him, of that she was certain, but she knew that she did not understand him at all. Oh, nonsense, she was being as romantic as she accused Joanna of being.

"It is not your scheme that upset her precisely. It was something else I said and most profoundly regret now." Oh, she sounded so maudlin. How foolish to be sad-hearted when tonight was made for gaiety. She looked at Lord Morgan, and looked away as quickly, when tears filled her eyes.

"If we have failed to amuse her then we must see if my brother can make her laugh."

How sweet of him to share the blame, when it is all my fault. She drew a deep breath and denied the melancholy.

"Look at your sister," Lord Morgan encouraged. "My brother Rhys has a charm for young ladies that totally escapes me."

Christiana saw Rhys handing a glass of lemonade to a laughing Joanna. "Oh, yes, that is so much better. It is how I truly love to see her. That gentleman is your brother? He must be charming."

"Let me introduce you to him and you may form your own opinion."

"But, my lord, we have not discussed—"

"And what is there to discuss? No matter how you wrested it from her, your sister has given her approval and neither of us needs convincing." He bowed over her hand.

It was all for show, of course, to prove to any curious observer that he was gracious and she was charmed. Then Lord Morgan straightened and smiled at her in a way that caught and held her heart as well as her eyes. It was a conspirator's smile, but there was enough of the lover in it to make her cheeks warm. "And so, my dear Miss Lambert, we begin."

Seven

By the time Sally was helping them out of their finery, Christiana's mind was filled with a dozen anecdotes for her journal, moments she wanted to remember even if Richard would not care about them. "Lord Rhys was so amusing."

Joanna nodded. "His imitation of Sally Jersey made me laugh aloud, but I was so afraid that someone would overhear him." Joanna yawned hugely. "You know if the patronesses knew of it, he would never receive a voucher again."

"Do you think he cares? I doubt it." Christiana sank into the slipper chair by the fire that had burned to coals, watching as Sally brushed Joanna's hair.

"Who else did you dance with?" she asked with carefully guarded curiosity.

"I think I enjoyed my dance with Lord Monksford the most."

She could see Joanna's considering gaze reflected in the mirror. It was not the name that Christiana had been hoping for, but her sister's tone caught her attention. Not dreamy, precisely. How could anyone be fanciful about a man as stuffy as Lord Monksford?

"He certainly has been dancing long enough to have acquired some skill."

"He does dance beautifully," Joanna agreed, "but

what I enjoyed the most is that he did not pay me one compliment. I detest compliments."

Christiana caught Sally's eye in the mirror and they shared a puzzled glance. It was the maid who spoke their common thought. "But, Miss Joanna, how can that be so? You be so deservin' of them and all."

Joanna shrugged, not sharing the smile the other two exchanged. That sobered them both immediately. Here was something that was really bothering Joanna.

"My hair is not the color of corn silk. Why do men think you need to hear that sort of thing?"

"Oh, miss," the maid answered again after a glance at Christiana, "I think that they are just looking for something to say that will please you."

Christiana nodded her approval.

"I would prefer real conversation like the kind I had with Lord Monksford and not idle compliments." Joanna warmed to her subject and spoke with true vexation.

"Yes, miss." Sally handed Joanna her cap and gathered up their clothes. She looked at her younger mistress with raised eyebrows, handing the subject off to her. This was a conversation that would be better finished between the two sisters, alone.

Christiana went to the bed and climbed up beside her sister as Joanna settled under the covers. "Remember that wide bed in the nursery we shared?"

Joanna nodded and smiled. "Covers pulled up to our chins with the moonlight coming through the gaps in the curtain. What did we talk about then?"

"What our dolls were doing while we slept. How annoying George and his friends were. All those things that are so important to little girls." She paused. "Sometimes I miss that."

Joanna reached over and took her sister's hand. "We are as close as ever, even if we do not share the same room or the same bed anymore."

"I hope so, Joanna; I hope that I did not spoil it all last night."

"Of course not. You shocked me, I will admit it, but then I can think of a dozen other times that you have shocked me and we are still as close as sisters can be, are we not?"

"That is such a relief." Christiana felt her heart lighten. "A dozen times, Jo?"

"Oh at least, Christy." She smiled and settled back against the pillows. "The time you put a frog in Miss Andrew's drawer and then let George take the blame. That was wicked, sister dear."

Joanna was grinning now and Christiana guessed that her shock then had been more pleasure than pain.

"Or the time you told Papa you were going to visit the sickly tenants and instead spent the hour spying on George and the Wiltons."

Ah, yes, she was fourteen then and beginning to realize her feelings for Richard were not at all sisterly. "But that time I was punished."

Joanna laughed. "If you can count being sent to your room without dinner when everyone knew Sally would smuggle you a tray."

"But it was missing the family's companionship—that was the true penalty. I was so sure that I was missing something wonderful. It really was a punishment."

"I love you for trying to distract me from my sullens." She settled back, pulling the covers closer to her. "We both know it is fatigue that brings on these megrims. A good night's sleep and even Mr. Bathright's silly suggestion that no lemonade would be sweet enough for me will seem more amusing than stupid."

"It is much as Sally says, Joanna, those absurdities are just a nervous young man's way of filling the silence."

"I know, and I must learn to be a better flirt, I suppose."

"There is a way of looking from under your lashes that can be very effective." Christiana paused to make sure she had her sister's attention and then demonstrated. "Have you tried it?"

Joanna mimicked the gesture and they both laughed.

Christiana climbed down and pulled the covers around her sister, happy that she was smiling again. Perhaps she would try one final time to get some information on the only name her sister had failed to mention. "Lord Morgan made you smile."

"He did." Joanna turned on her side and looked at her sister, propping her head on her hand, the ghost of a smile hovering. "He told me any number of things. One of them was that my wariness and concern for you was everything that was admirable. And that he would rely on me not to let him make a mull of your charade."

Christiana waited for more, but Joanna let her hand fall and settled back into her pillow. "Is that all?"

"All I have the energy for tonight." Joanna yawned. "Did you know he had a sister who died?"

"No I did not know that!" Christiana had been about to pick up the candle and move to the door, but that piece of information ended her thoughtful inclinations. "What was her name? Why did he tell you about her?"

Joanna turned away from the light and settled into the pillow. "Her name was Maddie and you remind him of her."

"Oh." She sat on the edge of the bed. "Well, that should be flattering but somehow it is rather deflating."

"I knew I should have waited until tomorrow to mention that." With a yawning sigh, Joanna turned back toward her. "You must admit, Christy, that his comparison is so much better than a more romantic analogy, for your whole plan hinges on avoiding such complications."

"Hmmm," Christiana acknowledged. "But, Jo, to remind him of his sister is so plebeian. You must admit, that you would run miles from anyone who reminded you of George."

Joanna smiled but otherwise ignored that comment. "The thing is, there is always the chance that one of you could mistake the game for the real thing. I worry that someone will be hurt in this."

"Are you doubting my devotion to Richard?" She did not want to argue again, but this lack of faith could not be borne.

Joanna reached out and touched her sister's arm as though trying to bridge a gap. "I would not doubt you for one minute, especially after what you told me last night. No, it's Lord Morgan I wonder about."

"Oh, Joanna, never worry about him. He has been at this game since before we learned to dance. The whole thing was his idea even if it does suit my needs perfectly. He only wants to appease his family. By his own admission he is not ready for a wife. No, if there is anyone who can control his emotions it is Lord Morgan Braedon."

This is a farce, a ploy to outsmart your brother and his ridiculous demands. Morgan had been reminding himself of that for the last twelve hours, but neither endless repetition nor a cold gray morning could destroy the sense of anticipation, excitement, even happiness, damn it, that had him smiling as he dressed.

As Roberts lathered him for a shave Morgan tried to convince himself that his elation came from his success at the tables last night. The game he'd found when he left Almack's had kept him up until dawn, but the money won would build the new stable and thatch his tenants' cottages.

Roberts straightened from his task. "If you keep grinning like that, milord, you will be making your calls with several cuts on your chin."

He managed to keep his face expressionless for the rest of his shave by recollecting the bottle of brandy he had drunk before play. The god of chance had smiled on him, for his fellow gamesters had been even more bosky than he was. The foolishness of imbibing when he had so much to win in so little time was enough to sober anyone, even a man anticipating a flirtation with the loveliest of women.

What should his next step be? He was certain of one thing. He was going to approach this false courtship with as much decorum as one Season would permit, his goal quite simply put: never to appear in the gossip columns again unless it suited his own ends.

By the time Roberts pronounced him fit for public appearance Morgan had considered being obvious and paying a morning call, going for a stroll, and relying on chance to bring him down the same street as the shop-loving Misses Lamberts or wager on the certainty that they would be in the park later in the afternoon. It was that rare night when no balls or rout invitations had been delivered, so that was not an option. A call, he decided, and for the sake of the gossipmongers, more than one.

He thanked the gods of good fortune for smiling on him and hurried downstairs for breakfast. The moment he walked into the breakfast room, he knew he had given thanks too soon.

James was at the table.

Sitting at his accustomed place, James was reading the morning paper as though he'd done it every day for the past week. He gave no word of greeting. He spared Morgan no more than a glance.

Damn, but he hated this kind of surprise. What was James doing in London? He had enough to keep him busy at Braemoor for the entire Season. He could ask, but it was unlikely that James would tell him. He did so favor intrigue.

Morgan sent the footman for fresh coffee and sat down. "Are your spies so unreliable that you felt the need to check on me yourself?"

James set the paper aside, favoring him with the smile he had learned from their father. The one that matched the cool distance in his eyes. "You flatter yourself." He sipped his coffee. "There was some business in Town and I thought I would tend to it myself."

James needed to get away from their father. From Braemoor. Morgan could understand that. He crushed the sympathetic thought. "How is father?"

James shook his head. "In some ways the marquis is better, in others not improving at all." He paused and, with uncharacteristic directness, answered the question Morgan was really asking. "I no longer think he is on his deathbed, but a full recovery is doubtful."

That must make your life hell, Morgan thought. The footman returned with the coffee and the two settled into more polite conversation.

"Have you seen Rhys?" Morgan asked. It was obvious from the depleted state of the sideboard that Rhys had been in the room recently.

"Watched him eat breakfast." The coolness disappeared and the brothers shared a smile. James continued. "I did manage to get a few words from him. He tells me that Almack's was a great success for the both of you."

"It was a pleasant enough evening and we both danced with a number of lovely ladies."

"Including a Miss Lambert?"

"Both Miss Lamberts, Miss Perry, Miss Halersham, and a dozen others whose names I do not recall." Morgan ignored James's smile and tried to control his own rising irritation.

"Morgan, I saw the betting book at White's."

Morgan looked at the footman, who nodded and left

the room. The staff knew every detail of Braedon life whether they were in the room or not. But for the moment, Morgan wanted the illusion of privacy.

"I noticed there is no bet from you entered against it." James pushed his coffee cup away and looked at his brother with suspicion. "If the wager were false I would assume a counterbet would be an easy way to make a few pounds. As far as I can see, gambling to win is your sole purpose when in Town."

James leaned closer to him. "What are you doing with all that money, Morgan? I heard that you won over a thousand pounds last night. It's not as though your lodgings cost you anything. So where does the money go?"

"I gamble, James." There was no way in Hades he was going to tell his brother what his hard-won blunt was for. Morgan was certain that James would do his best to sabotage his plans for the property if it suited his needs. "I play faro, whist, hazard. I win and I lose and I do occasionally pay a bill and loan money to friends."

James was unconvinced. "Is it blackmail, Morgan, some by-blow you refuse to acknowledge?"

"No it is not." He had been very careful on that score.

"Or perhaps you are actually trying to improve that property your mother left you in Wales?"

"Why would I do that, James?" Morgan allowed a small smile, just enough to reflect how unlikely James's all-too accurate guess had been. "Do you think I would actually live there?" He waved away the idea. "I would rather take my chances with the French; besides I can make twice what that property will earn in one Season at the tables."

"Hmmm. I never did think land management would have any appeal to you." James relaxed back in his chair.

He was safe. James would never guess how much

he had learned about agriculture in the past two years. Coke's progressive farming methods had been like a foreign language. Now he could talk knowledgeably about that and a dozen other innovations he was counting on to turn his property to real profit.

If he could ignore the fact that James was his brother and had once been his closest friend, he could treat him like the antagonist he'd become.

What he wanted to keep secret, James would never guess. He'd mastered the player's façade much earlier in life and with less effort than it took to understand farming techniques.

"But I digress. How or where you spend your funds will soon be of no concern to me. Since there is no answering bet on the books, can I assume that you have found yourself a match?"

Morgan laughed, a genuine eye-watering burst of sound. "Why is my social life everyone's favorite subject this Season? Oh, James, Braemoor must be sadly lacking if that is what has brought you to Town."

"Have you?"

"Why the hurry, James?" Morgan loved the edge of irritation that James could not quite mask. "The Season is under way and I am following the prescribed course. And no matter how boring life is at Braemoor I have no intention of reporting every dance and picnic to you."

James nodded. "Just so you are not trying to play some wily game, Morgan. I want you engaged by the end of the year, sooner, if you can manage it."

"Finding a bride is not as easy as buying a bottle of wine." This time Morgan controlled his mirth. "Surely you would give me some time to find a chit I can live with without contemplating murder."

"Why should you be any different from the rest of the *ton?*"

James's cynicism was damn irritating.

"I am paying a call this morning. That should make

you happy." Morgan rose from the table. He would get something to eat at his club later.

James tossed his napkin on the table and rose with him. "Excellent. I think I will go along with you."

"James, I do not need or want a nursemaid. You are not invited."

James shrugged away that detail. "Just one call or did you have several in mind?"

"I think two calls only, since it is so late in the day." For his own reasons he was anxious to get the scheme under way. Besides it would prove to James that he was making the effort. "Two calls, yes, the Lambert sisters and," he improvised, "Miss Perry."

By the time they were approaching the Lamberts' Green Street town house, Morgan was feeling a jolt of unaccustomed nerves. He was used to playing alone, relying on his own wits and no one else's. Now he must count on Christiana and even Joanna, to some extent, to play the game with him, without time to plan.

"Is he your competition?"

Morgan saw Lord Monksford approach from the opposite direction just as James spoke.

Not realizing he was being observed, Monksford stopped for a moment, straightening his jacket and checking his boots to be sure their shine bore up in the daylight.

As if a new coat and freshly polished boots would give him an advantage over much younger suitors. The little vanity made Morgan smile. Monksford saw the look as he caught sight of not one, but two Braedons. Morgan nodded from several feet away and Monksford returned the barest of acknowledgments.

"The Right Honorable Lord Monksford is not one of your closer friends?" James whispered.

"Is it me or all Braedons?" Morgan looked at James, who was trying not to smile. "I have no idea what I have ever done to earn his disapproval. The

truth is I like the way his mind works. I've heard him
at White's carry on, oh about the Cintra Conventions
for example, and the Peninsular campaign in general.
Except for his obvious disdain, I think we would find
that we share any number of the same opinions."

"How odd that you care." James touched Morgan's
arm in an unusual gesture of comfort that undid his
cynical tone. "He detests me, not you, Morgan."
James stopped abruptly. "I will tell you the story some
other time."

While they were being announced, the three exchanged the most civil of pleasantries. As they remained waiting in a strained silence, Morgan realized
that Monksford was not much older than James. It
was his thinning hair and sober manner that added to
his thirty-odd years.

When the butler returned and held the door for
them, Monksford stepped in first. The room was not
crowded precisely, but there were at least four other
young men and several ladies. Mrs. Lambert was
basking in her daughters' success, while those two
were receiving the attentions of their callers in ways
he could have exactly predicted.

Miss Lambert was seated on a small sofa, talking
earnestly with a young man who was flushed from his
efforts to be charming. Miss Christiana Lambert was
standing near the window, trying to entertain all of
her guests at once, and succeeding, if the light laughter was any indication.

Lord Monksford was greeted warmly by Mrs. Lambert, but nothing could match her effusive flattery
when Morgan introduced his brother, Viscount Crandall.

Mrs. Lambert turned her back to Morgan and took
James's arm, calling Joanna to her side instantly, making a pointed introduction. James was coolly polite.
As if that would put the oblivious Mrs. Lambert in
her place, Morgan thought.

Joanna saw it, though, and Morgan was intrigued to see that her ice matched James. Joanna Lambert was loyal, of that there was no doubt. And as equipped to best James as a dove was against a hawk.

Most of her would-be beaux knew when the game had gone beyond their purse. None would approach her after James had been given such singular attention by Mrs. Lambert. But John Monksford was not young or easily intimidated.

If Joanna was a dove then Monksford was a bantam rooster, used to his own superiority and unaware that he was hardly in the same league as James.

As Monksford approached them, Miss Lambert turned and offered him her hand with a welcoming smile. In those two gestures Morgan read more pleasure in his visit than relief at her supposed rescue.

Now Christiana was free and he turned to her, trusting that James could handle this social challenge without his help.

Christiana welcomed him with two hands outstretched and a smile that made her eyes sparkle with excitement. She was dressed this morning in a charming muslin, white and cut rather low. The shawl she carried was for show rather than warmth, a silk in a daring blue that contrasted with the white and helped to explain the *décolletage*. Christiana Lambert's sense of style mirrored her approach to life, testing the conventions, hoping to make the world dance to her tune. And a merry one it was.

He took her offered hands and bowed over them.

"Oh, Lord Morgan, I am so pleased to see you."

It was a conventional greeting, but spoken with unconventional warmth. He smiled in approval and she lowered her voice.

"My lord, I think I would have been quite a success on stage." Then she blushed. "Though I am quite pleased to see you, truly."

He pressed her hand gently and let it go. "Yes, I

can see that. And your voice does have a quality of projection that would rival any of our current actors. But let us be quiet a moment."

He turned slightly and she had to turn as well so that she could give him her full attention. It had the added advantage of blocking her face from James's view. "I can see I timed my call quite perfectly. You have had a chance to charm any number of young men and they have seen that I am among the competition."

She laughed, but it was a quiet, conspiratorial sound, no more than a breath against his cheek. "What is next?" she whispered.

"We will not stand here and plot. We will enjoy each other's company and set the scene for our future meetings."

"But what is next?" she insisted.

"A surprise," he insisted with a smile and turned so they faced the room again.

It was then that Christiana saw Lord Monksford talking with Joanna and his brother.

"Who is that with Joanna and Lord Monksford?" She spoke with an element of awe in her voice. James did have that effect on people. There was an arrogance about him that made him hard to ignore.

She turned toward him and Morgan leaned closer, closer than he should, and breathed in the youth and vibrancy she wore like a scent. "That is my brother, James."

She clapped her hands together and her grin grew twofold. "Oh, that is perfect, absolutely perfect. He is the one we want to impress, is he not?"

When had the gods of mischief been let loose? With sudden vehemence doubts assailed him. It was too soon to put their charade to this test.

Eight

Christiana looked toward James without making the slightest effort to disguise her curiosity. Morgan took her hand and hoped that her mother was not watching. "We will not overplay this, Sprite. Your mother and my brother need only see our interest in each other. No dramatics."

She nodded politely, but her beautiful eyes were sparking with the challenge. "Yes, I do understand, really I do. We must stand here a moment longer and chat." She paused. "Then you will introduce me?"

"I suppose I must." Morgan tried to imbue his voice with some enthusiasm.

"Thank you." Christiana spoke with finality and then turned briefly to look at the group. When she turned back, she was composed and amiable. She was everything a young lady should be. Her eyes had quieted, even her gown appeared more demure. Had she left her excitement with the blue shawl now draped across the nearest chair?

"Have you ever noticed, my lord, how lovely my sister is when she speaks with real animation?"

She spoke with such primness that he was the one who grinned. "How do you do that?" he whispered, breaking his own rule.

"I think of what is at stake," she hissed at him.

He nodded, properly chastised, and subdued his

smile. Glancing toward the group, he realized that she was right. At this moment Joanna Lambert was more than lovely. Her dress was as simple as Christiana's, muslin also but washed through with blue and of far more conservative cut than her sister's. It suited her slimmer figure and more serious mien and the color of her dress made her eyes more blue than gray. Was it the conversation that added the color to her cheeks and eyes? She was talking seriously to Lord Monksford and James. And both men were listening.

Christiana shook her head, her eyes brimming with disappointment. "I do not understand why she is so taken with Lord Monksford."

"You do not think my brother is the one responsible for that glow?" Morgan had been among the *ton* long enough to have witnessed more than one unusual alliance.

"Decidedly not. Your brother is too intimidating by far. It is Lord Monksford who has captured her fancy."

Oh, how he would love to use that in the betting book at White's, but if Monksford disliked him now, he would surely give him the cut direct if he became the butt of the kind of gossip that was routine for a Braedon.

"You think James is intimidating? Your sister does not look the least bit impressed."

"It is precisely because Monksford is there as a buffer." Christiana waved her hand. "Joanna says she likes Monksford best of all the men she has danced with, but I think he just makes her feel comfortable. He must be nearly as old as Papa. And I know Joanna misses Papa's kindnesses right now."

Morgan felt for the man. Monksford was not even five-and-thirty and at least one Lambert saw him as nothing more than a father figure. "He looks older because he favors all the wrong colors. That brown jacket ages his skin as surely as it would a woman with his coloring."

"Yes." She spoke in a considering tone. "That could be it, but we can hardly walk up to him and suggest a different tailor, can we?" She giggled, and then stifled it.

"I generally respect what he has to say," he said, wondering why he was defending the man twice in one day. "Apparently your sister does too."

Joanna was nodding at something James was saying and then turned to Monksford, following his words with an enthusiastic speech of her own.

Christiana's face grew more serious. "But she could have so much more than a suitor who can talk knowledgeably about . . ."

Her voice trailed off and Morgan supplied the subject. "Farming. He can discuss the latest farming methods with knowledge and is not embarrassed to admit that he cares about his tenants almost as much as he cares about his land."

Christiana looked at him with a teasing smile. "Just as Papa can."

Despite the smile, Morgan could tell that this was a debate he would not win. If he was going to defend Monksford, it would profit him more to do it within the hearing of Miss Joanna Lambert.

"Before they solve all the problems for this growing season, come and meet James." Morgan took her arm and nodded at the trio. Morgan congratulated himself on his timing. The twenty-minute call was at an end. There would be only a minute or two for conversation.

As they moved toward the group, Christiana paused and clapped her free hand to her mouth. "Oh, how selfish of me! Does your brother's visit to Town mean that your father is better?"

"James says he improves, but he is still abed."

"That must be good news for all of you." The statement sounded like a question. "It must be so difficult."

"It is, Sprite. It truly is." Difficult was only one of the words he would use and certainly the most polite.

As the introductions were made, Joanna and Monksford took advantage of the interruption to step aside for a few moments of more private conversation.

James bowed to Christiana with appealing deference. She summoned a smile that managed to be both serious and sympathetic. "Your brother tells me that your father is improving daily. I am so happy to hear that and hope he will be truly recovered before long."

James responded with the expected and Morgan watched as Christiana's grave smile turned impish. "Does that mean you will be in Town long enough for me to learn whether you dance with as much skill as your brother?"

Minx, Morgan thought. *Flirting is as natural to her as seduction is to James.* That could be an incendiary combination.

"Not on this occasion, Miss Lambert. But I will be happy to prove my dancing ability when next I come to Town." James's smile actually reached his eyes. "Surely I will be back to London before the Season ends."

"I will consider it a promise, my lord. You now owe me a dance. Though you do face formidable competition in your brother."

Morgan wondered if she might be overdoing it. It was singularly difficult to view this exchange with any objectivity. But it did seem that her flirtation was conveying just the right element of interest in him.

Then Morgan realized that she was genuinely enjoying his brother. That was much of her charm. Her flirting was only a thin cover for the sincere pleasure she found in almost everyone and everything.

James gave her a slight bow. "I look forward to it, Miss Lambert. Have you ever known brothers who did not enjoy the chance to best each other?"

Christiana laughed, not some ingénue's giggle, but

one of true amusement. She reached out and touched James's arm as if she wanted to be sure she had his attention.

She did. James was smiling at her with open admiration.

Jealousy welled up in Morgan and froze his smile into something less than benevolent. He did his best to tamp it down. His heart was not involved here, he reminded himself. Only a little pride.

Before Christiana could speak again, her mother noticed the cozy tableau. Mrs. Lambert moved across the room with all the purpose of a soldier who did not want to miss any of the action. Stepping between them, she smiled at James. "What a pleasure to have you visit, my lord. Will you be at the Ponsonbys'? Joanna and I will be there as will Lord Morgan I understand."

It was a heavy-handed attempt to divert his attention from the younger daughter to the older. And James could interpret that any number of ways, Morgan decided.

They were away within moments. Morgan gave the coachman the direction to Miss Perry's while noting James's silence. His brother sat very still, flicking open his snuffbox and then closing it again with a snap. He repeated the motion a few more times without taking any snuff. "It would be just like you to pretend attention to the younger sister when it is really Miss Lambert who has caught your fancy."

True, Morgan thought.

"But then again," James continued with the air of one thinking aloud, "the older sister has a brain so she could not be the one you are interested in."

Morgan ignored the insult. It was hardly worthy of James. Besides, he had seen James in conversation with both sisters. He would be willing to wager the enamel box in his pocket against the one James was worrying, that it was Miss Christiana whom he would seek out again.

Still opening and closing his snuffbox, James turned to Morgan. "It is the younger one, is it not? The cut of her dress alone would have insured my attention. And what is her shortcoming? You gave me a rather daunting list at breakfast. I saw none in her, beyond a charming inclination to flirt outrageously."

Morgan relaxed his expression, struggling for an answer. Then it occurred to him that he did not have to disavow her appeal. He merely had to buy himself time. He shrugged. "She is young."

James closed the lid with a final decisive snap and slipped it into his pocket. "Hardly a failing when you are not yet thirty."

"No, but her parents are anxious for her to have an enjoyable Season and make the most of her opportunities." There were at least three or four ways James could interpret that.

"Meaning that her avaricious mother hopes she will find someone with a more promising income than that of a gamester."

And trust him to choose the most cynical. That might work, Morgan thought. But if James believed her parents looked on him with disfavor, he would question Morgan's continued courtship. "The Braedon name will excuse any number of indiscretions. You know that as well as I do."

"Yes, I do," James drawled. He looked out the window of the coach as it moved slowly past Hyde Park toward the Perrys'. "The Lamberts could not do better than the match. And do not doubt Mama knows it."

What would it take to ease James's bitterness, Morgan wondered. "Why not stay on for the Ponsonbys'?" No sooner were the words out of his mouth than Morgan cursed his fraternal concern. The last thing he wanted was James's continued presence. Besides, he suspected it would take more than a few days in Town to cure what ailed his brother.

James dismissed his brother's suggestion. "I return to Braemoor as soon as possible. Even these few days away allows for too much mischief."

"Then perhaps you could return for the Hawthorne Masquerade at the end of the Season." He felt safe mentioning it for he could see James was taking his new responsibilities very seriously. Once he was back at Braemoor he would not come back to London without an urgent need. A masquerade was about as urgent as James's need for a new snuffbox. "James, exactly why *are* you come to Town?"

James looked for a moment as though he might actually tell him when the carriage lurched to a stop. "Here we are at Miss Perry's. Tell me, Morgan, does she flirt with as much grace as Miss Lambert?"

James came no closer to answering Morgan's question until they returned from the last of their calls.

"Do you have plans for the evening, Morgan?"

"I am going to find a game of faro and win myself enough for a new pair from Tattersall's. White's for dinner first, I think." Morgan realized as soon as the words were spoken that his plans should have sounded more definite. "I want the evening to myself. My plans do not include dinner with you."

"I want you and Rhys to have dinner with me and then I want to visit several of the haunts you so favor." James named four, completely ignoring Morgan's objection.

"Not one of those hells is in my usual style. If you want to gamble let me take you to—"

James cut him off with, "I have a specific purpose for visiting those four and a reason for wanting both of you with me."

Anger flashed through him. James was treating him like a flunky who he could order at will. He was not a puppet, damn it. "It would be easier to garner my cooperation, and Rhys's, too, I imagine, if you shared the supposed reason."

"You only need to be there and you will understand."

He almost refused, damn the consequences, but the gods knew there were a bare handful of times when James had sought his company, much less implied he needed help. He was not flattered, Morgan decided, but he was curious. He resigned himself to a tedious evening, trying to determine the answer to one of James's infernal intrigues.

The Braedon brothers encountered Peter Wilton at the second club they visited. Morgan decided that Wilton was as close as he would be to Christiana all evening.

He still had no idea why James had insisted on his company, but he had won enough at the first hell to appease his irritation at being led around like a tame dog.

Rhys had come along willingly. He was still young enough to be flattered by the invitation to join his elders. As the carriage clattered from home to the clubs beyond Mayfair, Rhys chattered on about applying some of the scientific principles he'd learned to gambling.

For a moment, Morgan regretted his unwillingness to fleece his own brother. James looked at him and smiled and Morgan responded with a shrug. Between the two of them they should be able to prevent anyone else from doing so as well. It had not proved too much of a challenge so far.

"I actually won at Barton's." Rhys patted his pocket, and the jingle of coins attested to his success.

The brothers settled into the carriage and it began its slow progress to the next place on James's list.

"We noticed," James said.

"Beginner's luck," Morgan cautioned. "Jolly Jack's is an entirely different kind of place."

James nodded. "Run by a former naval officer who used his prize money to fund the place. Have you been to Jack's before, Morgan?"

"Once or twice," Morgan admitted. "Given its location, it attracts as many wealthy cits as members of the *ton*."

"And," James added, "given the owner's background, tends to be filled with whatever members of His Majesty's Navy as can make their way to Town with money still in their pockets."

Rhys nodded, apparently considering their words as a source of information rather than an urge to caution.

Given the popularity of the place, Morgan was not at all surprised when young Wilton hailed them shortly after they passed their hats and capes to the porter.

"Braedon, I say, Braedon!" he called as he approached them. He grabbed Rhys by the hand and shook it with enthusiasm. "Well met. I was hoping to see you again before you left Town."

Pleasantries were exchanged as the foursome made their way into the first room. Here quiet prevailed. The card tables were set up for whist and at least twenty men were concentrating on their cards. Morgan paused to scan the faces, looking for acquaintances, and then stopped short.

He did not know the man, who was deeply engrossed in play, but felt as though he should. Rather than stare, he moved on, thinking he had found the reason for this evening's quest.

The next room was much noisier and they paused there as Peter turned to look again at James. "Have you a relative in the navy, my lord?"

At James's disclaimer, Wilton looked puzzled. "The thing is, there is a gentleman playing whist who could be your brother—the same hair though much bleached by the sun, the same eyes, and a deeply tanned face, which is what leads me to assume he is a navy man on leave or one who recently left the service."

James shrugged, but he did glance back at the whist room, his eyes narrowing as they found the Braedon look-alike. The cards still had the man's whole attention and he was so engrossed in play that he never once looked up. James shrugged and turned away. Morgan understood exactly what that meant. None of them would want an introduction to a man who was most likely an illegitimate connection of some sort.

Wilton accepted the snub with aplomb and then turned to Morgan. "I had a letter from Richard today. I have just taken it to Christiana as Richard suggested."

Morgan's polite smile froze in place. With a sidelong glance, he noted, with relief, that James was paying no attention to the conversation.

Wilton noticed it, too, and as Morgan struggled to name a god on whom he could call for help, Peter drew James's attention, explaining, "Richard is my older brother off fighting in Portugal."

James smiled politely. "With Wellesley returned to Spain, they should be ready to give Boney's troops a fight."

"You should hear what he has to say! I was not at all certain that it was something Christiana should see, but if she has hopes of marrying a soldier she will not be shielded for long."

Morgan swore mentally. Every creative curse he had learned from childhood on echoed through his brain while he tried to find a way to undo the mess Peter Wilton was creating.

"Indeed that is so," James murmured, looking directly at Morgan. "Miss Christiana Lambert, you say? I do believe I met her today."

Peter nodded. "We are neighbors from home. Known each other forever."

A particularly loud cheer from the roulette table drew Wilton's attention to the play at hand. "I say, my lord, will you excuse me? I should like to try my luck." Wilton looked at Rhys and the two were off to see if they could stir up some cheers on their own behalf.

Morgan had faced worse situations, he was sure of it. There was the time he had been accused of cheating by that fool Gordon and once he had been challenged to a duel for an imagined insult. On both those occasions he had honesty on his side for he had been guilty of neither. This time the truth was ever so slightly shaded. All right, he should at least be honest with himself; the truth was under the heaviest of clouds. Still there had to be a way to make it sound right.

James remained silent. He simply watched Morgan with a question in his eyes.

"Yes, yes, yes, I know about the soldier. But, James, there is no engagement and as far I know this is mere speculation on Wilton's part. As he said, the Wiltons and Lamberts have been friends since childhood, nothing more."

James laughed. "And you hope to convince her that some inveterate gamester is a more worthy match than a soldier, one serving in the heart of the action no less."

James made it sound as though she would be choosing between a deuce of clubs and the ace of spades. And he was not the ace.

"No, not a more worthy match. But perhaps a more . . ." He stopped then. He was not about to justify his behavior to his brother. "James, you only said that I must find a match by the end of the year. As long as I fulfill your ridiculous demand, what does it matter whom I choose or how I win her?"

James shrugged. "Very well, my brother, but do not doubt for a moment that this one Season is all the time you have to find someone eligible."

It will be all the time I need, he thought, but he merely nodded his understanding of James's ultimatum. He gestured toward the vingt-et-un table. "Shall we try our luck too? Or shall we rescue Rhys before he loses his quarter allowance at faro?"

Rhys lost, but not more than was acceptable. Despite that he was slumped with disappointment in the carriage as they headed home, apparently still trying to figure out the mysteries of faro. "I really thought I had the key to winning."

James punched his arm with brotherly superiority. "And that may be true but unfortunately you wear your prospects as well as Grimaldi does his clown's mask. There can be no doubt what you are up to. Give it up, Rhys. You will never make your fortune at the gaming tables."

His own success had cured Morgan's temper but he still wanted to confirm his earlier suspicion.

"James, I rarely find the kind of games you prefer entertaining. Riddles and puzzles are best reserved for children. But since I think I was able to solve at least the first part of this one I must admit to some curiosity as to the rest." Morgan held his brother's gaze and waited.

Apparently the prospect of a game he could win improved Rhys's humor. He volunteered his answer before Morgan spoke again. "It was the naval officer at Jack's, was it not? He was what you were looking for this evening. And you wanted us along . . ." Rhys stopped short and looked puzzled. "Why *did* you want us along?"

"Moral support?" James offered.

"To see if we saw the resemblance." Morgan knew that was it.

James nodded. "I had no idea the resemblance was so marked. I think a stranger would have mistaken us for brothers."

It was so rare to hear James sound unsettled that

Morgan thought support may indeed have been one of the reasons he wanted them along.

"Do we have any idea how that navy officer is connected to us?" Morgan asked, for he undoubtedly was.

"Only the obvious," Rhys supplied.

James shook his head, but without any great conviction. "What other explanation is there?"

Morgan could think of one or two. "He could be the perfectly legitimate child of one of your mother's relations. We have had no contact with them for dozens of years."

"It could be and I have no idea why the marquis was so set on me coming to Town to verify this man's existence. Now I can tell him I have. The hell of it is I suspect he will have forgotten all about it by the time I return home."

Morgan was out of the coach before he realized that James was not coming. "Are you going back to Jolly Jack's?"

James shook his head.

Then where was he going? The answer followed on the heels of the question. Morgan smiled and paused at the door of the carriage. "Does she have a friend?"

"No." James shook his head as if the one word was not discouragement enough. "And she no more wants a *ménage à trois* than you do." He sat back and reached for his snuffbox. "Besides, what would your provincial Miss Lambert think of such lewd behavior?"

James reached over and pushed his brother off the carriage step. By the time Morgan regained his balance, the carriage was well down the street. When he turned around he found that Rhys had hurried away to hail a hackney that was delivering passengers nearby.

There were no stars to watch in London. What exactly did an astronomer do when the night sky was obscured?

Morgan stood in the street, his eyes adjusting to the night and a moon that was older than it was new. He had no need of some friend of his brother. His mistress awaited his pleasure not very many blocks away.

Instead he walked up the steps of Braedon House and bid a surprised Brixton good evening. Settling in the library with a bottle of brandy, Morgan considered his future.

He certainly did not consider "his Miss Lambert" as provincial as James thought, but he was not at all certain how she would react to the knowledge of a town house he paid for occupied by a woman that he knew in the most intimate sense.

With a deep sigh and a taste of the brandy, Morgan decided it was time to give *chère* Celine her *congé*. He could accept a few weeks of celibacy in exchange for a lifetime of independence. He was almost sure he could.

Morgan grimaced as a more practical thought occurred to him. It was another way to save money, which was the main thing he hoped to gain from this farce.

Morgan moved closer to the fire, put down his glass, loosened his cravat, and wondered why he was the lone Braedon sitting at home with a bottle of brandy for company. *Oh, my dear Sprite, I hope you had a more enjoyable evening than I have.*

Nine

"Oh, how *can* Richard find pleasure in such danger!" Christiana tossed the letter aside for the fifth time and took a deep breath, trying to control the tears of anger that threatened.

Joanna rescued the much-read letter from the floor. "I think it was wrong of Peter to bring it to you even if his father did give him permission." She folded it with care. "I think it would be best if we sent it back to Sir Howard with our thanks for sharing it."

"No!" Christiana reached for the paper, walked to her bed, and tucked it under the pillow. "I want to keep it awhile longer. Richard wrote those words and folded the paper. It is as close to him as I can be for much too long."

Christiana wished that she had a miniature of Richard, for she found that she had difficulty remembering the exact color of his eyes. Were they as clear and blue as Lord Morgan's and was his smile as playful? No, it was not, she knew that, but she was hard-pressed sometimes to recall it at all these days. Surely that was because their trip to London had brought with it so very many new people.

"Tell me, Joanna, how is it that he can talk so manfully of the poor food and miserable tents? He makes that sound worse than the skirmishes they have encountered." She already had the most troubling parts memorized.

"To speak the truth, Christy, I think it would be more manly of him not to complain about the food and weather. It will make nothing but worry for those who love him."

Christiana was barely listening. Why had he not mentioned her name once in the entire letter? He had suggested that his family share it with "friends." Is that how he thought of her now that they were separated by a great distance and an endless war?

"As if we are not worried enough already," she said in frustration. "How can he treat it as though he were playing with toy soldiers? How can he say that the enemy is worse off than they are? How does he know that? They could have more guns, or better transport, and perhaps they are lying in wait for them."

Christiana began to pace the room.

"Oh, this is awful, Joanna. My nerves are making me so restless. If only it were still light, then we could go for a walk in the park. I need some distraction, some way to forget that he is in danger and loving every moment while I am here with nothing but fear for company."

"You have me."

"Oh, dearest, I am very bad, am I not?" She rushed over and knelt by Joanna. "Complaining about my trials when I should be praising all the wonderful opportunities I have while we are in Town."

"That would be everything that is admirable and entirely too noble. It is beyond human to think only of the good and not of the fearsome." Joanna reached for the dull-tipped page knife and began cutting the pages in the novel they had purchased that afternoon.

Christiana jumped up and began pacing again, not quite wringing her hands. "Why is it that on an evening when there are no entertainments, men may go out and find their own while we must stay home and content ourselves with cards or reading or needlework?" She made a face at the last as it was her least favorite activity.

"You could ride," Joanna suggested. "In the morning," she added hastily.

"Of course." Christiana stopped her restless pacing as she considered the suggestion. "That is perfect. We will be to bed early this evening and I will wake up at first light as I always do when the milkmaids call."

Joanna's pleased smile made Christiana laugh.

"Jo, if the front door did not creak so loudly we could sneak out and watch the carriages come and go."

"Too childish, Christy." But she stood up. "We can do that from your window."

The two hurried to the window and watched.

The fanlights on the houses across the street cast patterns of light on the sidewalk and one of the oil lamps was being tended by a linkboy as a man hurried down the steps of the house next door and into a waiting carriage. The passing traffic entertained them for a few minutes, and then the street was quiet again.

Christiana turned her back on the window. "What do you think Lord Morgan Braedon is doing this evening?"

Joanna laughed. "That does not require much thought. He is gambling whilst trying to avoid his brother's company."

"What exactly did you and Lord Monksford talk about with Viscount Crandall?"

"The prospects for theater this Season."

Christiana bit her lip. It was acceptable social conversation. But just once she would like Joanna to tell her that her conversation had been inconsequential or perhaps even flirtatious.

"What do you and Lord Morgan talk about?"

Christiana smiled. "We tease each other and . . ." Her voice trailed off as she recalled their whispered conversation that afternoon, the actual realization of their plan, and the wonderful distraction it presented to more weighty concerns. "We have a number of common interests."

Joanna leaned against the bedpost and looked at the ceiling. "Let me see"—she paused—"you both like to dance, to flirt, and to plot." She laughed. "The truth is, Christy, I suspect the two of you are connected by much more than a love of music and flirting."

"Oh, really?" She had made them sound so shallow that she was glad to hear Joanna's perspective.

"You both keep your deeper feelings to yourself for all your charm and friendliness. When I danced with Lord Morgan last night, I saw depth in him that I had never suspected."

"Tell me more." This was worth hearing. "How is it that you have seen this and I only suspect it?"

"Because, Christy, in order to win my support for your harebrained charade, he had to be frank with me. He had to convince me that he had something more than his selfish needs at heart and that he did not intend to seduce you and discard you to win some sort of wager."

"Joanna! Did you actually accuse him of that?"

"No, of course not, Christy." Joanna's voice took on the soothing tones a nurse used on an irate child. "But he knew your well-being was my main concern, however he wanted to interpret it."

"Is that why he told you about his sister? The one who died?"

"Yes," Joanna replied thoughtfully. "They must have been very close."

"So close that her death has changed him in some profound way."

"Hmmm, though that sounds a trifle theatrical." Joanna walked to the window and pulled the curtains shut and then turned back to her sister. "I think when she died he lost his closest confidante. And he has never found anyone to replace her."

Christiana blinked. "Do you think so?" she whispered, sinking into one of the chairs near the fireplace. They were silent and Christiana wondered if she might be the confidante he must long for.

There was a scratch at the door and Sally entered. The two sisters exchanged looks and Sally held up her hands. "Now, miss, I know the night's boring for the two of you, but I'm not wanting to be part of any trouble you are brewing."

Christiana pulled Sally into the room and closed the door. She put her arm around the girl's plump shoulders. "Not a bit, Sally. We were simply wondering if there was any of that delicious syllabub left from dinner."

"No, miss, there's none left. The housekeeper let us have it for supper. Said it would na' keep."

Joanna pulled out the ribbon that Sally had admired that morning. "Then perhaps the fruitcake from tea this afternoon?"

Sally eyed the ribbon and grinned. "I could bring it up to you. Everyone else is gone to bed."

That was the critical piece of information. "No, we would not want to trouble you, Sally." Christiana took the ribbon and tied it around the one already in the maid's hair. "We will find it ourselves. Now you be off to bed. We will be each other's maid this evening."

The maid scurried from the room.

As soon as she was gone, the two tiptoed from the room and down the backstairs. When the tread squeaked they paused and waited. "It is the barest adventure to steal to the kitchen for some unauthorized fruitcake," Christiana whispered in her sister's ear.

Joanna nodded in agreement.

"Suppose we sneak into the library with it."

Joanna stepped into the darkened but still warm kitchen and turned to her sister. "The library? Why?"

Christiana looked about the empty shadow-filled room as though she actually thought someone might be listening. "Have you not always wondered what brandy tastes like?"

By the time Christiana was deep enough into Hyde Park to smell the grass and forget the city the sun was fully risen and burning through the morning fog. By the time she cantered the length of the first path the hint of a headache that she had awakened with was gone. She was certain the headache was from her restless night's sleep. Richard's letter under her pillow had done nothing to make him feel closer or to ease her mind.

The headache was most definitely not from the brandy they had sampled. They had only taken one sip. It was like liquid fire and neither one of them wanted to prolong the experience.

No wonder her father was irritable the morning after those lengthy dinner parties her mother so favored. If port was anything like brandy she could not imagine how anyone could enjoy it, or the resulting effect.

However, *this* experience, riding in the morning, she would enjoy for as long as she possibly could. It was the one good thing about a night early to bed. She could rise at first light and spend an hour in the park. It was as close to real riding as one could find in Town.

She could almost believe that she was in the country. The park was almost empty. She could make out a few others on horseback but this was not a fashionable hour to be seen abroad. Christiana imagined that each of the other riders was here for the same reason that she was and it had nothing to do with the latest gossip or showing off a new habit.

Dare she try a gallop? There was a rider, a man, judging by the size of his horse and his seat, and he was galloping at the far edge of the trees, nearer to Rotten Row than she. She had heard it was considered *risqué,* but there was no one to see her except other less daring souls who surely would welcome a gallop as much as she would.

She turned her borrowed mare toward the farthest reach of the track and started off in a firm canter and as they passed from the sight of the entry gate and her groom she urged her mount into a gallop. Florrie's version of a gallop would have disappointed even the most nervous rider, but Christiana made the most of the dash and drew up at the end, a little breathless herself, more from the forbidden act than the exercise itself.

She looked around quickly to see if anyone had noticed the breach in etiquette, just as Lord Morgan, astride a lovely brown gelding, emerged from the wood. Startled at first, she thought about leaving without a word but then realized she really did wish to speak with him. She nodded formally to him and he rode closer.

"I will not tell a soul, Miss Christiana, if you keep my gallop a secret as well."

She smiled and Morgan drew his horse up next to hers. They turned and began a slow walk back to the gate. "I had no idea that you rode here in the morning."

Morgan smiled. "And I had no idea that you did. Do you think anyone will believe that?"

"No, I expect not." She turned to hide her grin, pretending interest in the other riders. Most were still enjoying the solitude, but over on the edge of the park still bathed in early fog she saw two riders move into the wood. "But surely no one will take exception to a few moments of conversation. After all we are not riding into the most secluded part of the park like that couple over there."

She nodded toward the spot where the duo had disappeared.

Morgan did not even glance at them. "Lady Edgmont and Mr. Hurman have been meeting here for so long that it would be shocking if they were *not* seen."

Christiana craned her neck to catch a glimpse of the pair but the mist already hid them.

"My dear, I think this will only add the tiniest spice to the gossipmongers while it will sweeten my entire day. But is it worth the risk of words with your mother?"

Christiana brushed that concern away with an airy sweep of her hand. "I can easily prove that I did not have any plan to meet you. I am wearing my least flattering habit. She understands my vanity completely since it is one of the traits I inherited from her."

Why had she worn this horrid old thing? Her new bottle green habit with the military look suited her perfectly, even Mama agreed. This was her oldest habit and while it had once been a beautiful brown, it was now faded and a wee bit too tight. She hunched her shoulders and hoped that the buttons did not pull too much.

Morgan raised the quizzing glass he so rarely used and tapped her hands very gently with his whip. "Sit straight, Sprite. The buttons will hold."

She pushed his whip aside, but straightened as commanded. "They may hold, but do not, under any circumstances, make me laugh."

Since that was precisely what threatened them both, she pressed her mouth into a tight line and turned her attention to his horse. "He is lovely."

"And yours is . . ." Morgan paused, clearly at a rare loss for words.

"My horse is borrowed."

"Ah." He nodded in understanding. "Next time let me loan you one from our stables."

"Oh, really?" At first thrilled, she quickly had second thoughts. "That would certainly raise eyebrows, would it not?"

"It would merely add fuel to the rumors of my courtship. If I *gave* you a mare, it would be a different story altogether."

Christiana sighed. "I understand the rules, but sometimes I think they were created to eliminate the fun from every possible adventure." She gathered her thoughts and began her list. "Why are clubs only for men? I should think it would be most diverting to meet daily with friends as you do. Why are men permitted to go to Tattersall's and not women?" She stopped abruptly when she saw that Lord Morgan was smiling.

"Is that your entire list?" he asked.

It was a patronizing smile that stirred her irritation rather than pleasure.

"No," she answered with an imperious lift of her chin. "But I can see you will not take these injustices seriously."

"Sprite, you make me feel ancient." He bit his lip, but the laugh escaped anyway.

Was he laughing at her? He *was* treating her as though she were a sister. And come to think on it, no gentleman would have mentioned her habit unless they were on familial terms.

What was the good of flirting with someone if they persisted in telling you to sit up straight and then laughed when you voiced your feelings?

"I ask you, my lord, who made up these rules?" *Men, that's who,* she thought and let him find a way around that.

"Is it the rules you are angry with or men?"

"Men," she spoke with a firm nod. "Most everything is their fault as far as I can see." She looked at him steadily and hoped he knew that she was not joking now. "Why do men think it is so entertaining to go off and fight in a war and leave those they love behind?" She barely breathed the last word as a knot formed in her throat and tears gathered in her eyes. She turned from him and looked beyond the park. Through the sheen of tears she could see that Park Lane was alive with people. Were any of them worried about their men at war?

Morgan saw the tears, heard them in her voice, and cursed her absent Richard for being so young and unfeeling. He could imagine what the young officer had written to his father and brothers. It most likely did not have a single reassuring word for his almost fiancée.

"I am sorry, Sprite." He could tell her not to worry but that would be pointless. Women excelled in worry, and a good thing, too. They were so grateful when their worry proved pointless. He could tell her Richard would be safe, but that was even more nonsensical. Young Wilton was in the heart of the action. With Wellesley in command and determined to make up for the previous year's debacle, Spain was a perilous place to be just now.

She sniffed. "And exactly what are you sorry for, my lord? Sorry that you are a man? Sorry that you are here to witness my tears?" There were no tears now, and while he preferred anger to upset, he would much rather have her smiling.

He leaned across the small space separating their horses and took her hand. "I am sorry that you are worried. I am sorry that I can do nothing to ease it. I am sorry that I can think of nothing that will make you smile." He held her gloved hand with both of his and was shocked at how much he longed to touch his lips to hers.

She held his gaze for a moment, then pulled her hand from his and spoke in a rush. "Why do men like brandy?"

Where in the name of Bacchus had that question come from? His horse danced restlessly and Morgan took a moment to control him before he spoke. "I do believe brandy is an acquired taste."

She raised her eyebrows. "Does that mean that you did not like it when you first tasted it?"

It was so long ago he could barely recall that first taste. Port had been his initiation into strong drink. He could still recall all too clearly how he felt the morning after that adventure. "Miss Lambert, exactly what did you and your sister do last night?"

She shrugged her shoulders. "It tastes perfectly hideous, like fire trailing down your throat, and then it settles in your stomach in the most sickening way."

Her expression was eloquent and Morgan was hard-pressed to hold back his laugh. He did, though. She was completely distracted from her misdirected anger and he had no desire to resurrect it.

"Are you laughing at me, my lord?" She narrowed her eyes, but he saw no anger there.

"No, never, my dear." He let his own smile show.

"Well, whom can I ask when I have questions like this? My brother is in Jamaica and Peter Wilton has forgotten we exist. You have grown as dear to me as a brother and I hope you think of me in the same way." She looked at him through lowered lashes and in such a way that he knew she was testing his reaction.

Morgan relaxed, surprised at the tension that drained away. This sort of conversation he could handle. "I have two brothers, neither of whom are particularly dear to me at the moment. No, Sprite, I refuse to think of you in that way."

"That is not what I mean and well you know it."

"Ahh, do you mean do I think of you as a sister?"

She gave no answer, but pursed her lips and waited.

Until that expression settled on her face, it had not occurred to him that there was a wrong way to answer the question. But obviously there was. "No, I do not think of you as a sister."

He looked at her face and then let her see his eyes travel down the length of her very close-fitting habit. He smiled at her blush. "A sister? Most definitely not."

He stroked his horse's neck to quiet him. The movement brought his horse closer to hers, so that her skirts were brushing against his riding boots. "I may have taught my sisters the steps to the minuet, but I never wanted to dance with them. I may have noticed their new dresses, but I never once admired the way they fit. I may have been sorry to see them crying, but never sorry enough to want to wipe away their tears."

With each phrase his voice grew softer, so that she had to lean closer to hear him. He could see the color rise in her cheeks, not a blush of embarrassment this time, but of awareness.

"I never once wanted to drink brandy from the same glass that their lips had just touched."

Her eyes were wide. They went from his eyes to his mouth and only then did he realize how very close they were.

He wished the prospect of a kiss brought pleased surprise. He had a sinking feeling he had answered the question incorrectly after all. And he could think of no way to change his response. Nor did he want to. He did, however, straighten in the saddle.

She moved away abruptly herself and looked straight ahead. "I . . ." she began, but her voice was hoarse. She stopped, swallowed, and tried again. "I can not . . ."

Now he thought there were tears in her voice, but she still would not look at him. She mumbled a word he was almost sure was "Richard" and turned her horse with a jerk that was another indication of how upset she was.

Morgan cursed his stupidity. For all her flirtatious ways, Christiana Lambert was young, as he had told James, and provincial, as James had reminded him. A few weeks in London might have given her some Town polish, but a lifetime of country living was not forgotten so quickly.

There was no denying his actions were the reason for the set-down today. It had passed just far enough beyond innocence to rouse guilt.

If he was not more careful, he would lose his chance with her and be left with no courtship pretense. He would have to think before he spoke. Simple enough, but when he was around Christiana he seemed to have an increasingly difficult time with that basic precept.

With real regret, Morgan turned his own horse toward the gates. In truth, a sincere courtship would hardly require more effort than this sham.

Ten

"What I wish to know now and can not possibly ask him is how you tell the difference between a flirtatious comment and something sincerely meant." Christiana was pleased with that phrasing. It was the essence of the problem. In truth, her feelings were at the core of it, but she was not sure she was ready to share her confusion with anyone, even Joanna.

The vast emporium that was Schomberg House rose before them. They had planned this expedition days ago. Until this morning the sum total of Christiana's worries had been whether the two of them could find a bonnet that would match Joanna's newest dress.

However, as a result of her morning ride, Christiana realized that she needed to clarify her mind before she could give the myriad of goods the attention they deserved.

"He did not seem to be flirting at all when he told me that he wanted to drink from the same glass that had touched my lips and I did not feel at all like giggling when he said that."

"What did you feel like doing?" Joanna asked, pausing inside the entrance, giving her sister her full attention.

Christiana stared at the furs and fans in the first shop and did not really see any of them. *What did I feel like doing? I wanted to kiss him. And that is pre-*

cisely why I hurried away. Christiana could feel a blush rising at the memory of his caressing eyes, his smile, the chance touch of their bodies as his horse moved closer.

She moved on quickly, stopping at the next display. "Oh, Joanna, look at this wonderful porcelain vase. Do you think it is French?"

Joanna took her arm and drew her away from the display. "Yes, it is precisely the sort of thing Mama would like."

Christiana was about to argue the point further when Joanna gave her a look. "Now why did you ask me a question and avoid the discussion? The difference between flirting and a sincere compliment? Exactly what did happen this morning?"

"Nothing happened." Oh dear, now there was no way to avoid telling the truth. Christiana looked around. No one was paying the least bit of attention to them. Still, she urged her sister into an alcove where they could pretend to examine some shawls. "I am being foolish. It remains a flirtation as long as I behave as a flirt should."

"Christy, you make flirting sound like a virtue." Joanna shook her head.

Any other time Christiana would have read disapproval but right now her sister was smiling. "Well, it is a skill at the very least. And there is nothing wrong with it as long as it is done properly."

"And you did not 'do it properly' this morning?"

Joanna's smile had disappeared and Christiana could hear the edge of alarm in her voice.

"No, no I was very proper." She paused and drew a deep breath. "It is only that my thoughts were not precisely proper. All I could think about for a moment was what it would feel like to lean closer, to touch his lips with mine." No blush this time, but guilt at her weakness.

Joanna laughed, actually laughed at her, and she

laughed so loud that a gentleman passing looked their way and smiled. Pulling her from the alcove, Joanna took Christiana's arm and urged her to the next shop.

"My dear heart, that is the very sign of a successful flirt and not some great wrongdoing on your part. Do you think that just because you have given your heart, you will never be attracted to another man?"

Well, yes, she had, Christiana realized. But even a bare moment's thought made her realize how naive that was. "I suppose you are right." Of course she was right, but Christiana did not like the feeling that an element of her long-held romantic conviction was so easily crushed. Did that mean that the other elements were as vulnerable?

That worry made it worth one last defending gesture. "No, Joanna, I take that back. I am not at all convinced you are right. A true love match would indeed make you oblivious to all others."

"That may be, if it is a true love match, but even the most devoted lovers must eventually notice the world around them again. Especially as their lives change and their family grows."

Christiana saw Joanna's blush now, but forbore to tease her about it as her words registered. *If it is a true love match.* That was exactly how Joanna had phrased it. Was she suggesting that her love for Richard was not a true love match? That was not something she cared to discuss right now. The very thought made her shiver. Not that she doubted her love for Richard.

Fortunately Joanna did not press the point. "Christy, I think that this is the issue: It is no longer a flirtation when the lady thinks the compliment is seriously meant."

"No, Joanna, part of the charm of an accomplished flirt is his very ability to be convincing. No, I think it passes beyond flirtation if the words make the lady uncomfortable." Is that how she would describe what

Morgan made her feel? Uncomfortable? She tried the word out and found it did not suit her reaction at all.

Pleased. Yes, that was it. She'd been pleased, flattered, and totally entranced. Then shocked at the feeling of intimacy that had surrounded them in an open field so early in the morning.

It was hours later and that feeling of pleasure was still hers to summon. Did Joanna have any idea exactly how entrancing true flirtation could be?

They walked on toward the shop featuring hats. The hallway was as crowded as the entrance had been. Everyone abroad seemed to be intent on shopping along Pall Mall and at Schomberg House specifically.

Christiana looked around again to see if they were overheard and then realized not a single person cared what they were talking about. Some much more august personage was moving toward the small furniture display and much of the crowd was following.

Joanna moved closer to her sister and Sally and the footman closed in behind them. "There is also a quality of credibility in a true flirt."

"Hair like corn silk?" Christiana asked, recalling Joanna's least favorite compliment.

Joanna laughed. "And creativity." She looked at her sister out of the corner of her eye. "I think Lord Morgan scores very highly on that point."

Christiana paused to consider a display of buttons. They were truly elegant and clearly beyond her allowance. Without discussion, they walked on.

"Perhaps that is where the awkwardness is. If he would use the tried and true compliments that would be acceptable, but to say 'I taught my sisters to dance, but never wanted to dance with them' is beyond clever and charming, you must admit."

"Yes," Joanna agreed, "and as beyond our experience as Mr. Harding's buttons."

"But you see, Joanna, we can enjoy the beauty of

his buttons, can we not, just as we should be able to enjoy a flirtation."

"And are you?" Joanna stopped and looked at her sister.

Christiana did not care for any of the stationer's wares, but she stared at the display. "Yes, yes, I do enjoy his company and his conversation and even his very elegant flattery. I do." She said the last almost to herself.

"If this flirtation with Lord Morgan is a pleasurable experience and you are enjoying yourself, then exactly why are we having this conversation when we could be examining any number of fine shops?" Joanna was not so much exasperated as confused.

They moved on, their attention drawn by the steady stream of people in and out of the milliner's shop a few steps ahead of them. "Joanna, my question is simple: How does one react to a compliment that appears more meaningful than flirtatious. Especially when I am not at all certain which it is?"

"How did you handle it this morning?"

Joanna asked the question so cautiously that Christiana was not sure her sister really wanted to know.

"I stammered incoherently and then left; actually I would say that I ran away."

Joanna pursed her lips. Was she thinking about her answer or trying not to laugh?

"I can tell you one thing, Joanna, that bit of truly gauche behavior guarantees embarrassment at our next meeting."

"It was an honest reaction though, Christy."

"You are sweet as can be to try to find a way to make it sound acceptable."

"I suspect, Christy, that there is no answer good for all such situations. It must depend on the people involved, their level of friendship, and their understanding of each other's minds."

"I suppose you are right: the level of friendship is the key."

"And as far as I am concerned, a direct response is infinitely better than a simper." Joanna looked genuinely puzzled. "What is a 'simper' anyway?"

Christiana knew that her sister was trying to distract her. And in truth, she was tired of attempting to puzzle it out. So she gave Joanna's question some thought.

"A simper? Let me see if I can describe it." She considered it thoughtfully. "A simper is an unspoken way of accepting a compliment that you know is your due." Christiana paused a moment. "Which is precisely why it is so unappealing. There is entirely too much self-conceit in it." She looked at her sister. "Miss Perry."

"Ahhh," said Joanna in perfect understanding. They were outside the millinery shop now. Despite the heavy custom, the display stands were still filled with an appealing range of hats and bonnets. As they watched, the prettiest of the lot was taken from its stand and into the shop. Christiana and Joanna looked at each other, sharing dismay.

They waited impatiently while several matrons made their way out of the shop as Christiana insisted, "We are not too late. There is no good reason in the world why someone else should buy that bonnet when it is so perfect for you."

In complete accord, the sisters turned their full attention to the cause at hand.

It was obvious to Morgan that until he was less distracted he would not be able to concentrate on play sufficiently to best his opponent. Cartridge was newly arrived in Town, flush with his winnings from some absurd bet and anxious to increase his stake for the Season. If he played on, Morgan knew that the money Cartridge wanted would come from his pocket.

There was nothing to do but withdraw and set out in search of Christiana Lambert, for it was their morning conversation that was keeping him from successful play.

He was certain that the gods approved the decision when he met John Monksford on the steps of White's, although he did not appreciate the opportunity at first. He merely exchanged a polite nod with Monksford and moved toward his curricle.

Come to think on it, James had never explained the reason for the tension between Monksford and all things Braedon. Though Morgan could guess it centered on a woman. With that thought Morgan realized that Monksford could prove useful in this venture.

After this morning, he was almost certain that Christiana might be inclined to ignore him if they passed on the street, but Miss Lambert would certainly acknowledge Lord Monksford and that would give him the opening he needed.

He turned back and hailed Monksford in the foyer, which was empty now except for the footman awaiting Monksford's hat and gloves. "My lord, I am bound for Pall Mall in hopes of finding Miss Christiana and her sister. I have word that they are at Schomberg House. Would you care to join me and attempt to search them out?"

Monksford's surprise was not particularly flattering.

"It is pure self-interest," Morgan explained. "I have particular need to see Miss Christiana and if you are with me, I will be able to have a private word with her as you will with Miss Lambert."

Monksford bowed to him slightly. "It would be my pleasure, sir."

His instant agreement was a surprise.

"The truth is, Braedon, I have been hoping to have a word with you since our meeting at the Lamberts' the other day."

Morgan was curious, but the street in front of the

club was not the place for a conversation that might be less than complimentary. He had fairly given up on establishing a cordial relationship with the man.

With unspoken agreement they mounted Morgan's curricle and he turned the horses west from St. James.

It was no distance to Pall Mall but the streets were crowded and Morgan was grateful for Monksford's silence as he negotiated his way past other equipages and every matter of conveyance bringing goods to market. Only one pedestrian was foolish enough to challenge his right to the road. The mud spattered on that unfortunate's coat was enough warning for all nearby.

As they reached the arcade Morgan glanced at Monksford, who was searching the crowded entry with some alarm.

"My machinations may be for naught, eh, Monksford? Is everyone in London shopping here today?"

"So it would seem. Even if we are able to locate them, we may not have the opportunity for more than a greeting."

Morgan tossed the reins to his tiger with a word to wait until they were certain they were staying.

Moving into the entrance, Morgan shook his head. "I did not think to ask which shop and I have never been here before."

"The convenience of Bond Street meets my needs better. This is so much more suited to browsing. I think the numbers could work to our advantage, though. Surely we will meet someone who has seen them."

As they moved through the crowd, Monksford slowed. "My lord, I would like to apologize for my rudeness the other day. I am never at my best when I am in your brother's company."

It was a stiff little speech and Morgan was afraid that he spoiled it by laughing in Monksford's face. "You are not alone, Monksford. James annoys the hell out of me five days of seven."

Monksford did not answer right away, but a slight smile acknowledged Morgan's frankness. After a considering pause Monksford began. "I want to explain, my lord. I understand that the viscount is not the easiest of men, but I feel I owe you some explanation for my incivility. What happened between your brother and me was a long time ago and one would think it should no longer rankle."

Monksford looked around him and then seemed to travel back in time. "It is simple really. We were both courting the same woman. And she chose me."

Morgan wondered if Monksford was aware of the note of astonishment in his voice.

He shrugged. "Marie loved Town life. She loved the Season, the shopping, and the people. She was happy enough in the country but she came to life in Town, rather more like Miss Christiana than her sister. Many people misunderstood that gaiety for something else. Your brother was one such and would not give up his courtship even though it was clear where her attachment lay."

He stopped a moment, as if sorting through the details. "It came to nothing. Marie was as loyal as she was flirtatious, but it embarrassed me. And in the end it embarrassed her."

He looked directly at Morgan, who was silent more in astonishment at this confidence than for want of words.

"I am not a city man, Braedon. Nor am I a sophisticate, I make no claim to be. You can use me to further your own courtship because I allow it, but if you interfere with mine out of some misguided sense of family loyalty then I will have no qualms about bloodying your nose as I did your brother's."

The last was spoken in a rush of defiance that took much of the power from his words. Morgan still did not speak. Amazing. So Monksford had bested James. Not only could this man be a friend, but a role model too.

"Monksford, you need have no worry on that score. My family loyalty does not extend to using a lady as a source for revenge." He bowed to Monksford, who acknowledged the courtesy with a nod.

The two of them became more aware of their surroundings, and realized that the intensity of their conversation had attracted the attention of one or two of the *ton*.

Morgan spoke slightly louder than absolutely necessary. "I have an idea for exactly the sort of costume you should choose for the masquerade."

"Ponsonby's masquerade?" Monksford rose to the occasion and followed his lead. "I have not given it a single thought."

Morgan had no doubt that was true. He lowered his voice again. "You do plan to attend?"

"Miss Lambert will be there."

Morgan nodded. It was all the explanation necessary. "Just so, but it is essential that our costumes compliment each other or the ploy will not work."

Monksford looked aghast. "We are to dress alike?"

"No. No. We are to dress to compliment the Misses Lamberts."

"Ahhhh." Monksford nodded with a slight smile of appreciation. "And you have a plan for finding out what their costumes are? Miss Lambert has made no mention of it and they do seem to be caught up in the need to surprise."

Morgan tapped his finger against his lip. "I'll find a way."

They were passing a shop that specialized in tailoring for gentleman and Monksford stopped to eye a jacket, seemingly well made but in an unfortunate shade of gray.

Morgan moved on and Monksford followed. "I would be delighted to introduce you to Weston, Monksford. His tailoring would suit you prodigiously."

By the time they spotted Christiana Lambert and

her sister, it was clear that the two men did not have a care for anything more serious than the cut of a coat or the set of a shoulder, unless it was whether dark blue or bottle green would suit Monksford better.

Morgan could only hope that Monksford was taking this conversation to heart. The olive green he was wearing today was not complimentary to his complexion, nor would it blend favorably with the green shade of Miss Lambert's pelisse. Fortunately he knew that her awareness might make note of the ill-suited shade, but her vanity did not extend to anything as small-minded as ignoring Monksford because his choice of coats would not blend with hers.

For Christiana, the millinery shop was a true test of her shopper's mettle and her new virtue of patience, but when they left, not thirty minutes later, Joanna handed the footman not one but two cumbersome boxes to carry. They agreed to go home immediately to make certain that the hat would match the dress as perfectly as they hoped.

As they progressed to the entrance, Christiana listened as Sally gave the footman every detail of their modest adventure, with an impressive explanation of her bargaining ability. She really must remember to use that when Mama began to fret about the expense of it.

They crossed the entire length of the floor, stairs, and front hall of Schomberg House. Sally was describing the hat Joanna had almost chosen instead, when Christiana heard her sister clear her throat and speak. "Good day, my lords."

Christiana did her best to keep her smile in place when she realized that Lord Morgan *and* Lord Monksford were standing close by. Lord Morgan was looking splendid in a dark blue though not quite navy coat and a beaver of shining black. His smile drew one from her, but it faded and turned crooked when she remembered the last time they had been together.

Why had Joanna acknowledged them? What was her sister thinking? She really was not ready to see Lord Morgan after her morning's embarrassment. The purchase of the hat had distracted her from further understanding of exactly what she should do, how she should handle this situation.

She did not even know what kind of situation it was. Delicate? Absurd? And how foolish to be feeling something close to panic at the thought of conversation with him. Shoppers surrounded them and there were enough distractions on display to make anything more than casual conversation unnecessary.

The surge of people moved around them with ill-concealed annoyance. By mutual consent the four began to move toward the doors as Joanna explained they were bound for the carriage and home but were in no true hurry.

Christiana was feeling quite calm, enjoying herself actually, until Joanna turned to tell her that she and Monksford were going to the shop where they had seen the porcelain vase. "It will be just the thing to distract Mama from the fact that we are coming home with more than one new hat."

Morgan nodded but made no move to follow. Christiana wanted desperately to join them and it was not because she had no faith in Joanna's bargaining ability. How rude of Lord Morgan not to ask her wishes in the matter. She most certainly did not wish to be alone with him again.

They were within sight of the shop nearest the entrance. The display table was filled with fans, artfully spread so they showed to their best advantage. She craned her neck to see one that was tucked behind a monstrosity of silk and feathers. "One can see why these are at the entrance. They are so tempting. What a lovely fabric combination!" She stopped short of clapping her hands, trying for a more ladylike demeanor. "I think that silver one would be perfect for my costume for the Hawthornes' masquerade." Never mind that it would cost more than their entire Season in London.

She chattered on, not even certain of what she was saying, but altogether certain that silence would be worse. Eventually she did have to pause for breath and Morgan made the most of it.

They still stood before the fans. She thought that he was examining her favorite, but when she tried for a casual glance at him, she saw that he was looking directly at her.

"D—do you think it would suit?" She blushed at the stammer and was even more embarrassed when he shook his head.

"Christiana."

For some reason his use of her given name, for the first time, made her even more nervous. It had nothing to do with the frisson of pleasure that swept through her at the sound of her name on his lips.

He spoke before she did, which was just as well since she was sure that all she could manage was a croak.

"Whatever have I done to so upset you?"

What should she say? He knew her well enough to know that her chattering was a way to avoid meaningful conversation. She knew him well enough to know that he would see through a lie. Besides, she hated the wretched self-consciousness that had plagued her since morning. She wanted to enjoy his company again, not dread it.

She looked at him and found she could not quite speak with their eyes engaged. She looked away and spoke on a sigh that imbued her words with annoyance and regret. "You offered to dry my tears."

Eleven

"I feared that might be the reason."

He spoke with such smugness that a bolt of anger shot through her. Did he know everything? "Oh, really?" There was an edge to her voice that she could not quite control. "Am I that transparent? Or is this sort of insight some superiority that comes to all men along with their vast experience of the world?"

She cringed at her burst of temper. Was he not trying to address the very question to which she wanted an answer? His smile was in place, but did he realize that she could read the annoyance in his eyes, the way they narrowed slightly, as though he were trying to contain his anger. She bent her head, knowing her bonnet brim would keep her chagrin hidden from him.

What was it about Lord Morgan that roused such extreme emotions in her, from totally distracting delight to a stubborn anger that she could not contain? Richard never irritated her that way.

They stood without speaking. Christiana was afraid to open her mouth, since she was still torn between distress and an equally desperate need to beg his pardon.

Morgan broke the silence, with a voice so quiet that she was forced to look at him directly to hear his words. "My dear, this is the second time in this still-young day that you have railed at me." He bowed slightly. "I apologize." He spoke the last words gravely. And then he smiled and when the smile reached his eyes, she could do nothing but smile back at him.

He pulled the ends of her bonnet's knotted bow. "Though in all honesty and like all men, I have absolutely no idea exactly what I am apologizing for." He nodded again, this time short of a bow. "In that, women will always have the advantage. But I must tell you one more thing." Now his grin disappeared from his lips, but the smile remained in his eyes and she could not resist leaning even closer so as not to miss his next insight.

"If you continue to vent your anger on me when I have not earned it then I shall do the same to you and neither one of us will continue to enjoy each other's company."

Well, Christiana decided, it might not be insight, but it certainly was the truth. "Indeed you are right, my lord." She replied with a firmness she hoped conveyed her understanding. "To bicker constantly would make us exactly like brother and sister." She looked at him from beneath her lashes, inviting his reply.

"Brother and sister?" His voice was filled with amused disgust. "Not at all, Sprite. I thought we had done with that possibility hours ago. No, indeed, it would be worse than that. More like a married couple." He paused and leaned closer so that she could feel his breath on the side of her neck. "Indeed, we would be bickering like a married couple and yet not entitled to any of the benefits of the married state. What could be worse than that?"

She clapped her hands. How could a set-down make her laugh? But this one did. "Oh, my lord, you are shocking and wonderful and both at the very same time."

Lord Morgan took her arm and began walking with her toward the entrance. He continued from his earlier observation as if their more testy words had not occurred, "I can see you have thought about this morning's meeting too much and not in quite the right way." He was not looking at her, but rather scanning the crowd, as though he were watching for Joanna and Lord Monksford.

"Sprite, if you will forgive my—what was the phrase you used"—he paused as if in thought—"ah yes, if you will tolerate for a moment my 'masculine superiority'—do please consider our meeting in this way."

He bowed to an acquaintance, but continued walking. He was not looking at her, but his hand on her arm, the feel of his longer step matched to her more delicate one, was as particular a contact as his eyes on her face.

"My dear Miss Lambert, I never once offered you my handkerchief to dry your tears. I did not even suggest that you lean on my shoulder for comfort. I did not take your hand and press it to my heart. In truth, it did not even occur to me to pledge my life to see you smile again." He paused and now he did look at her. She was not going to argue with him about this. Not when he was being so generous and gentle.

"My dear, I did not do a single one of those things that would carry us over the boundary of propriety the *ton* has so carefully set. I merely wished, as any man would, that you not cry." A smile colored his words, but there was sincerity behind the humor, not laughter. He made it sound as though his wish had been motivated by nothing more than a desperate self-interest.

"In short, Sprite, you must admit, that while it may have been the most loverlike thing I have ever said to you, it was hardly worthy of the set-down you gave me then or the nerves you are feeling now."

"You are quite right." She was almost convinced. "It is only that, despite how you make it sound now, it was so sweet a thing to have said. And, in truth, completely unlike any of our previous conversations."

Did his shrug mean that she was wrong or that the distinction was unimportant?

"Is it not natural as we grow to know each other better that we speak with less reserve?"

They certainly were now. Christiana looked around to see if anyone was watching them, but everyone entering seemed intent on their errands, and those leaving were engaged in groups of their own. Standing as they were, in an alcove near the entrance, they might as well have been alone.

She had not answered him. On purpose. If they continued to flirt with more and more warmth then where would that lead? Before she even dared ask, Lord Morgan pressed on.

"Certainly there is more to our acquaintance than endless flirtation?" He spoke with real caution and then waited for her answer with a serious face as though it truly mattered to him.

Friendship? Was he saying that there might be friendship between them? She tried to respond thoughtfully and ignored the relief bubbling through her. Oh, if only she could show him how much she appreciated his insight, his awareness of her sensibility. She curtsied slightly, never taking her eyes from his face. "Oh yes, my lord, friendship would be a lovely thing to share."

What would it be like to have a gentleman as a friend? Certainly it would be totally different from the kind of childhood friendships she had shared with the Wilton brothers. It was indeed exactly what she wanted. A gentleman friend to share her adventures with. A step beyond flirtation, but something far short of lovemaking.

She breathed deeply and felt happiness surge over the relief. "It is precisely the reason for my nerves. There was no one I could ask this morning, for you were the very source of my uneasiness and, at the same time, the only person who would understand if I asked about it."

"And what would you ask?" He smiled.

"Oh, I do not need to ask now for you have given me the answer before I was even fully aware of what the question was."

His smile held, but she knew he did not understand. Well, she decided, that was one difference between him and her female friends. They would have understood exactly.

Morgan considered pressing her for a more reasonable answer, but decided it would invite more confusion. Her renewed smile was his personal sun on this otherwise gray day, though perhaps it was best not to tell her that at this moment.

He offered her his arm. Even the way she accepted his support was charming. She put her arm through his and by doing so they became partners. The conventions of the Season, the routines he knew too well, became an exploit, a quest, an adventure. They walked in silence and then Morgan recalled one of the lesser reasons for this meeting.

"Grandmama is planning a musicale."

Christiana turned her attention from her examination of the crowd, her smile now merely polite. He knew her experience of London musicales had not been entertaining. Was she already planning her regret?

"I understand she is going to ask your mama to allow you to assist her with the invitations."

"How nice." She looked away from him between one word and the next with a slight pause between the two, and the exact opposite meaning was conveyed.

"She hopes that she will have your agreement to help as soon as possible. Once she lets it be known that she is planning something, no one else will dare encroach on that date with some other event."

"Well, yes, of course, that is absolutely true." Her response was less measured now, enthusiasm in her voice again. "I do believe everyone is consumed with the masquerade and their costumes." She reflected a scant moment. "But once costumes are ordered everyone will be restless again as the masquerade is still weeks away. A new invitation would be quite welcome." She stopped walking and sent him a mischievous glance. "But can you convince the dowager duchess that there is nothing entertaining about an imposing woman singing in German?"

He nodded. "Not one word of German? On that point we are agreed. I think I need only remind her that she asked for our advice." He waved his hand in complete dismissal of one of the most talented women in London. "Quite overdone and not nearly as diverting as what I have in mind."

When Christiana did not respond to the tease, he looked at her and realized he no longer had her complete attention. Indeed her eager smile was gone, quite suddenly, replaced by concern and urgency. Morgan looked in the same direction, trying to determine what had caused such an instant change in mood. What was there amid the throng of shoppers, carriages, and vendors on the street directly in front of them? It looked a commonplace enough scene to him.

"Do you see that soldier, my lord? The one with the crutch?"

Morgan saw the man and was rather surprised that she had. But this man could hardly be called a soldier. The uniform jacket he wore was torn and dirty and the pants were not a regulation part of any uniform Morgan had ever seen.

"Do you see him?" Christiana asked again.

When he nodded she continued, "I always notice

the soldiers. I've seen one or two wearing uniforms before, but never anyone as affecting as he is."

Yes, he thought, she would notice soldiers. But this fraud was moving slowly down the street, avoiding the better dressed pedestrians, who studiously ignored him. The wretch paused and looked around, then resumed his stolid pace, finally pausing directly across the street near a row of small shops. The man pulled a flask from his pocket, took a small sip, and then put it away. Best to avoid any conversation with this wastrel. He was no more soldier than Rhys was.

Morgan took Christiana's arm and made to move back into the entryway of Schomberg House, rather than closer to the rogue. Christiana refused to move, forcing Morgan to a halt.

"You do not understand, my lord. I have read about this." She pushed her bonnet back so that he could see her face fully. "You must listen. I am certain he is one of those soldiers injured in the line of duty and sent home without any pension. If he is still recovering from his injury he will be hard-pressed to find work. If the limp is permanent, he may well starve to death."

All the gods of love knew he did not want to aggravate her again, but at this moment her naïveté was drawing him close to an exasperation that was hard to mask. "Sprite, if this man can not find work it is because he drinks too much. Did you see his flask? He handled that none too discreetly."

"Can you blame him for turning to brandy when the country he fought for disowns him that way? It is a disgrace." She opened her reticule and pulled out a crown. She pressed it into Morgan's hand. "Would you please give this to him. Tell him it is but a small token of my respect and appreciation."

Morgan pressed the coin back into her hand, but she would not be denied.

"Truly, sir, I do not wish to argue, but can only hope that Richard would be treated with consideration if he were injured with no money and no family to return to."

"My dear green girl, this man is no soldier. I would wager a year's worth of neckcloths that the closest he's ever been to battle is a fistfight with a drunken sailor."

"That's even worse! People taking advantage of his injury that way." She thought for a moment and he dared hope that she had taken his advice to heart. "Besides, my lord, even if he is not a soldier, his life is a misery compared to yours and mine."

There would be no victory in oversetting that sensibility for there was truth in her words. When she held out the money to him, he shook his head. "I will take care of that."

Morgan nodded to the footman and the young man stepped closer, on guard for his mistress's safety. Trying to curb irritation and distaste, Morgan pulled his gloves tighter and settled his beaver as he walked toward the man who had settled on the far edge of the stoop outside a furniture shop.

When Morgan stopped before him, the man struggled to his feet. His eyes were clear but guarded. "Beggin' your pardon, sir."

The few words Morgan had planned to say faded from his mind as the man struggled to draw himself erect with painful effort. As he stood with his shoulders back and his hands stiffly at his side, he transformed himself into the soldier that she had insisted he was.

Morgan's aversion gave way to embarrassed surprise, and when the soldier made to move away, Morgan stopped him with a gesture.

At that moment, a clerk came out of the shop, his broom raised as though he was going to sweep both of them away like some pesky bit of fog-grown dirt.

The soldier turned and eyed the clerk with contempt. It would have done no good, but Morgan was standing next to him. His stare with narrowed eyes controlled the anger that was aimed as much at himself as at the weasel in the doorway. With a subservient bob, the flunky disappeared with flattering haste.

Morgan and the crippled man moved together toward the corner of Pall Mall and St. James. "With whom did you serve?"

The man looked surprised at the question. "I was with the First Foot Guards till Salamanca. I took care of the horses what pulled the guns, sir."

They had a fine reputation, but Morgan could not recall the chronology exactly. "Were you with them through Corunna?"

The soldier's eyes clouded and he shook his head. "I'd be dead as General Moore if I had to make that march. No, sir, I was sent home long before the end."

He spoke like an old soldier. As though he regretted the missed opportunity of that slow death march with his comrades. "What are you doing in this part of town, Sergeant?" The rank was faded and dirty and Morgan hoped that he read it correctly.

The man nodded. "Sergeant Thomas Tidwell, sir. Walking is the onliest thing that improves my leg. The doctor told me that if I keep walking the limp would pass. To tell the truth, guvnor, I live at Ratcliffe and I am as lost here as you would be there."

"I had planned to offer you directions and pay for a hackney," Morgan lied glibly.

The man shook his head.

Ratcliffe was on the north side of the Thames and some distance away, but if walking was his only road to recovery then Morgan understood why he would prefer the trek. He made to hand the sergeant a guinea and was not surprised that the gesture made him feel ashamed.

Sergeant Tidwell took a step back. "I know I look mean. But my daughter and her man are looking out for me until I can find work. It's the coat, sir, I know, but you see, it's as close as I can come . . ." He stopped speaking and set his mouth in a tight line, unable to go on.

Morgan nodded and handed him the coin again. "Then buy your daughter something special and use this coin as a favor to me. For I sincerely wish to impress that lovely young lady across the street. It was she who asked me to come and thank you for your service to our country."

Morgan understood completely when Sergeant Tidwell frowned in disbelief, for not one other of the *ton* passing close by had acknowledged his existence. He explained, "She has a young man with Wellesley in Portugal."

The soldier stared hard across the street, where Christiana was easy to spot. She stood watching with undisguised curiosity, her expression full of sympathy, leaning toward them as though that would enable her to hear their conversation.

Sergeant Tidwell looked back at Morgan and now his eyes did fill with tears. He accepted the coin, nodding. "My daughter and her family live crowded and tight. That's another reason for my walking. I will give this to her, I will." He pocketed the coin carefully and patted the spot. "And you tell your young lady, my lord, hearts as sweet as hers make it all worthwhile."

He stopped speaking, taking a moment to control his emotions. "But you best not tell her this, my lord. Wellseley uses his men like cannon fodder. We will beat the French, make no mistake, but it will cost, it will cost dear. Not like the passage at Douro, no matter what is said." He spoke without anger but in bitter acceptance of a truth he had witnessed.

"It is quiet there now. We will let that be a comfort. I will convey your good wishes, Sergeant Tidwell." What else could he say? What more could he do?

Morgan directed him back to Ratcliffe, again offering a hackney, though it seemed insultingly insufficient to a man who had devoted his whole life to the safety of the ignorant throngs parading by, himself included.

Even though it meant several more hours walking, Sergeant Tidwell refused a ride. He insisted that not only was walking good for his leg, but easier on London streets than marching had been in the rough terrain of Portugal.

For his part, Morgan digested a very large piece of humble pie as he worked his way through the crowd and back to Christiana. He'd thought her naïve and perhaps she was. But it was that very naïveté, still not covered by too much Town bronze, which enabled her to see beyond the façade. The sergeant had been exactly what she suspected, a cashiered soldier hoping for work and all Morgan could do was hand him a coin in thanks for his service.

By the time he reached her, she had dried her eyes, but emotion still echoed in her voice. "Thank you, my lord. Thank you very much."

He took her hand and bowed over it. She was all that was true and dear in his life right now and he was grateful to the gods for sending her to him. "His name is Sergeant Tidwell and he lives in Ratcliffe Highway and it is I who thank you."

Her smile faded as the silence between them lengthened. She searched his face with such unguarded intensity that he wondered if she could actually see into his heart. Not a happy thought. For it was filled with more dark than light.

"Have we kept you waiting long?"

Christiana was so startled by her sister's arrival that she jumped in surprise. Morgan controlled his reactions and forced his voice to calm, though his racing heart made that difficult. "Yes," he joked. "You have kept us waiting so long that we have run out of things to talk about."

The humor was lost on Joanna, who looked from one to the other with some concern. Did she think they had argued? He wanted to assure her, but the chaos of the moment distracted all of them.

The Lamberts' chaise stood ready, but it was soon apparent that it would not hold all their purchases *and* three people.

"We really did not buy that much," Christiana announced as much to inform the world as to reassure herself. "It is only that the items we did choose are so large and clumsy."

They milled about without purpose until Morgan took command. "I will call a hackney for Sally and she can proceed home with the parcels."

Sally looked delighted at the prospect and Joanna nodded her appreciation. Morgan gestured to Sally to follow him and they moved farther down the street, where several hackneys were waiting.

Monksford handed the ladies into the Lamberts' conveyance and watched it move into traffic. Morgan looked up from his conversation with Sally, but there was no farewell from the chaise.

By the time Sally was seated, he had paid the driver and returned to where Monksford stood, the Lamberts' chaise was out of sight. Monksford was still watching the mix of vehicles as though his concentration would keep the ladies from harm.

When finally Monksford turned to him, Morgan smiled, "Sally has given me exactly the information we need to surprise the ladies."

Monksford nodded with only the vaguest interest and turned toward the curricle. Morgan stayed him. "I think we will need a few particular items that would best be purchased here if our costumes are to be equal to our intent."

The older man closed his eyes and shook his head. Was it refusal or disbelief? "You actually want me to spend money so that I can look more foolish than Grimaldi dressed for a performance?"

"Exactly," Morgan laughed. "But there are three

consolations. The first is that you can afford it, for I am not speaking of gold and jewels. Second, we will be only one of a hundred who feel exactly the same. And third, and by far most important, appearing a fool to please a lady is a sure way to win her heart."

"I had hoped that Miss Lambert was above such gambits."

"Most of the time I do believe that she is, Monksford, but there is something in the London air that empties our brains just enough to allow for foolishness and fun."

"The very fact that I am considering this proposal is proof that it has affected me as well." Monksford looked toward the darkening soot-laden sky as though the rain that threatened was the agent of the god of silliness.

Morgan thumped him on the back. "It will pass. And with any luck and the consent of her father, you can contemplate a lifetime of enlivening discussion with Miss Lambert."

Did that sound like an insult? He hoped not.

Monksford looked at him with an unexpected twinkle in his eye. "You have no idea exactly how *enlivening* those discussions can be."

As they moved into the great hall of Schomberg House, Morgan decided that comment was as close to *risqué* as Monksford ever came.

What part of today's conversation would Christiana consider worth sharing with her sister. Their growing friendship? The thrill of the shops? The soldier? He would never know. The workings of her mind alternately fascinated and confounded him. As they moved toward the upper level and the displays of fabric that Schomberg was famous for, Morgan spoke with sudden inspiration. "Do you have a full staff at your house in Town?"

Twelve

The silence in the Lambert chaise lasted only as long as it took to move into the street and out of earshot of their escorts.

Both sisters spoke at the same time.

"Oh, Christy, I am so sorry."

"Joanna, I must apologize—" Christiana stopped. What was Joanna sorry for?

"No, indeed, it is I who must apologize, Christy. It was wrong of me to leave you with Lord Morgan. I was certain a few moments' conversation would set all to rights. Then I was distracted discussing the masquerade with Lord Monksford. I suppose I should not have left you alone together for so long, but I was so sure that seeing him as soon as possible was the solution to your awkwardness."

"Rather like getting back on the horse right after one has fallen off?"

Joanna relaxed a little at the silly comparison. "I suppose you could think of it that way, Christy. Was I wrong?"

"I think that different feelings are involved." Christiana warmed to the debate. "With a fall from a horse, one has to deal with fear, but in a personal situation one must confront"—she paused—"embarrassment."

"And what is embarrassment, but fear based on social error?" Joanna waved her fan in emphasis.

"I can never win a philosophical discussion with you, so I am not even going to try."

"But, Christy, I would so prefer it to an argument."

"There is no argument coming, though I can see why you would think so. It appears that I have picked arguments with my two dearest friends today." She bit back a smile. Would that all disagreements could result in a truer friendship the way her words with Lord Morgan had.

"You and I were not arguing, Christy. It is merely that your nerves were overset." Joanna dismissed that casually, but leaned closer with wide eyes and an uneasy smile. "Did you really argue with Lord Morgan?"

"Well, yes, but only for a moment. Then he found some silly way to tease me out of it."

"Then everything is all right between you?" Joanna spoke with a hopeful nod.

"Why of course." Though in all honesty that wordless communion they had shared before Monksford and Joanna had interrupted them did stir a vague discomfort. For a moment, she felt as though she were the only person in his world. Was that disloyal to Richard or simply a part of Morgan's charm?

"Everything is well between us, but oh, Joanna"—she drew a deep breath—"men can be so difficult to understand."

"Indeed, so Mama always says. But is it that surprising? They see the world from an entirely different perspective. The very fact they go away to school and come to London on their own guarantees that."

The chaise bumped up against a curb and both of them reached out to brace themselves. The sound of some vehicle approaching too fast and with obvious carelessness drew their attention. They could hear more than they could see, though, as a much larger carriage pulled close to theirs blocked the view. Voices raised in anger followed the racers but soon the street was back to the usual hubbub of a late afternoon.

Christiana very much wanted to know what had happened, but not without someone to protect her. "Would you truly like to be in Town on your own, Joanna?"

"Of course not. I was never prepared for it. There are other things, though. Opportunities George had that Papa never even thought to offer us. I would have liked more schooling, to read languages besides French, and see the great art in Italy. I would have liked to go to Jamaica, too. I think I would have preferred to learn more about architecture than needlepoint."

She stopped speaking, but Christiana could see the list continued on in her head for a moment. Joanna looked up and tapped her sister on the arm with her fan. "What would you wish for?"

"If I had the same opportunities as a man?" Christiana mulled it over and was hard-pressed to come up with something she wanted that she did not already have. Then she remembered Richard. "If I had the same opportunities then I could be in Portugal right now."

"Exactly."

"But, Joanna, only to you will I admit that I have no desire to be in Portugal, not right now. I want very much to be exactly where I am. Here in London for the Season." It was the truth. Why did it sound so shallow? "Of course, I would be enjoying it much more if Richard were here and safe."

"Would you really?" Joanna asked with a knowing smile.

"Well, no, because then I would not have met Lord Morgan and Richard hates to dance and he would lose money gambling which we need to establish our household. But to admit that I am happier here without Richard is shockingly selfish, is it not?"

"No." Joanna made the single word a long, considering sentence. "Or at least no more selfish than Richard is. He had the choice. He had no need to purchase his colors at this precise moment. He could have waited until the Season was over, but he dislikes the city and he only dances when you insist.

"And because he is a man, he could choose to do whatever he wants. He had to know sharing the Season with you would have made for a lifetime of memories, but he chose to go early to Portugal instead. Which proves my point completely."

Christiana sat in awed silence. Joanna made it sound as though Richard was the selfish one. It was the second time today that someone had made her failings seem virtuous.

"You are too kind, Jo." She raised her hand when her sister would have spoken. "Do you have these sorts of discussions with Lord Monksford?"

"Oh yes." She answered promptly. "All the time."

"That is a part of Lord Monksford I do not know at all." She must make an effort to see beyond his awful coats and his thinning hair. Those elements were no more an obstacle to his real self than the sergeant's ruined clothes had been. She was able to see beyond that façade, why was it so difficult with Lord Monksford?

Oh dear, she thought with a flash of insight, *that is easy enough to answer.*

"I am quite jealous of him, Joanna." The words were out of her mouth before she could hold them back.

"Lord Monksford?" Joanna was genuinely astonished. "But why?"

"I have only just realized it, Jo, and I mean to have no more of it. To be selfish is one thing, but to add jealousy is to be vastly unbecoming."

Joanna was clearly unconvinced and Christiana leaned closer.

"You must see. Before you met him, I was the keeper of all your confidences. It was you and I who discussed whatever concerned you. Now, I have to learn to share those dearest parts of you with someone else."

"I am not sure Lord Monksford and I are at that point, at least not yet, though I suppose close attachments will change our lives in many more ways than we know." All gaiety was gone from her voice.

"Your melancholy is totally unjustified, Joanna, dearest. You are my sister. Only you can be that." Christiana looked at the window, amazed at the start of tears in her eyes. "You are the first and most important confidante I have. Richard is a wonder in many ways but understanding my worries is not one of them."

Lord Morgan does, she realized suddenly. *Sometimes he understands my heart before I do. Perhaps he is more worthy of Joanna's jealousy than Richard will ever be.*

They were within two blocks of the house on Green Street. Christiana recognized the park at Grosvenor Square just before they turned onto North Audley.

They would be home shortly and there was one more thing disturbing Christiana mightily. "Joanna, I must tell you about the soldier I saw, but first you must be honest with me. You did not tell Lord Monksford about our costumes for the masquerade, did you?"

Despite the dozens of rooms that made up Hale House, the dowager duchess used no more than four on a regular basis. One such was a receiving room that she had converted into an office. It was overfurnished and so stiflingly warm that the sun god would have called for ice. Morgan stood as far from the fire as he could and considered opening a window.

Only her family and close friends were allowed here. This morning, he noted, one of each was present, the two of them come to help with the musicale his grandmother was so fixed on. He was the relative and Christiana Lambert could be considered nothing less than a close friend.

In fact it was months since the dowager duchess had introduced him to Christiana, but it seemed yesterday and centuries ago at the same time. It was ages since he had thought of her as nothing more than an amusing dance partner, but only yesterday that he realized how much she truly meant to him.

Sergeant Tidwell had brought home to him, full force, exactly what he was willing to do in order to make her happy. It was some consolation to his new-found feelings that she had so appreciated his efforts. Not that this was love. No, not even a shadow of it. Best not try to define it, simply enjoy the way she had of making him feel an equal to any god on Olympus.

He watched Christiana now as she listened to his grandmother, her lips pursed in concentration, which under other circumstances might invite a kiss.

He turned away from them. He understood what it was that his grandmother so valued in her much younger friend. Christiana genuinely cared. She did not see his grandmother as someone whose time had come and was almost gone. She truly listened as she was listening now, answering even the most common-place conversation with thoughtfulness.

And not only with the people of the *ton*. So it was with everyone from Sally, her maid, to Sergeant Tidwell. She noticed people and even better than that, acknowledged them beyond a perfunctory courtesy.

He could tell by the way her brow was furrowed that her conversation was not a happy one, though the distress seemed to be all on his grandmother's part.

As much as he loved his grandmama, Morgan had

no desire to hear whatever it was. The gift of a generous ear was his Sprite's virtue and hers alone. Instead of joining them, he walked toward the desk.

He noticed that the invitation cards were already made out with date and time, awaiting only the addition of the guests' names. Had Grandmama already made all the decisions? Then why did she need them?

At that moment the intense conversation between the ladies ended. The duchess settled in her chair a few feet away from the table, right next to the well-lit fireplace. "You sit there, Miss Lambert." She pointed to a chair near the stack of invitation cards and envelopes. "Morgan, you sit on the other side."

He hesitated. Did she actually expect them to handwrite the invitations? "Perhaps I should go to the music room and see if the pianoforte needs tuning."

The duchess waved away the attempt. "We have to move it anyway. I'll have the tuner out once it is placed properly. But we cannot determine where to put it until we know the exact number we can expect. Now sit down!"

Christiana turned her head slightly toward Morgan and with expressive eyes wide urged his cooperation.

Rapping her cane on the floor, his grandmother called the meeting to order. "We are agreed that this will be held on Monday, not too late in the evening."

He and Christiana both glanced at the prepared invitations and nodded.

"Now, you two will tell me whom to invite." The dowager duchess looked expectantly at them.

"I did bring a list of the people I know who truly do enjoy music." Christiana was almost apologetic as she pulled a paper from her reticule.

Very good, Morgan thought. *I have not given the guest list a minute's thought.*

She read the names aloud and Morgan watched as his grandmama's smile grew. "Excellent, my dear Miss Lambert. A very nice mix of young people balanced with some of more mature years. But I do believe that we have room for almost twice that number."

She turned and cast a penetrating eye on him. "Morgan? Whom would you add to this group?"

He tossed out all the names he could think of, including young Peter Wilton and Rhys, who was almost certainly unavailable. He wished he had taken a moment to write down the names, but when he glanced at Christiana he saw that she was busily adding them to her list.

"Hmmm," was all his grandmother said, obviously not as pleased with his choices as she was with "dear Miss Lambert's."

"Your gaming connections are showing, my boy. Not Druson or Powers. They have passed beyond eligible: too many losses and too many fights. But the others will do."

It made for a large group for a musicale, but small enough for comfort if they were indeed to be situated in the ballroom. He stood and bowed to his grandmother.

"Sit down!" She spoke in a huff and Morgan hurried to obey.

He caught Christiana's worried expression. As he sat down he whispered, "Smile, Sprite, and pretend this is fun. Do you have any idea what I have done to irritate her?"

"Eh? What did you say, Morgan?"

Christiana looked directly at Morgan but answered the dowager duchess. "He said that he did not realize the planning was so complicated."

He touched her hand in appreciation and turned to give his grandmother his full attention.

"Just so, it is complicated," the dowager duchess agreed. "And success is in the details. The whole purpose of this exercise is to give you some idea of what it will be like to run your own household."

Morgan looked at Christiana. Neither one of them was smiling now. Was that what this visit was about? Matchmaking?

She rapped her cane on the floor again. "Listen to me, and stop looking as though marriage had not occurred to both of you. I have arranged for Monsieur Delacorte to play the pianoforte and his wife will sing."

That piece of news did distract Christiana and she brought her hands together in the lightest clap. "Oh, but how perfect! They are the most sought-after performers this Season."

"I still have some influence."

Was the dowager'd pleased smile satisfaction at her enduring authority or Christiana's pleasure?

"Now, I want the two of you to list your favorite foods, and any ideas that you may have for decorations. Then I can review them and see if they are acceptable."

Christiana nodded and took up a pen. Morgan did as well and they both began writing. Morgan stopped to watch Christiana. Where was her smile? She was taking this too seriously. Finally, he asked sotto voce, "Why are we not simply telling her?"

"Because she might not remember and almost certainly will not hear everything we have to say." She gave her own version of his grandmother's exasperated huff and went on. "You do understand that without our help an entertainment such as this would be completely beyond her. She does so wish to be a part of the Season and not just an onlooker."

No, of course he had not realized that.

"Please stop complaining, my lord. Her Grace is not asking too much. It is only a few hours."

"As you wish, Sprite. But I do have other commitments."

"Commitments that are more important than me

and your grandmother?" The distress in her voice was all tease.

He grinned at her. "Never more important than you."

"Or your grandmother," she prompted coyly.

He leaned a bit closer. "You know, I see something new in you."

"Really?" She sounded pleased. And interested.

"You no longer blush." He sat back and thought. Not since that afternoon at Schomberg House and that was days ago.

She laughed and leaned back in her chair. "You are as charming as ever, my lord, but I do hope I have learned something this Season, even if it is only how to handle extravagant compliments. Besides, we are friends now and that places your compliments in an entirely different light."

She thought these months in Town had changed her? Not completely; her Town bronze was only a veneer. Her smile was still so genuine. It reached her eyes and invited him closer than he had ever been to a woman. Did she have any idea of the effect she had on him? No, clearly not, or she would, indeed, be blushing. The only person who would approve of this was his grandmother.

He turned toward his grandmama, expecting to find her watching with measured interest, but found her eyes were closed and that she was close to sound asleep.

Following his gaze, Christiana rose. Taking a shawl from a nearby chair, she draped it gently over the dowager duchess, careful not to disturb her rest, then walked silently back to her seat.

She continued their conversation in the same near whisper, but his flirt had gone into hiding again. *Oh, come back and play,* he thought, and then heard what she was saying. "Your grandmother did not sleep last night and is upset with all Braedons. She has had a serious disappointment."

"I was wondering what had taken your smile. Was that what you were talking about earlier?"

She nodded with apology.

He grimaced. "Something I did?"

"Oh no, my lord. You are above all her favorite. I am sure of that."

"As much as I care for Grandmama, I find that 'favorite' is a dubious honor, one which I believe my brother Rhys holds with singular distinction."

"Certainly she makes all her grandchildren feel treasured."

He laughed. "We are not still five years old and I do believe you are avoiding the subject."

"Not at all." Christiana spoke with such indignation that he bowed an apology. Whether she had been trying to avoid the subject or not, she gave it her attention now, folding her hands demurely in front of her, glancing at the dowager duchess as if for permission to speak.

"Last week Her Grace wrote to your brother, suggesting he attempt a reconciliation between your sister and your father. Yesterday evening she received a letter from the viscount. He refused to consider it and gave no explanation."

Morgan closed his eyes and groaned. "I can imagine James's letter. Most likely one word. 'No.' "

"I think it was couched in a phrase or two of concern."

"But no regret, no explanation. It should not have come as a surprise to her. While our father is alive James will follow his direction, even if the marquis is too ill to watch over his shoulder."

Christiana spoke on a sigh. "She knows that now and she worries that this may be her last chance to effect a reunion given the precarious state of the marquis's health."

He nodded, not knowing what else to say. Christiana was tactful enough to return her attention to the party planning and leave him with his thoughts. He watched her bent head and felt a wrench of guilt that concern for his family was the reason that the sunshine was gone from her day.

A few moments later she looked up from her sober list-writing. "Do you think it would be a good idea if Her Grace invited some of the young ladies to perform?"

He considered it a moment. What did he know? But he owed her some help. She was the one doing all the work while he had all the pleasure of watching her. Even earnest she was all charm. The light from the window—he stopped himself. Ye gods, he was in danger of waxing poetic about the way the light encircled her hair. He cleared his throat and dispelled the poetry. "There are certainly several young ladies whose play is creditable. But they must play before the Delacortes or they will suffer by comparison."

With a firm nod Christiana made a notation.

"Now if my sister Mariel were here"—he paused, summoning the memory—"it would be different. She can play both pianoforte and harp with a skill that brings tears to your eyes. She would be received with pleasure and applause."

He pulled that thought closer. Could Mariel come to Town? Would she? He hitched his chair nearer to Christiana's and with a quick glance at his still-sleeping grandmama he spoke. "What do you think of this idea? I write to Mariel and invite her to come and play at the musicale. Do you think Grandmama would be pleased?"

"Oh, my lord, that is a wonderful idea."

She was smiling at him as though he had hung a star for her.

"It must be a surprise." He lost his train of thought for a moment, lost in the pleasure of easing her worry, in that smile that made him feel equal to the tasks of Hercules.

A soft snore from nearby pulled his thoughts back from that abyss. "Uh, a surprise, yes, it must be a surprise. If only because I am not sure I can convince Mariel to leave her two darlings behind, much less Charles and on such short notice. Could I rely on you to find some reason to ask that a room be prepared?"

Even as Christiana began to make notes, Morgan considered the possibility. It would only be for a few days. Travel from Kent was easily done in one day. She would be home in less than a week. And if he wrote now, there would be enough time to plan it all.

He made to rise. "Excuse me, my dear, I am going to move to the library and write to Mariel immediately." Before she could protest, he was out of the room, already wording the note. It would be much less distracting if a room separated them. His side of their friendship was teetering precariously. And Christiana was completely oblivious.

Thirteen

Christiana watched him leave the room and then glanced toward the duchess, whose snores were gentle but unmistakable. The list was as complete as she could make it. Should there be more savories than sweets? Was her idea for simple greenery intertwined with a white flowering vine distinctive enough?

Carefully replacing the pen in the holder, she drew a deep breath and considered what was really on her mind. Was she the only person in her world who had never known true heartache? Never known disappointment so deep that it changed your life? Her grandfather had died not much more than a year ago, but he was old, ill, in pain. The vicar insisted it was a blessing and she could only agree.

If she were being completely honest, it would grieve her more when the dowager duchess was gone. She loved her as she would have loved her own grandmothers, had they not died before her birth. Grief was the cost of loving.

Heartache came in other guises as well. The duchess and Lord Morgan and all the rest of the Braedons shared loss that was not grounded in death but in one person's determination to control his world. Christiana thought of her mama, who seemed inclined to manage. Then a guilty thought struck her. Her pretense of courtship with Lord Morgan was nothing less than their mutual attempt to manipulate the world to their satisfaction.

There you are, she thought, *I suppose all of us are inclined to make the world dance to our tune.* But for the first time she realized that it was a dangerous game to play. One could not ever completely control another or even one's own feelings.

From the corner of her eye, she saw the dowager duchess stir. With a guilty start, Christiana considered the party plans they had been working on before Lord Morgan had abandoned her.

"All done without me, eh." The dowager duchess's voice was a bit hoarse, but it cleared as she straightened in her chair. "And where has Morgan run off to the minute I close my eyes?"

"He is in the library, Your Grace, composing a letter he thought urgent." Christiana stood. "I can get him for you."

"You do that, my dear, and I will order some tea for us and then we can discuss the lists you have made." She drew the shawl from her lap and draped it over her shoulders. "It will take a few moments for the tea tray to come up, so you need not hurry. Morgan can finish his important letter and then show you the artwork."

Christiana forbore to explain. It probably did seem as though she was anxious for time alone with him, when all she really wanted to do was avoid a family argument.

She left the room in such a hurry that she forgot to ask directions to the library. A footman on duty in the hallway escorted her up a floor and to the front of the house. He scratched on the door, but did not wait for permission to enter before opening the door for her. Christiana stepped into the dimly lit room and found Morgan seated near a window, impatiently tapping his fingers on the desk, two ruined sheets of paper before him.

His relief upon seeing her was very gratifying. "Do come here, Sprite, please, and help me write this confounded thing."

"How difficult can it be, my lord?"

He put the quill back in the stand and pushed back slightly from the desk and made to rise.

Christiana hurried over to him and put her hand on his shoulder to keep him from standing. He looked at her hand, then up at her with such a pleased smile that she returned it with a grin quite unequal to the task.

She looked away for a moment and tamed the smile to something less tender while a cascade of thoughts crowded her brain. Was it normal that she should feel such pleasure in his company, such joy in seeing him when they had only been apart a few moments? What would it be like when she saw Richard? Why did the thought bring more worry than pleasure?

She picked up one of the crumpled sheets and scanned it. "Oh no, I am sorry, my lord, but this sounds like a royal command. Even a much-loved sister would have to refuse on principle."

"Yes, and as you can see I threw that sheet away."

"To your credit, sir." She picked up the other one. "Much better, sir, but perhaps 'beg' is a bit too abject."

"And your suggestion would be?"

"Tell her the truth. Your grandmother is longing to have her family close and has no hopes for a Braedon reconciliation. If your sister would come for a few days, it would be a comfort far beyond the effort involved."

He nodded with grudging approval. With a fresh sheet of paper he began. Christiana set her lips together so she would remain silent while he worked. After a moment she moved to the other side of the room, where she tried to examine a portrait of the current duke and his family, but the room was in such shadow that it was difficult to see more than a man in full court dress and a woman holding a baby against her elaborately bejeweled bosom.

Were they happy, she wondered. Were they well matched? Was their world filled with temptation? What kind of loss had they faced? Did it bring them closer together? More light would not answer any of those questions. Portraits were so unsatisfying. They raised questions and could not answer them.

The next painting was smaller. A family group, all children, which in itself was unusual. There were four, no, five, if you counted the oldest, who stood nearby with a fond smile that looked decidedly silly on a young man.

With a spurt of pleased surprise she realized that the standoffish young man was the viscount and this must be the Braedon offspring as they were at least fifteen years ago.

Indeed, one of the children held a small child-sized telescope. That would be Rhys and the girl with the flute would be Mariel. One more boy and girl sat close together, looking at a book: Maddie and Morgan. Not twins she knew, but very close in age.

She stared at young Morgan. There was so much about his youth she did not know. And she wanted details, hundreds of them.

"Are they telling you all the Braedon secrets?"

Lord Morgan came up from behind her and turned his back to the painting.

Despite the question, Christiana realized that he did not want to talk about it. His arms were crossed and although he was smiling there was a defensive look in his eyes. She struggled for the most innocent question.

"Your brother Rhys has been interested in astronomy since childhood?" She took his arm as she asked her question and moved toward the windows.

* * *

Morgan hated that painting as much as he loved it. They had sat for it only months before his mother died and their whole world changed.

Christiana looked lovely today. This dress was definitely new for the Season, a delicate green with twining leaves around the bodice, sleeves, and border. It was as springlike as the flowers just arrived from the Braemoor succession houses.

She let go of his arm as they stopped before a large globe of the world and he let her step away.

"My brother Rhys has had a telescope in his hand since he could walk. He could read before he was out of the nursery. Intellectually, he is quite impressive and the fact that he uses his brain for something besides his own pleasure is not at all typical of Braedons."

"We each have different skills, my lord. And judging someone else's particular talent as exceptional does not diminish the talent of another."

He looked at her with a little surprise. It was a compliment worthy of a diplomat.

"That insight is not a truth unique to me." With a slightly embarrassed shrug she explained, "I do listen to the vicar's sermons on occasion."

"You actually listen to sermons?" He gave her a slight bow. "My dear, that is one of your lesser acknowledged talents. Alas, daydreaming through them is only one of my shortcomings."

"But why do you dwell on your shortcomings?"

There was a touch of indignation in her question. It was charming and now Morgan was curious. "Let me see, Rhys is our intellectual, Mariel can claim music as her talent. But what is mine, I wonder?"

"A generosity of spirit, my lord."

"Suitably vague."

"I can give you examples: Your willingness to help me with my charade, your willingness to dance with all those least likely to find partners."

At his surprise, she added, "Oh yes, I have noticed that." She thought a bare moment more. "Oh, and your refusal to fleece the more foolish gamblers. How many times have I heard you decline play with Peter Wilton because he was foxed?"

"I am beginning to sound positively virtuous."

"You have your moments, my lord, but I think I will stop there, lest you think I hold you in too high a regard."

He was grateful for that. Few things were more annoying than having someone list your admirable qualities. Usually the list was a figment of their imagination and as accurate as Cupid's arrow after a drunken orgy. And generally aimed with the same intent. This was flirtation and nothing more.

Christiana gave the globe a delicate spin. "Does your brother Rhys have the use of a telescope?"

Morgan shook his head, remembering. "On this most recent visit, he and my brother James came close to a physical fight about some property on which Rhys wants to construct one."

"No, really?" She looked shocked, but she pressed her lips together to keep from laughing. "I would imagine that any argument with the viscount rarely results in a win for the other whether the fight is physical or verbal."

"That insight, so obvious to us, my dear, is something Rhys has not yet grasped."

This time she did laugh and shook her head. "But why does the viscount object? Is it valuable property or cultivated?"

"The thing is, the property that Rhys wants to use belongs to a neighbor, a hilly piece, useless for farming and not much better for grazing. There is even an old foundation that he insists he could use for the observatory. The problem lies in that Rhys wants to trade some prime Braedon land for it."

"Even if your older brother agreed, would that be possible? Surely the land is entailed?"

"No, not this parcel. Trust Rhys to research all this quite thoroughly."

"And Lord Rhys is hoping to talk your brother into the trade? I am sorry to sound cynical, my lord, but he is an incredible optimist to think any man would give up good productive land for useless, even in the name of science."

"He is worse than an optimist, he is a dedicated scholar." Morgan shook his head. "And right now he is living in a fantasy world. You are right. James giving up land is as likely as Bonaparte accepting an invite to dine with the King."

"I understand completely. In my family, the Lamberts and the Wiltons have been arguing over a piece of property for at least four generations. It is quite unusable land really, good only for hunting, but you would think they would be able to mine gold there if only one family or the other could establish ownership."

Ah, yes, the property that young Wilton had told him about so long ago. "Have they ever been close to agreement?" It was an innocent question, he insisted to himself. He was only curious to know if Christiana realized how nearly her own future was tied to the resolution of this dispute.

"It could be. There is some antique proviso that when a Lambert and Wilton marry the property will go to the male half of the union."

"Then, when you marry Richard, his family will secure the title to the property?"

"I think that the land is the only reason my father has been so hesitant to agree to our engagement." She spoke with a casual nod, totally unaware that this information amazed him.

She *knew* about the agreement? So much for young Wilton's assumption that her sensibilities would be offended by the knowledge. Not only Wilton, he, too, had been certain that for Christiana Lambert romance was of paramount importance in any married relationship. "Forgive me if I am indelicate, but the pragmatic aspect of this land transaction does not dilute your own conviction that Richard's attachment to you is purely romantic?"

"No."

The single word could have been firmer.

Her second no was much more firm. "He is a second son and gains no financial benefit from it, my lord. His attachment to me is of the purest and most noble."

He wanted to laugh, but restrained himself, with effort.

"I can see that you do not believe me. And, in all honesty, I am not as convinced of it as I once was."

"Really?" Now that did surprise him, which surely showed that her naïveté was contagious.

"If he was as passionately devoted to me as I would like then he never would have left for Portugal so soon. He would have come for at least part of the Season. Then perhaps we could have become engaged and letters between us would have been possible."

"A young man with a commission is not entirely at his own command. He must respond to his orders." *Good, Morgan,* he thought. *Defend the man. Remind yourself that she has interests elsewhere.*

She sighed and on the next indrawn breath claimed a bit more Town bronze. "At first I thought I would miss him unbearably, far more than he would miss me. But now I am not so sure. There are days that go by when I neglect to write in the journal that I plan to share with him. I do check the papers daily but there has been little fighting since Douro in mid-May. There are whole hours that go by when I do not give his hardships a thought."

"London is a city built to entertain and distract."

He took a step closer, and reached out to raise her chin so he could see her face. There was self-reproach in her eyes and he wondered if he should feel guilty. "London can even undermine our most cherished beliefs." He let his hand fall and took a step back. "That is something I must remind myself daily."

Christiana gave the globe one last spin before she turned toward the windows. "I now realize that it was an incredible conceit on my part to think that I would be immune from those temptations."

Was he the temptation? Best not to pursue *that* at this particular moment. They were alone, the conversation intimate, but the mood was all wrong. He stepped behind the large desk that stood in the middle of the room. "So you have given up some innocence and gained some wisdom."

"Wisdom? I am not so sure, my lord. Perhaps self-knowledge is a more realistic phrase?"

Perhaps it was best that she lost some little bit of her innocence. At seventeen it was charming, a way to retrieve his own youth, but at thirty would it be so appealing? He doubted it.

Not that he would be around to see.

"Yes, self-knowledge is a better term. In truth, I have always thought wisdom could only come from pain."

She turned back to him and smiled. "And this Season has been a hundred different things, but not one of them is painful."

"I will accept that you have gained self-knowledge or, perhaps understanding"—he bowed to her—"and hope that it does not inhibit your laughter or still your longing to dance."

She smiled into his eyes for a long moment and then sobered suddenly. "Do you think perhaps, my lord, we should return to the duchess?"

He offered her his arm. She was right; it would be best to return to the subject at hand, though he doubted that his grandmama needed their help as much as Christiana insisted. She had invited them today so she could see how they were getting on. Had she learned as much as he had?

As if to reinforce her suggestion, a footman scratched at the door and announced that tea was awaiting them. With his letter sanded, sealed, and slipped into his pocket, Morgan bowed Christiana ahead of him and escorted her down the hall.

"My lord, who are you going to ask to deliver the letter?" There was doubt more than question in her voice.

"You know, that could present a problem."

He settled her arm through his as they walked down the hall to the stairs and down them. "Time is a factor, but if I ask someone from Braedon House and he is found out, it could cost the man his job. And if someone from Hale House is sent, Mariel's invitation would not be a secret for more than a day."

As they reached the bottom of the stairs, she stopped their progress and stood facing him. "I have an idea, my lord. You could hire someone to go, someone with no connection to either family."

"And that would be?" Her question was tentative but surely she had someone in mind.

"Sergeant Tidwell?"

"An excellent notion! I even have his direction." The man was at Monksford's, working in the stable, not more than six blocks away. Surely Monksford would agree to the errand and Tidwell could be on his way before dark.

Christiana tucked her hand back into his arm as they moved along the hall to the back of the house. She walked very close to him, more closely than necessary when you considered they were walking down a hallway where frayed carpet was the only possible hazard.

He was not going to complain. He could only feel. Her head close to his shoulder, her lithe young body soft against his arm. No one could see them but the footman and if their promenade generated gossip below stairs it would be nothing that had not been reported a dozen times before.

This moment was too precious to sabotage with the *ton's* notion of appropriate. It was a rare day that he was regarded as both hero and confidante, though he was not entirely sure he liked either role. He would have preferred lover, but since that was denied him, hero would do.

Fourteen

"Was I awful?" Emily Perry's question showed a rare insecurity. The amateur segment of the musicale had gone quite well, but Christiana understood that there was always a need for assurance.

"Your piece was quite lovely." Christiana reached out to still the fan Emily was waving frantically. "You have a light touch and you chose a piece that was familiar but not overplayed."

Emily relaxed and began to recount each note of her performance. Christiana listened patiently, all the while praying that Joanna would rescue her, but the room was filled with guests and Joanna was nowhere in sight.

After a time Emily's beau approached and Christiana left the two discussing the manifold merits of her performance. Christiana nodded to several others, but moved purposefully to the knot of people gathered around the harp. Mariel Whitlow stood beside the instrument, as though she felt the need to share praise with it.

Morgan's older sister had the look of a Braedon, but kind eyes and a mouth made for smiling softened the strong jaw and high cheekbones. She wore her hair in the latest style and her dress was au courant. Despite the latest fashion, there was something about her that set her apart from this social milieu, as though she felt she was no longer part of the *ton* and not unhappy with that distance.

"It was kind of my grandmother to plan it so that I was the only harpist."

How sweet, thought Christiana. As if that was the reason she had sounded so extraordinary.

"Mariel, she could get no one else to play!" There was general laughter. "Too many remember your skill. It was only a few years ago."

An older woman added waspishly, "You would have to have more ego than sense to play the harp when Mrs. Whitlow is on the program."

Harshly said but true. The notes of the piece still echoed in her head. Mariel played with a rare talent and she played with heart. The harp, which usually looked so awkward, seemed like an extension of the musician, or maybe she was an extension of it.

"But no encore, Mariel." The man who chastised her spoke with a coy reproach that was surely meant as flirtation. Christiana watched the response with interest.

"No, my lord, the applause was very gratifying but it is, after all, the Delacortes' evening." She nodded to the corner of the room, where the professional musicians were talking with a group of admirers. "Do please excuse me, I have only a day or two in Town and want to spend as much time as possible with my family."

Oh, nicely done, thought Christiana. She managed to make his comment part of the whole and rid herself of the lot of them.

Instead of moving to where the dowager duchess stood surrounded by a small group of friends, Mariel came to her.

"Miss Lambert"—she nodded slightly and smiled—"do you know where Morgan has got to?" She scanned the room while adding in a lower voice, "Actually, you are the one I would like to speak with."

Since it was exactly what Christiana was hoping for, she answered with a total lie that would give them both an escape. "I think he went to the yellow salon to find the shawl your grandmother left there."

"Excellent. Come with me, will you, while I find him?"

It took a few more brief conversations before they were out of the room, but Morgan did accommodate them by remaining wherever else he was.

It was cooler in the salon. The room was painted wood with yellow highlights, very much in the decor of the last century, but it had aged well. Chairs lined the wall in the old style, but neither of them wanted to sit. Instead they walked closer to the fire.

"Grandmama is full of praise for you and tells me that you are exactly what Morgan needs."

Christiana blushed and tried to return the compliment. "He is a charming escort." Oh no, that was all wrong. Oh, heavens, it was one thing to fool the *ton*, but lying to Morgan's family was not at all appealing.

Mariel looked down, pausing for thought, and tried again. "Miss Lambert. I am talking about more than dancing and the theater."

Did she know how much she sounded like her older brother James: very Braedon, very in charge? Unsure how to answer, Christiana remained silent.

"If I seem rude, Miss Lambert, I apologize." She spoke without the slightest hint of apology in her voice. "I have so little time and the happiness of my family is important to me."

Now there was a hint of anger in the way Mariel fisted her palms at her sides. "I thank God daily that Morgan is not"—she paused, her mouth a tight line as she searched for the right word—"that Morgan is not constrained by Papa's dictates."

"Mrs. Whitlow, I enjoy Lord Morgan's company." Christiana took a step closer to her. "I am not sure what Her Grace has told you, or indeed what she may hope for, but a match between us is not possible."

"Then what game is Morgan playing? It looks very like a courtship."

"We are friends." Christiana spoke with as much firmness as she could summon. "I know the idea of friendship between a man and woman is unusual, strange even. But it is what we both want."

"And Morgan agreed to it?" She stopped and shook her head. "Even friendship is more than he has had these last few years. That is why Grandmama had begun to hope. He has allowed so few people close to him."

"Oh, exactly, ma'am. That is the heart of the matter, is it not? He so rarely speaks of family and when he does there is such regret in his voice."

They heard the babble of voices increase as the ballroom doors were opened and the small crowd of people proceeded down the hall to the dining room, where refreshments were waiting. Neither Christiana nor Mariel moved to join them.

"Morgan refuses to accept that there is no hope of a reconciliation. He and Grandmama can command, ask, and beg and Papa will not give in."

Christiana had only some little knowledge of this, but she nodded in sympathy.

Mariel looked at her in a considering way. "You know, Miss Lambert, that I am happy and content, but I will tell you that marrying without my father's approval was the most difficult decision I have ever made."

Mariel reached over and took her hand. "I know that you say there can be no match between you and my brother, but I feel that I must tell you, because of my own experience, that if you should decide to accept his suit, despite your parents' disapproval, you will have my support."

Their joined hands and her pledge of support made

Mariel's words more a caution than a warning, but her reasoning was so misguided that Christiana stammered, "Is that what Morgan told you?"

"Oh no, he never discusses his personal life with anyone. It is only what I have surmised." Mariel let go of her hand with one last pat. "What else could keep you from the match? He has such a reputation as a gamester that I can understand any parents' hesitation. He has so perfected the façade that sometimes I think he believes it."

"A façade? It is?"

"His gambling is only a means to an end." Mariel walked closer to the fire. Christiana followed a few steps and then stopped. Finally Mariel turned back to her. "Morgan inherited property from our mother when he turned twenty-five. Papa never told him about it before that. Not that Morgan would ever have saved as much as a farthing, mind you, but still it was so managing of our father. So like him."

Mariel shook her head slightly. "Now that Morgan has control of the property, he is trying to raise enough money to make it self-sustaining. And the only way he can do that is by gaming. Even Papa and James do not realize why he is so devoted to faro."

"Oh dear." Christiana put her hands to her cheeks. "His tenants were depending on him and all the while he was dancing attendance on me at Almack's!"

"Then it must be love, Miss Lambert. Almack's is a dead bore."

Christiana forced a laugh. "I trust you mean that as a joke, for I assure you our appearance of courtship is as much a game that we both are playing as any played at a table."

"You think to fool all of society, up to and including our grandmother? To what end, Miss Lambert? How will either one of you benefit?" There was an edge of suspicion that made Christiana cringe.

"Mrs. Whitlow, there are very few people who know

this and I trust your confidence." She waited, her silence insisting on an answer.

"I have been involved with the church for years now and excel at keeping secrets." Her smile was reassuring.

"My parents insisted I come to London for the Season and from the beginning I hoped to find someone who would escort me but expect no lasting connection. You see, I am quite determined to marry my neighbor from home."

"Determined?"

"Well, perhaps that is not the best choice of words. I love him, of course. We have known each other forever. Richard is fighting in the Peninsula and I have every intention of joining him to follow the drum."

"That is very noble of you"—she paused—"but is it wise?"

"Not noble or wise, ma'am," Christiana responded earnestly. "But when we are married I will go where he is and right now that is Portugal."

"How biblical." Her expression shifted from self-assurance to worry. Sitting on one of the chairs near a window, she gestured to the chair beside her. "Please do come sit with me for a moment."

Christiana did as she was asked even though she felt a lecture was coming.

"Christiana, I find my concern is now for my brother. You say he agreed to this sham?"

Christiana nodded.

"I will concede that it may have begun as sport, but are you certain that his feelings are not engaged? It is so unlike him to indulge in the courtship ritual and I can not think what would induce him to do it, except perhaps the hope that he can replace the absent Richard in your heart."

"Oh, but you see, Lord Morgan has his own reasons for the game." She was so relieved that she rushed into the speech without considering it was not her secret to share. "Lord Morgan told me that his father demanded he find a match this Season. Morgan said he would prefer to find a bride at a place and time of his own choice and given what you have told me of his property in Wales, I can understand even more fully his reasoning."

"Oh, Papa!" Mariel spoke the two words with the vehemence of an expletive. "Will he never learn?"

Mariel stood abruptly and began to pace the room. "Ah, well, now I see that it is the two of you who are playing a game. Both of you trying to convince your parents and the *ton* that you are fulfilling their wishes and very determined to honor your own."

That was the truth of it, but she made it sound foolish.

"Christiana, do bear in mind that it *is* a game and there are very few games where both the players win."

"You think we are closer than we should be." Christiana stood, uncomfortable because she knew it might be true.

"That is for the two of you to determine. But before it goes any further be absolutely sure that you are content with friendship."

"His friendship means everything to me. I would not hurt him for the world." Christiana's eyes misted with guilt. She loved Richard. She loved Richard. But if that was the truth then why did the thought of hurting Morgan make her want to cry?

"You mistake me, Christiana; it is not Morgan's feelings I am worried about. It is yours. You must remind yourself that this is a flirtation with a very experienced man, a heady experience for any girl in her first Season."

Christiana shivered. Put that way it sounded more delicious than mean-spirited. "Then everything is all right for I know that Lord Morgan is as careful of my feelings as I am of his."

"Very well then." Now Mariel sounded exactly like

a priest. She straightened her skirts and smoothed her hair.

"But, ma'am, what will you tell Her Grace?" Christiana stood where she was, anxious to have this one last issue resolved.

"I will tell her that she knows you and Morgan better than I and that I hope and pray the two of you know what you are about. It will be nothing less than the truth."

"Thank you, ma'am." There was something left unspoken, but Christiana was so relieved to have the interview end on a happy note that she did not pursue it further. Did that make her a coward or wise? She opted for sensible.

"Shall we join the others and treat ourselves to the wonderful sweets the duke's chef promised?"

And where *was* Morgan, Christiana wondered. Out loud she asked, "Do you think there will be any left? I can guarantee that Peter Wilton alone is capable of demolishing the entire buffet. And he was only one of a dozen young men invited."

"Aha, the chef understands this very well, but he has know me from childhood, and I can equally guarantee that he has set some aside for us."

The chef had indeed set aside a plate for each of them. Christiana accepted his offering with appreciation and when no one was looking, set it down on an empty table already filled with plates and glasses.

Searching the crowd for Lord Morgan, she finally located him talking with Peter Wilton and several other young men. He was listening to them with indulgent interest. As if he could feel her gaze, he looked up. She smiled at him and he smiled at her, and then returned to his conversation. *There,* she thought. *Everything is fine. He did not rush over to me and I am perfectly content to let him talk with his friends. There is nothing to worry about. Nothing at all.*

* * *

Christiana awoke early. With her eyes closed she smiled at the sense of anticipation that was her first waking thought. What was so exciting about today? The masquerade. Finally. Today was the Hawthornes' masquerade.

The last few weeks had been diversion enough but finally it was here. This party was the climax of the Season. There might be grander balls and finer dinners, but a masquerade was her idea of the perfect entertainment.

Everyone had a chance to be someone else. She and Joanna had spent hours, days even, perfecting their costumes of Starlight and Sunshine, but that was only half the fun. Who would Morgan choose to be? Would she be able to recognize him or would his disguise be so deep that she would dance three dances before she knew?

She snuggled down into bed. Oh no, it could never take three dances to know him. The thought of three dances made her smile as well. Would more than the conventional two be allowed? That was another secret pleasure of a masquerade. Not only could you appear different, but you could carry the game deeper and behave differently.

Of course, it would be difficult to fool anyone for long. They were all so well known to each other now. The guest list would include the same circle they had spent the last few months with. Had anyone thought to change the way they walked as part of tonight's charade?

Christiana jumped from her bed and pulled a bit of the curtain aside. Was that sunshine? She could barely see the sky for all the tall houses that lined the street, but she thought it looked promising. Would the day hold fair into the evening and allow for walks in the Hawthornes' garden? She dove back into bed, snuggled into the covers, and turned her pillow so it felt cool against her cheek.

It was going to be perfect, absolutely perfect.

"You look perfect, Joanna, absolutely perfect." Christiana looked to her mama, hoping she would add her assurance.

"You look lovely, dear."

Christiana breathed a sigh of gratitude as a tentative smile replaced Joanna's frown.

"It seemed like such a good idea at the time, Christy." Joanna turned to her mother. "Do you think anyone will know what I am pretending to be?"

Mama's generosity faded. "Do not intellectualize, Joanna."

"Dearest, a masquerade is for amusement, not edification." Christiana had to agree with her mother. "With your mask on you look exactly as one representing the bright light of day should."

Joanna's half mask included a diadem of golden rays that framed her face. Her golden gown showed off her lovely skin and completed the illusion of bright sunlight.

Christiana brushed an imaginary speck of dust from her sister's skirt, then reached for her fan. "Now we must hurry so we are not too late. This is one time when I want to be among the first to arrive so that I can see what everyone is wearing." She dropped the fan on the bed and reached out to straighten Joanna's skirt just once more so that it would lie perfectly.

"Stand still, Christiana. Stop fidgeting."

Christiana refused to be annoyed by her mother's testiness. Nothing was going to spoil this evening. She stood still while her mother inspected her up and down and then nodded.

"Oh, Mama." Joanna spoke with amused annoyance. "Say it, Christy looks wonderful."

"She does." It was sincerely meant and her slight hesitation was understood by all three of them.

Joanna stepped closer to her sister. "You are still not sure she should be wearing black? But, Mama, sprinkled with brilliants the way it is and with her tiara of stars one could hardly mistake her for anything but the Night Sky."

Mama allowed herself to be convinced. "You look wonderful, both of you. A credit to your family."

It was such an unusually generous thing for their mama to say that Christiana could think of nothing less than a curtsy in thanks. Joanna followed suit, and in rare accord, the three of them made for the hall and the waiting carriage.

They did not arrive as early as Christiana would have liked. The train of carriages wound around the square, each occupant waiting with varying patience for the chance to alight at the grand entrance of the Hawthorne residence.

Once inside, the Lamberts made their way to a withdrawing room along with every other young lady and all spent at least another half hour admiring each other's costumes with singular sincerity. Most friends were easily recognized, though the youngest Miss Westbourne was well disguised as a shepherdess and had even changed her voice to match her outfit.

They discussed Miss Westbourne's costume as they made their way to the grand staircase. "It is an excellent idea. She has no particular beau and this will leave her free to entertain anyone who might ask her to dance."

"You know," remarked Joanna, "I do believe that a masquerade comes as close to making us the equal of men as any entertainment I can think of."

"Do you know what Lord Monksford is wearing?" If Joanna found him early then she could discuss the point with him. As far as Christiana was concerned, this evening was made for frivolity not debate.

Not three minutes later, Louis XIV, the Sun King, invited Joanna to dance. Christiana was dumbfounded. This man was wearing a suit made from the same fabric as Joanna's dress. His wig was a modest replica of those lately favored and there was no mistaking that he had come up with the outfit to compliment her sister's costume.

Was it really Lord Monksford? Every unkind thought Christiana had ever entertained about him disappeared, replaced by an affectionate admiration for a man who was willing to go so against his natural inclinations just to please her sister.

The golden couple moved to the dance floor and Christiana looked around for her mother, eager to share her amazement.

"Lady Starlight?" The quiet night-darkened voice came from behind her. "May I have this dance?"

It was Lord Morgan. He had gone to no great lengths to hide his face, though a half mask did cover his eyes. His voice was more seductive than usual, but it was very much in keeping with the costume he wore.

His clothing was the darkest black velvet and very formal, virtually unrelieved by white. Even his shirt and cravat were a black silk that made him look mysterious rather than menacing. He had draped a cape from his shoulder, this in satin, shimmering against the velvet of his suit.

"You look wonderful!" Christiana clapped her hands and would never ever admit that she was not exactly sure what he was supposed to be.

"But you have recognized me."

"Well, my lord, we have spent the entire Season together. By now I know your laugh even if I am half a room away. I can tell it is you even when your back is to me by the set of your shoulders and the tilt of your head."

"As I know you despite the mask."

She smiled as he stepped back to take in the elegance of her costume, though his eyes never left her face.

"But someone must have told you what I was wearing, my lord. Someone surely told Lord Monksford what Joanna's costume was going to be."

"No, no. Your eyes give you away and the way you bring your hands together." He covered her two joined hands with his own. "Just like this."

Who knew how long she would have been content to stand with him like that? But the orchestra's opening notes drew the attention of the entire crowd gathered in the outer room, and Christiana and Morgan were swept along with the rest of the guests as they all moved toward the ballroom.

As Morgan took her arm, Christiana realized that while he might not be anything more than a night-driven spirit, his costume was a perfect background to her brilliantly spangled gown.

"This is going to be so much fun! And how did you find out what I was wearing? Was it Sally? But when did you talk with her?" And then to design his whole costume to complement hers. Was there a more wonderful man in the world than Lord Morgan Braedon?

Fifteen

"Oh, the quiet in this garden is lovely." Christiana turned to look back into the ballroom. "I think everyone is dancing. Someone has even convinced Mama to take the floor."

Morgan watched her with unabashed enjoyment, drawing his pleasure in the evening from hers. She seemed pleased with the attention they drew—among the brightly colored costumes their black and sparkling outfits drew a dozen compliments.

After their first dance she had confided, "It is grand, just once, to be the belle of the ball. And the disguise gives us the freedom to enjoy every moment of it."

When she suggested a walk in the garden after their second dance he would have been a fool not to agree.

At first they walked in silence along the path, nodding to other couples they passed. As they moved farther from the house, there were fewer people and more dark corners. Christiana insisted there was a fountain at the end of the path and so they walked deeper into the garden as the sounds of the party faded behind them.

They hurried away from one dead end, holding their laughter until they were out of hearing, though as far as Morgan could tell the couple was so engrossed in each other they would have not heard any interruption less than a fireworks display.

"Who was it?" Christiana grabbed his arm as she barely saved herself from tripping over an uneven paving stone.

"That is the wonder of a masquerade, Miss Starlight. I have no idea who that was." He kept hold of her arm and led her to another path, this one more brightly lit. "It could be that they do not know either."

"You mean that woman might be kissing a complete stranger?"

"Yes. Does that shock you?"

"A little. How very daring." She shivered.

Was that a shiver of awareness or was she chilled? He took off his cloak and wrapped it around her. She stilled and he wanted desperately to turn her into his arms and enfold her as closely as the satin of his cloak held her. Instead, he let his hands linger, caressing her shoulders lightly through the fabric. She leaned back into the gesture for the briefest second, and then pulled the cape around her with murmured thanks.

Now they both were clothed in unrelieved black.

She stopped abruptly. "Do you think people suspect that is why we came out here?"

"Undoubtedly." The idea had certainly occurred to him. Had it only now struck her? Better late than never.

"Oh my." She stood with her back to him and spoke quietly but with animation, as though she were playing to a full house of one. "The *ton* can be so foolish." She turned back to him. "They refuse to believe that we may have simply wanted some air, some conversation. They think that friendship between a man and woman is impossible."

Christiana took his arm, humming the last tune they had danced to. She was in high spirits tonight and it was contagious.

They looked down a short path and then turned back as another couple had claimed the stone bench.

With a sigh of annoyance, Christiana whispered, "They think that all men and women are good for is some sort of endless mating ritual."

There was a touch of irritation in her voice now. He loved it and wondered just how to bait her a little more. "They just do not understand." Actually, he never had either. If this was friendship then it was one of the most exquisite frustrations of his life. He had been friends with women before, but it was always after an intimacy that made anything less absurd. "The true benefits of friendship are beyond their grasp."

"Yes! Friendship can be so rewarding. Good conversation, no need for games or pretenses, a true understanding that makes good manners natural."

Is that how she viewed what they shared? He would not have described it the same way. Did she really believe it or was she being coy? "You are, my dear, so delightfully, incredibly, wrong." Any insult was effectively eliminated by the low-voiced intimacy of his words.

"Me? Wrong?" The words were a squeak caught between amusement and flirtation.

"Yes. Friendship between a man and a woman is never as simple as good conversation and no pretension. For the simple reason that men and women do not ever understand each other fully."

She did not deny it, so he continued. "One is always wondering what the other really meant. For instance did you truly mean what you just said or are you, perhaps, fishing for more of a declaration from me."

She watched him, but still had no answer. Was she tempted?

"Sweetheart, do you really think in all these weeks, in all these charming afternoons, and softly scented nights, that friendship might have changed from an end to the means?"

He held her hand lightly in his. He had done that often enough before, but always to an end, to assist her down a step, to direct her to some sight, never just holding her hand for the sheer sensuous pleasure, the way he was now.

Her smile was cautious but he saw no censure, no shock. Touching her chin with a gentle finger, he raised her face to his. "Have you never realized how much I long to touch those sweet lips, those lips that charm and laugh and gossip with me, only with me?"

Running his thumb over her mouth, he felt the little gasp slip from her. Had Richard ever seen her eyes this green, totally focused on him, on his eyes, on his mouth? He was hardly fool enough to ask when he was so close to what he had wanted for so long. He stepped closer so there was hardly room for a breath between them. "Do you know how many times I have thought of caressing that sweet spot between your cheek and neck? That spot is so inviting when you wear your hair that way."

He trailed his hand down her cheek, resting his palm at the curve of her neck. The smile faded. Her pulse sharpened.

He needed no answer. He did not need to read her eyes. How could she not long for the same kiss he had dreamed of for weeks?

Holding her face with his hands, he touched her mouth with his. The small kiss he planned disappeared with the first feel of her. He had waited so long and had so much to give. Morgan kissed her with a passion he could barely control, teasing her lips with his tongue, using his hands to stroke the sensitive cords of her neck, eager for the response that meant surrender.

His own yearning masked her first response, but he recognized the softening of her mouth against his, the slight opening of her lips. But after a moment he realized that was all the response there was.

He felt the tension in her body. Hands that should have been clutching at his coat were pressed against him, urging them apart. He allowed himself to be pushed an arm's length away and realized at once his mistake.

Her eyes were bright with tears or anger. She looked at him as if he were a stranger. No, it was worse than that; she looked at him with a gaze of shocked disbelief.

"No!" Christiana had enough control not to shout the word, but he heard the vehemence despite the whisper. The joy was gone from her eyes, the color faded from her cheeks. She looked old all at once, not in years, but in experience, experience garnered from one kiss, from him.

He put out his hand, hoping to apologize, to talk some sense into her, to make amends somehow, so they could return to the ballroom and forget his grotesque blunder.

She slapped him and he knew there was no hope of a reprieve. Turning, she all but ran to the door. Shock held him for a moment and then he realized that her hurried entry into the ballroom, alone and distraught, would be ruinous.

He ran after her, reaching her a few feet from the doorway. Thank the gods that the black of their costumes made them all but invisible to the couples inside.

Taking her arm, he pulled her back into the shadow. He could feel rage throb through her. He would deal with that later, or maybe never. Now he would do his best to save her from herself.

"No!" It was his no this time.

She raised her free hand to slap him again, but he grabbed it before she completed the arc.

"One slap is deserved, two is excessive."

"Let go of me," she hissed.

"No. Not until you listen."

"There is absolutely nothing you can say that will excuse your behavior."

As if she had nothing to do with it. As if her teasing and temptation was not finally more than he could bear. He would leave that for later as well.

"I have no intention of apologizing." That caught her attention. She stilled, even some of the trembling eased. "Christiana, you can not go back into that ballroom looking as you do now."

She looked at her dress, her bosom, as though she thought it was something about her costume that was out of place. When she saw nothing amiss, she glared at him. "What do you mean?" With a jerk, she tried to shake herself free of his hands.

He let one go, but held the other, the one he now thought of as her slapping hand. He was sure anyone looking at them would suspect some sort of declaration. Tomorrow's *on-dit?* Perhaps, but better than a scandal, he decided.

"You are upset. You must take a moment, calm yourself, school your expression before you go back inside."

She was silent, but he heard understanding in the huff of breath she released.

A group of three dressed as minor Greek gods walked by them with barely a glance, clearly intent on their own debauchery. Christiana did not so much as glance at them, but the presence of other people gave them both time. Morgan could marshal his thoughts and Christiana, hopefully, could control her emotions.

"Well," she said on another huff, "since this is all your fault, I can hardly pretend gratitude, but you are right." She glared at him. "I hate it that you are right."

He nodded cautiously.

"Almost as much as I hate you for ruining everything."

He held her gaze and denied the pain that grabbed

and held his heart. There were tears in her eyes and
that made his burn too.

"I will walk through the doors with you, my lord.
You will take me to my mother. I will plead a headache. She will be very annoyed but she will take me
home."

He nodded since it was exactly what he had in mind.

"And then, my lord, I never want to see you again."
There was no mercy in her voice, no hope of forgiveness.

I never want to see you again. The words hung in
the silence that stretched between them, a sampling
of the rest of his life. *I never want to see you again.*

"If that is what you truly wish, Sprite." He used
the nickname on purpose, hoping for some softening,
for some sign of hope.

She stared at him, unmoved. "It is exactly what I
want."

He bowed to her, anger filtering through remorse.
Offering her his arm, he wondered how long she
would be able to control her emotions. Long enough,
he prayed, begging the god of mercy; let it be long
enough to save her reputation and ease his sense of
responsibility.

She laid her arm ever so lightly on his, as though
closer contact was abhorrent. Her stiff composure was
infectious. The smile he contrived was a mockery of
happiness. Hers was more convincing, but a far cry
from the merry look that usually lit her eyes and dim-
pled her cheek.

As they moved through the room and toward the
outer hallway, Morgan decided that he was dressed
perfectly for his trip to Hades. He was bound for the
netherworld. He was at the end of his parole. It was
the way it should be, he decided. It was easier not to
feel. So much easier not to risk this again, not ever
again. No woman was worth it.

He deserved the punishment, for the gross misunderstanding of his own emotions. Christiana had made him feel again. He had thought it was an amusing flirtation, tinged with freshness because she was so sweet. He had managed to convince himself that it was lust carefully tempered, to entertain and tempt them both.

How wrong. How stupid. He read it as lust, but that touch of sweetness made it love.

Mama's harangue all the way home in the chaise did give her a headache. Or maybe it was the effort to preserve some semblance of normalcy when her world was a shambles. To Christiana's relief, Mama returned to the masquerade so she could escort Joanna home. With eyes half closed against the now real pain in her temples, she allowed Sally to undress her and then sent her off as well. It was a shame to disappoint her, but Christiana could not bear to relive the evening, not just yet.

The first thing she did was grab the journal from her night table. She held it against her breast for a long moment and then with a vehemence born of self-loathing, she ripped each page out of the book and into tiny little pieces.

Her head ached so much she thought she might be sick. She collapsed onto the window seat, pressed her forehead against the cool glass and tried to distract herself with the activity in the street below while she waited for Joanna.

Tears trickled down her cheeks and her headache eased as though the tears were leeching away the pain.

It did not seem all that much later when Joanna and Mama returned. Christiana glanced at the clock, surprised to see that it was close to morning. How odd that she could sit so still for so long, random scenes playing through her mind like a play she had been in, one that had the last curtain rung down without the proper ending.

She could hear Sally and Joanna chattering and suddenly it was near impossible to wait for Sally to leave. Jumping up from the window seat, Christiana began pacing the room. The moment Sally left, she was through the connecting door.

Joanna was combing her hair and turned with some surprise. "I thought you were asleep."

"Sleep?" Christiana was shocked at how brittle her laugh sounded. "I am not sure I will ever sleep again!"

Rushing over to her sister, Christiana fell to her knees next to her and grabbed Joanna's hand.

"Oh please, Joanna, tell me what to do. Help me. Oh, sweet heaven, how could I have been so stupid! How could I not know?"

Christiana stood up as quickly as she had rushed over and, with her back to Joanna, burst into tears. They came in a steady stream with deep, gasping breaths. "How could I think that it was nothing more than a silly flirtation, something to make the Season go by more quickly?"

It was the truth. It was the truth. How could it hurt so much?

"How could I think that what I felt for Richard was love?" She turned back to Joanna, still sobbing. "It was vanity or make believe, or something equally appalling, but it was never love."

"Christy! Control yourself!" Joanna commanded, moving from her chair to stand in front of her sister, panic sharpening her voice.

She'll slap the hysterics out of me unless I calm down. With a deep breath Christiana controlled the sobs, taming them into small hiccoughing breaths. Joanna nodded approval as she took her sister's hand, leading her to the small sofa near the fire.

"Now sit here with me and start at the beginning."

"Lord Morgan kissed me." Christiana sank down onto the sofa, even though it would be difficult to stay still.

"Oh my." Joanna's words were a whisper. "Where did this happen?" She asked the question not with curiosity, but as though she were trying to draw a careful picture.

"In the garden. We went out for a walk." No need for Joanna to know that it had been her idea that they leave the ballroom for some air. Her idea that they walk to the fountain that was at the far edge of the property.

"So no one saw you kiss?"

"Oh, heaven, I hope not." She thought a moment as she drew in a huge breath. "No, no we were quite alone and we were both in black. I was wearing his cloak because it was cool outside, especially after the closeness inside."

Joanna raised her eyebrows a bit, but that was as close to censure as she came.

"So, Christy, no one saw you. Good." She puzzled it out to herself then spoke. "Then your only real concern is not propriety but your"—she paused before adding—"reaction to the kiss."

"I slapped him and ran away." The last made the tears flow again. "He stopped me and insisted on escorting me to Mama so there would be no gossip and then Mama brought me home."

"Christy, do stop crying." Joanna spoke with asperity. "You will not get around me that way. And tears will only make your eyes swell." She moved away for a moment, taking a coverlet from the foot of the bed and spreading it over the two of them. The fire was nothing more than a few guttering coals. "Of course you slapped him, but I am not talking about what you did, but your first feeling, your first reaction when he kissed you. I trust it was not disgust."

"Oh, Joanna, the word 'reaction' does not describe

it at all." She did stand up now, leaving the coverlet with her sister and reaching for Joanna's robe. "A reaction is something you feel when you see a wonderful painting or hear beautiful music. It is much too tame a word to describe what I felt." Her voice trailed off and she had to struggle mightily not to smile.

Joanna did smile. Then raised her hand to cover her mouth. "Oh, I see. I think I know what you mean. Rather like a sweeping wave of emotion that you can relive at will simply by remembering the kiss?"

"Yes!" She did not mean to sound so surprised that her sister should understand. Of course this feeling was not hers alone, even if it felt rare and treasured. And terrifying. "Joanna, what should I do?"

"About what, dearest?" Joanna pulled her back onto the sofa. "About the way you feel? About Richard? About Lord Morgan?"

"All of it, Joanna. I have made such a mess." Tears threatened but she swallowed them whole. "The way I feel? I do not even know how I feel. At first the most marvelous sense of coming home, never wanting to be out of his arms or out of his sight. And then not a second later I was sick at the way I was betraying Richard. I hate Lord Morgan for doing this to me and then I realize it is all my own fault for being so naïve about love and courtship in the first place, right up to the moment that I suggested we go outside."

Joanna grimaced. "It was your idea?"

"Yes, taking the air had seemed like a good idea at the time. Now I realize that I had been beyond flirtatious all evening. It was the costume, do you see?"

When Joanna looked uncertain, Christiana shook her head.

"Well, I see. The stupid costume let me be someone else for the night, let me admit that I was attracted to Lord Morgan as more than a friend, let me invite him to escort me outside for a few moments alone." She buried her face in her hands. "Exactly what could we do outside that we could not do inside? Now I know and I have ruined everything."

"And you are certain that Lord Morgan does not share your feelings?"

"Of course not. He told me from the outset that for him this was a way to protect his own interests."

"But you felt the same way and your feelings have changed."

"Have they?" She turned away and brushed at the tears that threatened. "The truth is that I do not know my own heart any longer. And I certainly do not understand his. I have never understood him and now I never will."

Her head drooped and she suddenly felt exhausted. "Joanna, what I do know is that I have nearly forgotten Richard's existence. I cannot even remember exactly what he looks like. Does that sound like true love to you?"

"No, my dear." Joanna smiled in sympathy.

Christiana felt calmer now. It was still a disaster, but if she could clear her head enough to think, she might be able to decide what she should do. She got up and walked to the window even though the curtains were pulled shut. "I feel more when Lord Morgan smiles at me than I have ever felt in the dozen times that Richard and I have kissed."

She whirled from the window and looked at her sister. "Do I need to say anything more than that?"

Joanna shook her head.

Christiana walked over and gave her sister a long, hard hug. "Thank you for always being here, for helping me to understand. I am not sure I can sleep but I will rest and think about what I am to do."

She walked to the door, already thinking out loud. "I must decide how to tell Richard, when to tell him, even what to tell him. I must think about how to smooth over my stupid behavior with Lord Morgan. There is only a little while until we go home. Surely

I can survive until then." She turned back to her sister. Joanna would have spoken but Christiana spoke over her. "I could have laughed it off. I *should* have laughed it off, or reacted in a dozen ways that would have been infinitely less embarrassing." She stamped her foot. "He has always been the sensible one. He is older and is supposed to be wiser. How could he! Oh, how could he ruin everything this way?"

Sixteen

By the bright light of day, Morgan Braedon was asking himself the same question, but his only audience was a half-empty bottle of brandy. It was not inclined to give him any answers. Bacchus knew he had done his best to find wisdom there last night, but even with half the bottle circulating through his brain no answers came.

What insanity had gripped him in Hawthorne's garden? He had kissed Christiana and in less than a minute a friendship he valued was ruined. From her perspective they had no future and it appeared she would just as soon forget their past.

It had only been a kiss. A passionate kiss, it was true. That had been his fault. He was generous enough to admit that, but the temptation of that mouth had been with him since she first smiled at him at the Westbournes' ball, months ago.

He was human. If she would not allow him one small indiscretion then perhaps their friendship should end.

That reasoning had been acceptable for all of six hours. Home for a change of clothes and then to his club for some deep play. It had been just the thing to distract him.

He won at first, his sobriety a distinct advantage. He won great golden amounts of money and his humor was well on its way to being restored. Whole minutes would go by when he did not think of her face, her mouth, her outrage.

Then the brandy he had been sipping began to infiltrate his mind and fill it with memories. The present moment faded in importance. He managed to cut his losses and come away with satisfactory winnings, enough to meet his steward's demands for the next few months.

First light found him sitting in his bedroom, still dressed, swilling brandy in an epic and futile search for oblivion. A few hours of restless sleep had not solved anything.

He rang for Roberts, going through the usual morning routine without enthusiasm. He finished breakfast and moved to the library to prepare a letter to accompany the draft to his steward in Wales. It was routine correspondence; he had sent a dozen like it in the last two years, but he ruined three sheets of paper before he was satisfied with it. The letter was sanded and sealed just as a caller was announced.

"Monksford. Welcome. It is good to see you." The man was a sea of rational thought, which was what he needed desperately at the moment.

Morgan waved him to a seat and joined him by the fire. With a sentence or two they covered the weather, likelihood of success in the Peninsula, prospects for a good growing season, and the latest offerings at Tattersall's.

After insisting that nothing would induce him to buy the matched bays currently offered, Monksford cleared his throat. "Have you been to Green Street this morning, my lord?"

"No," he replied, surprised at the turn of conversation. "I had not decided on whether to make a call today." He kept his expression as bland as he could.

"I have just come from there." Monksford leaned

forward in his chair. "The Lamberts are not home to anyone this morning."

"Ah, then you have saved me a trip." He tried for a tone of finality and even made to stand, hoping that was the end of the conversation, but Monksford did not take the hint.

"You were with Miss Christiana last night were you not? Was she well when she left?"

"Miss Christiana went home with a headache last night." Now it was Morgan's turn to clear his throat. "Perhaps they hope to keep the house quiet until she is recovered."

"Can I guess without giving offense, that you are the cause of the upset and not some unwelcome news from home?" The blunt question was rare and the smile that unaccompanied it even more unusual.

"Monksford, there may be no connection between us except for the courtship of two sisters, but I suppose I should tell you . . ." His voice trailed off as he struggled for the right words. "The truth is you will be made to suffer the consequences of my actions, especially when sisters are as close as the Lamberts. I am sure Miss Joanna will know all."

Monksford encouraged him with a nod. His expression turned grave.

"Miss Christiana interpreted some, er one, of my actions last night as an insult."

"Lord Morgan, I can count very few times when I have seen you discomfited or at a loss for words." Monksford took pity on him. "Did you perhaps rush your suit?"

"Rush my suit?" Morgan gave it a moment's thought. "Yes, I suppose you could say that."

"And is it hopeless?" Monksford shifted slightly in his seat. "Forgive my impertinence but since we are being frank, I think I need to ask if this is a true courtship. I had understood Miss Christiana's feelings to be otherwise engaged."

The answer to Monksford's question came to him so abruptly that Morgan wondered how long the gods had been shouting it at him. He wanted a future with her. He had fallen in love, single-handed and one-sided. And he wanted to find a way to make it mutual.

Morgan was silent for so long that Monksford's grave expression gave way to concern.

"Monksford, this is more than infatuation. I am too old for that game."

To his way of thinking, infatuation implied perfection and he well knew that Christiana Lambert was not perfect. She had a way of wanting the world to turn at her command and her spontaneity was as much a burden as a joy to anyone who wanted to see her safely through the Season. He cared as much about her well-being as he longed for her arms around him. If that was not love, then what was?

"Then, Braedon, the next question would be: Is it hopeless?"

"Only Miss Christiana knows the answer to that."

"One thing I have learned from watching you this Season is that if you want something then you usually contrive a way to make it yours. I suppose the truest question is: What do you want?"

"My first instinct is to do as she asked." He fingered his cheek, remembering the slap with a wince of indignity. "Oh, Hades, Monksford, to do what she *demanded,* and never see her again. Count this Season as a lesson learned and well over." Morgan looked away from Monksford. "But I feel differently now."

"Then you must find a way to repair the damage. Regret and self-recrimination are hardly productive without the lady's attention."

When Morgan looked at him in some surprise, Monksford laughed. "I did learn something from my first marriage."

"What do you think? Should I write her?"

"Too easily discarded," said Monksford with a glance at the papers crumpled on the floor by the desk.

Morgan nodded. "Yes, and that was merely a letter to my steward. Flowers? No, they are entirely too superficial."

"I am afraid, my lord, that you will have to wait for a social opportunity and hope that you are not rebuffed."

"But the Season is almost over. She could easily avoid me if she wanted to." Morgan considered his options. "I think I must call on her. At least make an attempt to speak with her."

"They are not at home today to anyone, Braedon."

"Now you turn cautious on me!" Morgan stood up and straightened his coat. "You said yourself that if I want something I can find a way to make it happen. You inspire me, Monksford. There must be a way to be heard."

By the time he reached Green Street, Morgan felt like a schoolboy intent on his first seduction. He had come up with a dozen scenarios that would prevent him from seeing Christiana and had dealt with each of them. Indeed, he'd decided that even if she had gone so far as to leave Town he would follow her. He raised his hand to the knocker, but the door was opened before he could let it fall. The butler stood before him, solemn and determined.

"I am sorry, my lord, but the Lambert family is not receiving visitors today."

Morgan nodded curtly. "I understand that Miss Christiana is indisposed, but could I please speak with Miss Lambert." Yes, that would work. Joanna could be his emissary.

"I'm sorry, sir." The butler made to close the door and Morgan stuck his foot out to keep the door from latching. There must be some peddlers' blood in his background. Desperation made for harsh measures.

The butler looked down at his highly polished boot

with some regret. A long ugly scratch ruined the sheen.

"You misunderstand, sir." The butler struggled between dignity and humanity. Humanity won. "It is not you personally. Miss Christiana refuses to see anyone. She had word today of her neighbor. Richard Wilton died in Spain near Talavera, these ten days past."

The door closed even as Morgan murmured all the right platitudes. His words faded as an iron band circled his heart and squeezed until it physically hurt. He stood staring at the door a moment longer.

Oh, God help her. He knew how this hurt. He could remember all too well. He remembered the horrible disbelief, the powerlessness; the rage he could barely control when his mother died and especially when Maddie was gone.

He moved to his curricle and took the reins, relieved that there were so few abroad this morning.

He remembered the guilt that had overwhelmed him, for being the one still alive when it had been all his fault.

He remembered something else too. The resolve he made then to never feel that kind of loss again. He vowed to never let anyone close enough to cause that kind of heartache. He would protect himself from pain by shielding himself from love.

Christiana had rescued him from that isolation. He wanted to tell her he knew how loss felt. He wanted to help her. He wanted to ease her pain, hold her and comfort her, but he knew that right now his presence would only make the pain worse. He turned back to his curricle and set out for Monksford's town house to report the news.

It was such a comfort to be home. As the carriage moved up the drive, Christiana looked out the window and absorbed every familiar detail. The roses that climbed the wrought-iron gate were still in bloom and she caught the fragrance on the breeze. She could see the glint of sunshine on the lake, barely visible through the trees. To the north she saw the gentle rise of land behind the house, which protected it from the worst of winter storms.

She had never talked with Morgan about the country. Was he committed to life in London or did he plan to spend time in Wales. Did he even have a house there?

She had never asked because she thought it made no difference to their relationship. Until that one kiss, she had been completely blind to her growing feelings for him. And now she would never have the chance to test those feelings, to see if they would grow. And that guilty truth brought tears to her eyes as readily as any other grief she felt.

Papa came out the front door as the coach drew to a stop. He had the coach door open and was reaching in to help her down before the coachman could jump down from the box.

"Welcome home, daughter."

Tears filled her eyes as he took her arm, patting it with a gentle reassurance she had longed for.

"Your mother tells me that she and Joanna will only be five more days at Lord Monksford's and I am to join them for the last two days of the visit. I am not sure I should leave you alone."

Oh, she knew she was home. Papa wasted no time on chatter, but began with exactly what was on his mind.

"I will be quite all right, Papa. I think some time by myself is exactly what I need."

At his doubtful look she could not help but smile. Indecision was so out of character.

"Papa, I am just come from Monksford and have no desire to return before the engagement ball. Please, I am not made of glass. I am more likely to die from the shock of you being so accommodating than I am to go into a decline."

He looked her in the eye for a long moment and with a nod his indecision vanished. "Just so you know that I am as mindful of your grief as I am of Joanna's happiness."

She nodded, not trusting her voice.

"If you want to talk with me——"

She interrupted him. "Not yet, Papa. Not now." She squeezed his hand. "But thank you."

With her arm in his, Papa escorted her to the door. "Since you are home, you must explain to Mrs. Purdy how to prepare that dish we had in London those few days while I was with you. The fish dish with some kind of white sauce. It is the one thing from London that I miss." He rethought that. "Besides you girls and your mother."

"Turbot in oyster sauce." She handed her pelisse and bonnet to the butler and smiled at him. "How is your grandson, Purdy?"

"Ben is a wonder, miss. We think he will be walking anytime now."

"Oh, but that will keep Hannah busy. May I call on her tomorrow, perhaps?"

Purdy bowed. "It would be her pleasure, miss."

Christiana moved toward the stairway leading down to the kitchen. "Papa, I think between the two of us, Mrs. Purdy and I can contrive, but first I will have some tea, if you please. It may only be a day's travel from Lord Monksford's, but my thirst is just as real for only being a few hours old."

She turned the corner and proceeded slowly down the stairs, her body stiff from the long carriage ride. Her father's voice carried down to her. "No, no, Purdy, keeping her busy is the surest way to heal."

So Papa and Purdy had plans to keep her occupied. Perhaps Papa was right. She had filled her last days in London sitting in the window seat in her room on

Green Street, watching life go on. It had not really eased her heart. Nor had the one or two engagements she had managed. Being surrounded by gaiety was infinitely more difficult than being alone. It was all so meaningless. And there was always the fear that she would have to see Lord Morgan.

At least here at home she cared about the people, knew their lives and their worries. Please, heaven, here she would feel something besides the aching empty loss of Morgan and guilt over her faithlessness to Richard.

Christiana walked into the kitchen. There was the long scarred wooden table lined with benches, the familiar earthenware teapot the servants favored, and a plate of the wonderful biscuits that were Mrs. Purdy's specialty.

The cook herself stood nearby, her eyes doubtful.

Christiana barely looked at her, but walked over to the table and picked up a piece of the shortbread. The smell of it was everything that was home. With a shaking hand she tried to take a bite but tears overcame her. She dropped the sweet and covered her face with her hands. A moment later the redoubtable Purdy pulled her into a hug, rocking her back and forth as if she were still a child. Christiana wanted to stay there forever.

Putting her at arm's length, Purdy nodded. "You sit and drink some tea and tell me."

"Tell you what?" Christiana smoothed her skirts as she sat and Mrs. Purdy poured the tea.

"Whatever you wish."

That included every detail she could summon of Joanna's pending engagement and her travels in Monksford's very elaborate coach. Everyone was being so kind to her.

Mrs. Purdy recounted the well-being of each of her children, all destined for service at Lambert Hill.

Neither one of them mentioned Richard and it was

as if the London Season had never happened. It was
a pretense but at the moment a welcome one. There
was nothing here to remind her of Morgan and no one
who knew that she had been such a fool. For the moment coming home meant leaving her more painful
memories behind.

She did her best to eat dinner, to reassure her father
and the Purdys, but eating the food was like stuffing
sawdust in her mouth. Bedtime loomed. But even the
invitation of her room and familiar surroundings was
not enough to induce her to sleep.

It was a warm evening, so she decided on a walk
toward the stable, where there were rumored to be
some new kittens. She had missed this in London: the
quiet, the security, the freedom to wander about in the
moonlight.

She smelled the tobacco before she saw him. Sergeant Tidwell was seated on a stump just outside the
stable.

He stood up when she approached and she walked
closer. "Good evening, Sergeant."

He nodded and made to move back to the stable.

"I meant to thank you for bringing me from
Monksford. You will return tomorrow?"

At first she spoke to his back, but he turned to her
and nodded.

"How is your leg?"

"Mending better now that I have work, thank you,
miss."

"You're quite welcome." She hesitated. "But you
know it was Lord Morgan and Lord Monksford who
found you employment."

"As you say, miss." He smiled and bobbed his head.

She turned to walk back to the house and then
glanced back. He was on the stump once again. "Sergeant?"

"Yes, miss."

She walked closer, looking at the paving stones at

her feet. "Would you tell me, please, what was it like in Portugal?"

He looked hesitant so she explained a bit more. "I know no one who has been there. I thought perhaps knowing a little of the life there would make it easier to understand."

"Beggin' your pardon, miss, but understand what?"

She breathed a laugh and shrugged. "Life?" She paused a moment. "And death."

The sergeant shook his head. "Oh, miss, it's not my place."

"Oh, I suppose not in the ordinary course of things, Sergeant, but you do know more about such things than I ever will."

He relented. "It was hot in the summer and cold in the winter and had more rocks on the roads than any god could have created."

"Yes, I can imagine that made for long, long days." But that was not really what she wanted to know.

"Miss, I can tell you about the officers and their lives. They train and lead in battles but they spend a good part of their days doing the same things they would do at home, they gamble and hunt and ride."

She nodded, expecting that he would say it was hardly his place to give any more details.

"I will tell you this though, beggin' your pardon. The good and the brave are not only on the battlefield. Your Lord Morgan Braedon did more for me in one day than any officer ever did in my twenty years of wearing the King's uniform."

"Oh, Lord Morgan is not 'mine.' Not in the way you mean."

"Yes, miss, he is." He was so intent on his conviction that any obsequiousness was gone. "He came up to me that day only because you asked him to. That makes him as much yours as any man who would leave you to fight in Portugal. He knew it was important to you and so he went beyond what you asked him to do. He found me work and he made sure my leg was tended to. He did it all when he never knew you would know. He is a brave and noble gentleman, miss."

Was he saying that Morgan was more worthy of her admiration than Richard? She could hardly ask him.

"Miss, I am being bold and I beg your pardon, but it is the only way I know. I spent too many years with men who wanted the nub of the thing and nothing else."

She nodded her permission.

"I see you grieve and want you to know that he died doing what he wanted. Could a man ask for more?"

She shrugged.

"We all have somethin' we regret. We learn to live with it."

Was he talking about himself, her, or Richard? Perhaps it applied to all of them.

The sergeant stood taller with his own military version of polite humility. "No insult meant, miss. I best be leaving now."

"No insult taken, Sergeant. Thank you. I thank you for your insight."

He nodded with a jerky bow and turned, and moved quickly back to the stable.

Watching his hurried progress actually made her smile. It was an unusual conversation, but in its way a small gift from a comforting God.

Everyone has something to regret. The phrase echoed in her mind as she walked back to the house. She knew that, had grasped it sometime ago but lost sight of it lately. Now she was part of the group who faced a loss that would change her life. It was hardly an exclusive club, though some of her dearest friends were members: the dowager duchess, Morgan Braedon.

She found some solace in that. If only because other

people went on and built lives of meaning and purpose. Why should she be any different?

Christiana walked into the front hall. It was dark and quiet. She was so tired her head ached, and for once sleep came with a welcoming oblivion.

To her surprise work helped as well. The second night at home she actually slept the night through, having exhausted herself by working with young Purdy in the kitchen garden. And for the two nights following she slept better than she had in weeks.

That ended the day she went to Wilton Way to pay a formal condolence call on Sir Howard Wilton. Papa had been to see Richard's father before, but he insisted on coming with her this time as well. She was not about to object. It would be a difficult enough visit with his company; without him it would have been hideous.

Sir Howard did not keep them waiting. When he came into the room, Christiana wondered if he was leaning more heavily on his stick than he used to. Was his face more lined? After conventional greetings, she took a deep breath, though her voice came out little more than a whisper. "Sir Howard, I am come to tell you how very sorry I am to hear of Richard's death."

He bowed and took her hand. His shook a little, but it was the only emotion he showed. "I know you must feel it as sorely as we do, Christiana."

She nodded and bit her lip to still the trembling.

"We all know that he died in happy anticipation of your engagement."

She nodded again, not trusting her voice. "I am glad that gives you comfort, sir." She felt so false but knew it would not ease his fatherly grief if he knew the truth.

"He will be buried where he fell, but I have com-

missioned a marker for the cemetery here, near his
mother, I think."

He walked over to a desk, picked up a paper, and
handed it to her. The plan was for a small obelisk, not
much taller than a rosebush with Richard's name,
rank, regiment, and dates of birth and death. The
words "loyal soldier" were crossed out, and another
word added that she could not read through her tears.
She stared at the paper until her eyes were no longer
full and then handed it back to Sir Howard. "Lovely.
I know it will serve his memory well."

The visit was over a few moments later. She and
Papa rode away in a strained silence, Sir Howard's last
confidence echoing in her head. They reached the end
of the drive before she had to vent her anger.

"He died so stupidly, Papa! A horse race. He died
trying to win a bet!"

"Awful."

"Oh, Papa, 'awful' is a nice word for it. There is
nothing noble or worthwhile about the kind of acci-
dent that happens on the road to London almost every
day."

"Not every day, Christy."

"Well, then it happens more often than it should.
Awful is much too generous. Stupid, foolish, useless,
ridiculous. And even worse, Richard died because he
was trying to win money to pay off his gambling
debts."

"Sir Howard seemed to think that made it more
honorable."

Papa was not any more convinced of that than she
was.

"Even Joanna could beat him at whist." All at once
her anger evaporated and she sank back onto the seat.
"Why would he even try to win at cards? Why was
he not saving for our future?"

"I can understand that. He wanted to fit in."

"It makes me so angry!"

"It angers us all, Christy. It seems such a waste."

She nodded and then turned to her father. "Papa, please, I will walk from here."

Without complaint he knocked and the coach stopped. Christiana climbed down, watched the chaise move on, and then set off across the field toward the copse of trees that was the boundary of the two properties.

The grass was long, a deep rich green. It was dry underfoot and she walked quickly at first and then slowed as her outrage faded.

How foolish of Richard to try so hard to be something he was not. A soldier he might have been, but never a gambler. She stopped suddenly and looked blindly back toward the woods that had been a favorite meeting spot. Had Richard been any more foolish than she had been to build a fantasy of a childhood friendship into true love?

Oh, surely Richard was more foolish, for his game had cost him his life. Her game had only cost her heart.

Where was Lord Morgan? What was he doing? What had his brother done when he found out that there would be no engagement?

Seventeen

Morgan tossed off his fourth attempt at a letter when the door opened with a singular command and his brother came into the room.

"James!" He stood up and tried to summon some vestige of welcome, but the gods knew that this was the least wanted arrival in a fortnight.

"Yes, Morgan. Your brother James stands before you, eager to hear every detail of your pending engagement."

"You must be eager. There is plenty of water if you want to change and wash the smell of horse off you."

"Later." He walked over to the table that held any number of bottles and poured a drink. He offered the glass to Morgan and when he declined, James tossed back the liquor and then poured more.

Not like James, Morgan thought. He watched his brother with narrowed eyes and a little worry.

"Sorry to disappoint you and Father, but I still have four months. You did say I must be married 'by the end of the year.' "

"Did I?" The uncertainty was compounded by the way James rubbed his hand along his brow.

"Yes, you did. More than once." Morgan spoke with conviction but was growing more distracted by James's distress. He was doing his best to hide it, but it was unlike James to be less than subtle. "James, you must at least give me credit for knowing the terms of anything that smacks of a bet."

With an oath, James turned back to the brandy. "Then give me something, anything, to take back to the marquis."

"Are you here at his request?" If so, then his irritation made sense. Certainly he had more pressing affairs than humoring a sick man's whims.

"Request? If the ranting tantrum he threw could be considered a request. Parkner had to dose him with laudanum to get him to quiet. I came as much to escape as to honor his wish."

Morgan considered the revelation. He was not the only one being pushed. It must be hell having two autocrats under one roof. The gods well understood that even Mount Olympus was big enough for only one Zeus.

Morgan walked over to James, took the glass from his hand, and urged him to a seat. "Sit down, let me order some food for you—"

James swung at Morgan's hand, pushing him away. "I have no time for London. My usually sensible land steward has taken it into his head to marry and is away for a fortnight. Morgan, just tell me what I want to hear and I will be away."

"All the more reason to order up some food."

"All right. All right." He brushed a hand through his hair again. "Maybe it will get rid of this confounded headache."

Cook was a genius and there was a cold collation before them both in less time than it took for James to disappear and clean up. He sat down and made serious inroads into the food, talking with his mouth full. "Is it Miss Christiana Lambert?"

Oh, how he wished it was. How he wished he could say a truthful, unequivocal yes and send James home happy. Even more, how he wished it were true.

"Yes, yes, it is. Or it will be."

"What, your charm did not persuade her within a sennight?"

"My kiss frightened her away." Now why had he admitted that? Because he was desperate for advice from anyone and because it made James laugh.

"Dear God, tell me, you have found a virgin and have spent so long with your mistress you forgot to treat her like a lady."

"No, James, I made the mistake of letting too many of my feelings show, much too soon." *Before even I fully understood them.*

The confession silenced his brother's laughter.

"I have been trying to write to her for days now." He gestured to the pile of crumpled paper.

"Letters never were your strong point. Why not call on her."

"She has gone home."

"That does not bode well."

"I appreciate your sympathy."

"I am sympathetic, Morgan. The urgency comes from the marquis. It obsesses him, but at least I can go back and report that you are indeed on the verge of a proposal."

"That optimism suits Rhys more than you."

"I trust you will make it the truth." James stood up and nodded firmly. "Make it work, Morgan. Find her and make it work."

His brother left the room as abruptly as he had entered. The door clicked quietly behind him and silence filled the room as completely as James's presence had.

Most any other time Morgan would have tried to puzzle out exactly what was upsetting his brother. Certainly more than the unsettled state of his supposed courtship.

Morgan walked back to the desk, well aware that his plate was already filled with confused emotions that he desperately needed to understand. Not his own.

He knew his heart as surely as the gods knew man's every failing.

No, it was the confusion of Christiana's emotions that he longed to understand. He picked up the pen, wondering what he could say to her that would convey his heartfelt remorse and his desperate longing, and wondering, too, if it mattered to her at all.

Light filtered through the thin gauze curtains her mother favored in the summer months. The morning room was Christiana's favorite this time of year and she sat with her sister in companionable silence.

"Have you had any word from Lord Morgan?"

Joanna's question was so unexpected that Christiana set her teacup down with an audible rattle.

"Letters you mean? No. He never called on me while we were still in London, why should he send a letter now?"

"He did call. More than once."

This time Christiana did spill her tea. She brushed at the spot on her skirt with some annoyance. "He did?"

"Yes, but Mama would not let him be announced. At the time I thought it was the right thing to do, you were so distraught and not thinking clearly. So I did not try to convince her otherwise."

"I told him that I never wanted to see him again and I meant it."

"You do not. Perhaps then you did, but only because you did not know your own mind. You have had time to grieve now and I can not believe that he is not foremost in your thoughts."

"Do you think that I am so shallow that I can overcome my sorrow in a month and move on to my next conquest? Or is that since you are engaged you think you can read my heart too."

"No, I could do that before I was engaged." Joanna

spoke with a complacent confidence that was mildly infuriating. "Before I was engaged and understood true happiness I was willing to wait until you understood your heart for yourself. Now, Richard's death has complicated everything and I think I must take firmer action."

"I do not want to hear this, Joanna." She stood up to leave the room and was halfway across it when Joanna spoke again.

"You never loved Richard."

If Joanna had hit her with a cane, it could not have hurt more. She whirled around. "I did love Richard."

"Christy, be honest. You told me yourself that you were not going to marry him. Now, because you feel guilty for not realizing it sooner, you are willing to marry his memory."

"I did love Richard, Joanna." Her voice was wooden. "Just not enough."

"Oh, please, Christy. You loved him as much as he would let you. You know as well as I do that he was selfish and self-righteous and once you saw a little more of the world you realized that there were other matches that would suit you infinitely better."

It might be true. It was true, but the callous assessment of her feelings pinched her heart. She expected more sympathy from Joanna.

"I suppose you are an expert on courtship now that Lord Monksford of the thinning hair and middle years has proposed. Is he your heart's delight?"

Joanna was shocked at first, then angry. "Never ever belittle him again, Christiana." Joanna's eyes filled with tears. "I have not spoken to you of him because—because I did not want my happiness to make your pain worse, but now I am angry enough not to care."

Joanna walked over to Christiana and led her back to the sofa. "Life goes on, Christy. Sit down."

Christiana did as she was told, already regretting

her meanness. Joanna did not sit but began to pace in front of the sofa.

"First, Lord Monksford is only thirty-two years old." She took an angry breath and expelled it, managing to calm her voice. "He has two dear daughters who need a mother and hopes to have a son one day. He has a wonderful estate not more than a day's journey from here and it very much needs a lady's hand. He is wealthy and does not bet on horses or keep a mistress. He is everything that is good."

The anger disappeared completely with the last phrase.

"But I am not marrying him for his house, his children, or his wealth." Joanna stopped pacing and came back to sit down beside her sister.

"Christy, he actually listens to me when I talk. He never scans the room for someone more important or prettier to talk to or dance with.

"He brings me nosegays because he has found out that they are my favorite sort of flowers. While we were visiting, he had his cook prepare my favorite dishes. He actually knows what they are. I am not sure Mama knows what they are."

She leaned closer. "Christy, he does not know the color of my eyes. I love him for that alone. He is looking for someone to share his life and not someone to adorn it. Yes, Christy, he is my heart's delight. I cannot imagine happiness without him."

They were both crying now. That lasted all of a moment before Joanna brushed at her eyes. "And this crying has to stop! It is ruining our complexions."

"Very generous of you, Joanna, but I am the only one who is a watering pot these days."

"Perhaps, but look at the frown lines I am getting from worry over you."

Christiana did look and could see nothing but happiness beneath the tears. "I am so sorry, Joanna."

"Yes, I know you are. Now you can prove it by not

letting it happen again. John Monksford is the world to me and I want you two to love each other as sister and brother."

Christiana nodded. "Of course I will. How could I not, when he has made you so happy?"

"There is one more grace I will ask of you, dearest." Joanna pulled a letter from her pocket and handed it to her. "I am going to consult with Mama about dinner."

She walked to the door but turned around once more. "Do think of him kindly, Christy. He does care, I am sure of it."

"More love-dazed wisdom?"

"No. I watched the two of you for most of a Season. Do read his letter and begin to think about the future at least a little."

Joanna closed the door softly and for a moment Christiana stared at the envelope. It was addressed directly to her, with the Braedon frank in the corner. What room had he written this in? How many sheets had he ruined before he had it exactly as hc wanted it? Holding it gave her no insight so she broke the seal and read.

Dear Christiana,
    The London we shared is cold and lonely without you. But I know that it is not nearly as empty as your world is right now. To lose someone loved and longed for is an immeasurable loss. I send my deepest sympathy to you and Richard Wilton's family and hope that his death in service to King and country will, in time, bring comfort.
                                        Morgan Braedon

She read it five more times. How thoughtful. How sweet. But Joanna was wrong. It was a sympathy note, not a declaration.

She stared at the ceiling, refusing the tears. It was

something that Joanna, aglow with her own personal happiness, could not understand. Not only was Richard dead, but she had lost Morgan Braedon too.

Was it the warmth of the day or perhaps the way the sunlight spread across the façade? Morgan was not sure but whatever the reason, Monksford was one of the loveliest houses he had ever seen. Large enough to impress, but not grand, it was a building that time and family had made into a home.

Any number of the leaded windows that marched across the front of the house and rose for three stories were thrown open to catch the summer breeze. It added to the welcoming feel. A maid was shaking a rug from an upper window, but ducked inside the moment she saw him.

It was most likely that the other guests were outside, perhaps by the folly he could see in the distance, but he went to the front door, to present himself formally and change his clothes before joining the company.

He watched the cricket match from his bedroom window. The teams were well matched though of varying ages from youngsters to grandfathers. The ladies sat nearby. He thought he could pick Christiana out. Had she cut her hair? He supervised Roberts as Roberts supervised the unpacking, and then rejected two neckcloths before he was satisfied with the knot.

Suddenly in a hurry to join the company, he rushed down the stairs, then changed his mind. It would be better to see her for the first time at tea, indoors where she could not easily leave. He decided to stop in the library and choose a volume to help him to sleep later on.

That was where John Monksford found him. His welcome was effusive and Morgan was impressed at how happiness took years from Monksford's face.

"Braedon, put that book down and come with me. You have put off this meeting long enough."

"What is it about the newly engaged, John? Do you think you have all the answers or do you want the reassurance that you are doing the right thing by urging others into the same state?"

"Both."

"That's another thing about happy couples. They almost never allow themselves to be annoyed."

"Whereas, the unhappily single want to argue with anything that moves."

"How is she?"

"Better than she was"—Monksford considered his answer a moment—"but not anything like she used to be. Joanna tells me that she is too calm. At first she was angry and upset, now she is little more than quiet."

"I suspect that at least part of the change is permanent." Morgan shook his head. "You know as well as I that loss like that changes one."

"As it should. When my wife died, I determined that the best way to honor her memory was to make the most of the rest of my life. I think that is true for all of us. And I think that Christiana needs you in her life before that change for the good can take place."

That was a large order. He tried to shake off his insecurity. "Enough melancholy, John! This weekend is a celebration. How many will be here for the engagement ball tomorrow?"

"Most every family for ten miles and about twenty or so from London. Our close friends and family are staying here and the rest are at near neighbors'. It makes for an engaging house party."

Monksford seemed to relish the idea of spending the small fortune it would take to entertain them all.

His host walked to the doors that opened onto a terrace. "Come this way. Later I can show you the results from that new seed I used this year. Very satisfactory."

Morgan followed him, relieved that some things did not change.

He knew the exact moment that Christiana realized who he was. Joanna rose from her seat to come and greet them, and Christiana turned to see where she was going.

He could have looked away, but he was so hungry for the sight of her that he held her gaze. Before Joanna claimed his attention he decided that Christiana looked thinner and much too serious.

"Welcome, my lord. It is so lovely to have you join us. It reminds us both of the best parts of this past Season."

Joanna and Monksford were a pair of smiling fools, Morgan thought, but their happiness was near irresistible. He held her hand a moment and then kissed it.

"Thank you, Miss Lambert, for including me. I trust your wisdom completely."

Her smile dimmed a little. "Never say it will be easy, my lord."

"Nothing worth winning is."

In complete understanding the three of them turned back to the garden party. The cricket match was over, or at least suspended, and the group gathered in the shade had more than doubled. Youngsters hurried to the trees and began climbing the lower limbs, trusting that their parents were sufficiently distracted by conversation.

Christiana stood up, her face pale, and walked toward the three of them as though she were accepting a fate decreed but not desired.

He had longed for this meeting, but now that it was upon him he had no idea what to say. All he could remember was her demand that he never darken her door again.

Joanna Lambert rescued him. "Christy, I am so

happy that Lord Morgan could join us. He was able to change his plans at the last minute."

Someone called to Monksford and he and Joanna both stepped away with entirely too much alacrity.

"I very much wanted to share this celebration with your sister and Lord Monksford."

"And so do I." Christiana nodded, her face much too composed.

"I can only hope their happiness is contagious."

Christiana looked at him as though he were asking for the moon. Then she smiled. Not her familiar gamine grin, but one that was more practiced and much less sincere. "The happiness they share is rare, my lord. That is something I have come to understand most clearly of late."

He had no answer for that. Should he express sympathy again? He had done that once already. Now he wanted her to know how he felt, but this was not the place for a declaration.

Right now, even the easy friendship they had shared seemed beyond his grasp. Civil conversation was the most he could hope for. He had two days at least. He was not going to rush his fences again.

"My lord, you must excuse me. My father asked to have a few moments with me this afternoon." With a slight curtsy, she turned and walked slowly across the grounds.

Morgan watched her until Monksford came up from behind and spoke. "I am sorry, Braedon. It will, I suppose, take time."

The meeting with Papa had been more than a convenient excuse. When she had come early to breakfast, he and Mama had been in a close conversation that ended the minute she walked into the room. As he'd left the room a few moments later, Papa had asked her to meet him in the library before tea.

It was a bit early. Tea was not for another hour, but she would find something to read and wait for him. She sat by the window with a book of fashion plates and turned the pages without looking at a single illustration.

He looked wonderful. If his eyes seemed strained that could well be because of the long ride in the bright sun. A good night's rest would take care of that.

He did seem a trifle formal, but that could easily be blamed on the awkwardness of their meeting. Joanna had insisted that he had called while she was still in London. And his denial there would account for some uncertainty now.

Of course, if he had managed to win all the funds he needed for his property then he had no need to pretend anything with her anymore. There was even less to regret. One kiss.

Had he not made it clear that he had come for Joanna and Lord Monksford? So, his friendship with them would be their only contact.

That meant he would be at the wedding, too, she supposed. Well then, after that it would be over and she would never have to see him again. She would not have to worry that he was being polite for all the wrong reasons: to ease his embarrassment, or worse, her own. Did he feel sorry for her? Please, heaven, let his good manners come from more than that.

She would not go to London for the Season this next year. Her heart was not ready for courtship. If she went up to London again in two years then most likely he would have found a match and would spend his time at the tables.

When her father came into the room she was still debating the wisdom of claiming a headache to skip dinner.

"Christy, my girl, are you all right?"

"Oh yes, Papa, just a little tired."

"To be sure, watching cricket is an exhausting exercise."

She smiled at his silliness. "Papa, what were you and Mama discussing this morning before I came into the breakfast room?"

"Exactly what I wanted to talk with you about now." He sat down in the chair, put his hands on his thighs, and nodded firmly. "There was too much chance of interruption at breakfast, and since then there have been enough activities to distract a wooden horse."

He stood up, walked over to the beautifully carved fireplace screen, and then back to his chair. There was no laughter in his face now. If anything he looked upset.

"Daughter, your mother tells me that she has it from Joanna that you are still upset about the influence your London Season had on your feelings for Richard."

Christiana nodded, miserable at the thought that her father probably knew the whole sorry tale.

"Your mother says that Joanna says that you say that you were disloyal and dishonest to Richard."

"I think faithless is the word I used."

"You are too hard on yourself."

She shrugged. He was her papa. Of course he would think so.

"Hear me now. I can tell you something that may help you see your relationship with Richard differently."

"You know something? What could that be?" She all but laughed at the thought of her father as an adviser to the loveless.

"Yes, all right." He rubbed his forehead with his hand. "You recall the acreage that has been in dispute between the Lamberts and the Wiltons? It must be a hundred years that we have been arguing over it."

"Of course. And I know that if Richard and I had married the land would have gone to Sir Howard, to the Wiltons."

"Good, but what you may not know is that Sir Howard promised his son a goodly amount of money if he did contract an alliance with you and the land did come into the Wilton holding."

She clenched her hands and made a conscious effort to not let her jaw drop in amazement. She was more than surprised. She was shocked.

"Now, there are always settlements, you know that, so I am not sure that this is all that much different." He pulled out a handkerchief and began mopping his brow.

"It is completely different, Papa, and you know it. The money Richard's father would have given him was not part of my dowry unless your accounting is extremely convoluted." She jumped up from the chair, ignoring the book when it fell to the floor. "Papa! Do you mean to tell me that the courtship was not about love or passion, it was about land and money?"

"Christiana, calm down. All marriages are about land and money. Most of them are very satisfactory. Look at your mother and me."

"Do not try and distract me, Papa." She spoke each word with rigid clarity. "Whatever other marriages are based on, I wanted mine to come from love. You see how happy Joanna is? That was what I hoped for, what I thought I had found with Richard. I learned in London that I did not love Richard, but I still believed that kind of love was possible even if it is as rare as snow in May. And now you tell me that for Richard this was never about loving? It was only about money!"

"Yes, all right. I told your mother this might not be the best time to tell you."

"Oh, Papa, yes, it is. My mourning is over. He has had all the tears he is ever going to get from me." It was as thorough a purging of her guilt as anything could have been.

They both heard the gong announcing tea. Christiana took a deep breath, walked over, and gave her father a hug. "Thank you, Papa, I know how hard that was. You go to tea. I think I must sit here a few moments and gather my composure."

He held her at arm's length and stared at her. "All right." He kissed her on the cheek and moved toward the door. "Do you think Monksford will have something stronger than tea?"

"Papa, he will if you ask him."

"Yes, yes, he will." With that assurance he hurried from the room.

Christiana tried to let the silence of the room calm her. She picked up the volume of fashion plates and set it on the library table. She walked to the doors and pulled them shut. Then she went back to the chair and sat down, folding her hands in her lap. Deep breaths eased some of her anger but did little to assuage the hurt.

Richard never wanted me. Never. Not even when I begged him to make love with me. Bitterness combined with the hurt. *Oh, I thought he was so stalwart and noble, but it was all a lie. He never wanted me. Not that way. Not at all.* With a deep sigh she accepted the truth. *All he really wanted was the money.*

If the pain of his death had brought insight, then she would gladly accept wisdom from this betrayal. Tears welled in her eyes. She was not crying for Richard. She was done with that. These tears were for her ruined dreams.

Eighteen

"Joanna, the house is filled to the rafters. Am I not right, Sally?"

"Yes, Miss Christy." The maid nodded vigorously as she combed Joanna's hair into the upswept style her sister preferred for the evening. "We are so crowded that some of the servants are sleeping on the floor."

"Oh, dear." Joanna twisted her head to look back at Sally but the maid turned her mistress back to the mirror and spoke to her in its reflection.

"We are on an adventure, Miss Joanna. No one is complaining, well, except for that old biddy who waits on Mrs. Cartwright. Does she ever put on airs! It galls her that I outrank her even though I have no London training." Sally giggled. "I never sat at the head table before."

Christiana and Joanna shared a glance. Joanna nodded as Sally put the last comb in place. "Sally, it will be like that every day when you come here with me after the wedding. Remember that now and do your best to establish an easy relationship from the beginning."

"Yes, Miss Joanna, I am."

When Joanna stood up, Christiana took her place at the dressing table, but waved Sally away. "I had best get used to doing my own hair. You help Joanna dress."

Christiana combed out her curls. Sally's move to Monksford was only one of the ways her life would change. Soon a conversation like this would mean a day's travel. "You will be missed, Sally. No one to bring me treats from the kitchen, no one to run messages to Hannah when Mama sends me to my room to read sermons. Thank heaven I still have Mrs. Purdy for I vow I would not be able to endure it without her shortbread!"

Joanna came over to stand behind Christiana. She took her brush from the table and began to comb out her sister's afternoon coiffeur. "Sally, go to Christy's room and find that garnet necklace. It would look wonderful with this new gown."

"Yes, miss." Sally slipped from the room.

"Joanna, I left that necklace at home."

"Yes, I know, you left it home because Mama insisted you bring it. All to the good; it will take Sally even longer to find it and give us privacy."

She began to arrange Christiana's hair, but kept glancing at her sister's face in the mirror. "You seem more, uhm, cheerful, since you spoke with Papa."

"I am for some reason. You would think that finding out about Sir Howard's maneuverings would have hurt more than healed, but somehow the opposite is true."

"It has nothing to do with Lord Morgan's arrival?"

"No. Not at all." Christiana met her sister's gaze in the mirror so Joanna could see that she meant what she said. No more fantasies for her.

"Christy, please, do give him a chance."

"Give him a chance for what? He is here because he and Monksford have become friends. He is not here to see me. And the last thing I ever want to do again in this life is give my heart to someone who will not value it."

"He is here to see you. He watches you every moment you are in the room. I know he cares for you."

"You do not see clearly these days, Joanna."

"No, dearest, it is you who are looking at this in entirely the wrong way. Please, please, at least talk with him."

"Of course I will be civil to him. I will even dance with him."

She could do that much. He was such a fine dancer and she could ignore the implied intimacy. She had danced with dozens this year without any of the heart-lightening thrill she felt dancing with Morgan Braedon. "But bear in mind, Joanna, that the sort of happiness you and Monksford have is uncommon. You had best accept that."

Joanna put down the comb and came around to look at her handiwork directly. "You look lovely. If Lord Morgan no longer holds your interest, perhaps that young cousin of John's would be worth getting to know."

"Joanna, love has made you hopeless."

"No, darling, it has made me ever hope-*full!*" Joanna walked over and began to shake the wrinkles out of the pink and gauze confection that Christiana was wearing to dinner. "I am hopeful, confident even, that you will find laughter again, that you will find love again, that you will find someone to make your life complete."

"Find laughter again? I laugh." Christiana got up from the dressing table, annoyed that she did not feel at all like laughing at the moment. She clamped her newly mastered control over her downcast feelings and held very still while Joanna lifted the dress over her head. "I do laugh, Joanna."

"Yes, you do, but not like you used to. Part of you is still in hiding."

Sally tapped at the door and came into the room, holding the necklace. "Your mama had it. She said she brought it along because she was certain you would forget it."

The group standing by the fireplace broke into laughter. Morgan sipped the port and wondered how long it would be before they rejoined the ladies. You would think the newly engaged Monksford would be anxious to return to his fiancée. The clock chimed and he realized that it had been less than thirty minutes since they had finished dinner.

The whole evening seemed interminable.

He had watched Christiana during dinner, flirting with Monksford's cousin, who was seated next to her. He was sure she was not the slightest bit interested in the jackanapes. His clothes were outlandish, his laugh bore a close resemblance to a braying donkey, and he talked as though each of his words were a pearl of wisdom. Of course, Christiana appeared to be hanging on each of those pearls, so perhaps the idiot was entitled to the feeling.

She was so quiet. Not that she did not partake in conversation, but even her demeanor was quieter now, as though her grief had drained her enthusiasm. He missed that the most. It was one of her most endearing traits. Had she really changed that much? He hoped not, for he so missed the Christiana Lambert he had come to love.

Monksford's suggestion that they rejoin the ladies was met with some teasing and Morgan held himself still so as not to be the first to leave the room.

"Gentlemen," Monksford hailed them as they began to move to the door, "there are some whist tables set up, if you would care to play. And billiards."

Good, Morgan thought, *if all else fails I can look for someone eager to lose a few guineas.*

Most of the conversation in the blue salon came to a halt when they walked in. Morgan scanned the room, but could not see Christiana. Had she gone to bed? Not long ago, she would have been the last to leave a party.

He circled the room, chatting with each of the ladies, spending a little more time with the crippled daughter of Monksford's sister. She would be old enough for a Season next year and this was her first social outing, by way of rehearsal for her visit to Town. Her shyness was understandable, but within ten minutes he had found her passion: horses. She was as familiar with the stables as any man he knew, explaining that, "It hardly matters if one of my legs is shorter when I am on a horse."

Too bad there were not more opportunities for riding in Town. Perhaps her best hope for an alliance would be at house parties like this.

He moved on to talk with Mrs. Lambert, in hopes of finding out where Christiana was. It was an endless ten minutes but his reward was her insistence that he go out to the garden and "tell Christiana to come indoors." With a prayer of thanks to the god of protective mothers, he stepped out onto the stone walkway that led to the garden. He could see her sitting on a bench at the foot of the steps, where it led into the formal garden.

She turned at the sound of the open door and shrugged when she saw who it was. Hardly welcoming.

He came down and sat beside her. "Your mama wants you to come inside. She instructed me to tell you that she is too busy to nurse you if you take sick."

"Very well."

To his utter surprise, she stood up and started toward the house. When had she ever obeyed her mother? "Please do not leave because of me."

She looked at him and then at the garden, aglow in the light of a full moon, as haunting and lovely as his memories of her.

"It is beautiful out here. Quiet and peaceful."

"Romantic?" Now why had he said that?

"With the right person, it would be irresistible," she agreed.

He closed his eyes a minute and tried to convince himself that was not rejection. Standing up, he moved closer to her.

"Richard? Is that who you were thinking of out here?"

"Richard?" She laughed with genuine surprise. "No, my lord, Richard was more interested in money than he ever was in marriage to me."

"He was engaged to someone else?"

"Oh no, but I found out from my father that he was being paid to marry me."

"Oh, Sprite, that's absurd." He leaned against the back of the bench and folded his arms across his chest. "Who would need money to be convinced to marry you?"

She gave him a real smile. It was small and self-conscious, but as real as he had seen in the twelve hours he had been here. "Lord Morgan, I do believe that is one of the nicest things you have ever said to me."

"The truth." He bowed to her.

"For some perhaps, but why would my father make it up? Sir Howard was going to pay Richard to marry me and bring that old land dispute to an end."

"Ahh, I see." It did make sense and it would be devastating to her.

"Yes, well, it is over now. I would be foolish to mourn for something that was nothing more than an illusion."

"You seem so calm, too calm." It was almost a question. Indeed he did wonder how deep it went.

"I think I have matured. Life is not one long endless entertainment."

He stepped closer and took her hand. "It could be vastly more entertaining than it has been."

She pulled her hand from his. He saw a flash of anger, but it was soon gone. "Whatever you may think, my lord, I am not given to dallying in gardens."

"To my knowledge, you have only done it once before. It is one of my most treasured memories."

She looked at him in some confusion as though she was not sure she could trust him. "Is that meant as flattery, my lord? I want you to know that I am not as susceptible as I used to be."

"You wound me, Sprite." He tried for a light tone, but she had almost convinced him.

"I trust I only wound your ego, my lord."

"What about our friendship?" In the old days he could have easily teased her into a show of temper with this interchange.

"A social friendship perhaps, but not a personal one. No, our London months were a game which both of us played very well." Her answer was cool and slightly amused.

"Neither one of us was playing." He spoke sharply. That was going too far. He smiled gently and spoke more quietly, as he reached for her hand again. "You are as dear a friend to me as any I have ever known."

"Speak for yourself, Lord Morgan." But her hand curled around his. It was the one sign he needed. Dare he call her bluff? "You can prove our friendship is meaningless."

She was silent for a long moment. "How?"

"A kiss." It was a gamble, and he hoped the long odds favored him, favored them.

"Kiss you! Absolutely not."

There was the anger. Oh, how he missed it. "You are a coward."

"I am not a coward." She stamped her foot.

"Prove it," he taunted.

With an angry start she moved to him and raised her mouth to his, her eyes open, defiant.

He watched her until her eyes drifted shut and then she touched his lips with hers. They were cool at first, as cool as her false front. But they softened and warmed and he had his answer. She might mistrust her feelings, might be afraid they were not shared, but they were there underneath a most fragile poise.

He would have ended the kiss and begun to build a future, but she would not let him. Suddenly her façade cracked and exposed a desperate torrent of emotion.

Her mouth ravaged his as though passion could erase the pain of reborn feeling. She clutched at his shirtfront. The rest of her body was tense, her mouth was moving over his, her lips open to his. She did not use her tongue, but would have welcomed any move on his part.

He could feel her desperation. He understood the loneliness that made sex seem an easy answer. He never thought for a moment that she wanted anything but escape from weeks of confusion that had held her silent for too long.

She had no interest in the love he had come so earnestly to offer. She would reject the commitment he'd been willing to make. It was humbling. It was maddening.

As he tasted the soft perfection of her lips, he thought of settling for what he could have. He considered for just a moment what it would feel like to kiss her back fully instead of controlling his response as he was, to use his hands to ease the tension in her body, to bring her to a sweet, liquid warmth that would welcome him and bring them both pleasure. He wanted to, with every tiny moan that slipped between her lips, he wanted to. He was a fool not to.

He called on his considerable if rarely used control. He would stop her now, but he would not give up. He loved her too much to abandon her, but he was going to play this hand as carefully as any in his life. There was more than money involved.

Pushing away from her he used his body to shield her from anyone else who might happen onto the patio. The brick wall was behind her, cool in the warm night. He welcomed the roughness against his hands where they circled her. It helped distract him from the fire she had so very effectively lit.

He looked at her intently, not sure if censure was what she needed, but sure it would bring her back to her senses.

"Oh, God," she moaned and deep racking sobs followed. She looked down and made to move away, but Morgan knew exactly how to handle this. He pulled her close and held her closer, murmuring wordless encouragement. The tears were a far safer release than a kiss and he held her until the sobs ended and her breathing evened.

"There, my love, are you feeling better?" He tried to see himself as a kindly uncle and ignored the ache that cast him as a lover.

She pushed out of his arms with an abrupt energy he had not expected. She turned from him and faced the wall that surrounded the garden. Summer bloomed all around them and even though the flowers were shrouded in the darkness, their fragrance bathed them in an evocative scent.

"You sound like some doddering guardian, my lord. I am feeling better, thank you. Mortification has an uncanny way of erasing more meaningful feelings."

He smiled at the row of buttons on her dress and reached out to turn her just a little. "Christy, my dear, sweet angel, confusion makes us do things we'd never contemplate in our saner moments. And confusion mixed with grief you are certainly allowed."

He turned her around to face him. She turned willingly though she would not look him in the eye until he tapped her nose. "No, no more tears." She took a deep breath and a small smile replaced the tremble of her chin. "Your mother has shown admirable restraint in sending no one to look for us, but soon even your father will look up from the card table and wonder where you are."

"You give me far more credit than I deserve. It would take more than a missing daughter to take Father from his evening cards." The smile grew, a little cynical when he would have preferred happy, but he would not worry over details. "And Mama is so caught up in Joanna's engagement that she'll not think of me until she wants to release every pent-up feeling . . ."

He knew why her voice trailed off. Like mother, like daughter. The thought passed through his mind as well. "No, no. No more regrets. It was a kiss to end all kisses my dear. Let me hold on to that thought."

She blushed now with pure embarrassment and he seized the moment to satisfy himself. So much nobility could be wearing.

He deserved a small reward.

He pulled her closer, ever so gently, and whispered against her lips, "Now kiss me sweetly and not like some desperate spinster."

Despite his invitation, it was Morgan who kissed her this time. First his lips touched hers gently, as gently as a butterfly lands on a rose. A caress, all softness and delight, he moved his lips over every inch of her mouth, lifting then settling again, a light tasting that renewed pleasure with each touch. Finally, he settled his mouth on hers, deepening the kiss just a bit until he tasted the soft inside of her lip. He stopped one brief moment before the kiss became more than he planned, but he stopped considerably short of satisfied.

She was smiling when he lifted his head, her eyes soft and shinning. "Thank you," she whispered.

He wanted to ask her what she was thanking him for, but decided it would be better if neither one of them knew. Instead, he offered her his arm and escorted her into the drawing room. They parted as soon as they entered the room and when he looked about a moment later she was listening to her aunt and mother as they chattered on about some nonsense. If they noted she was a little disheveled they did not comment. But then no one noticed what he saw now for the first time in a long while.

He recalled the night they met, the way she had flashed that smile at him, the smile that invited him across the room and shocked him into awareness. She might never be quite that bold again, but her love of life was back; he could see it in her eyes, in the way she responded to her mother, in the way she glanced around the room for someone to share a private joke with. He caught her eye and the smile became a laugh, which disappeared as quickly as her mother questioned her levity.

He could not hear what she said, but he watched her suck in her cheeks to hold back the laughter. He turned away, afraid if he watched her much longer he would lose all sense. He walked toward the card room but he moved slowly, letting his imagination do what he could not.

Nineteen

"Why does it have to rain tonight of all nights?" Joanna stared out the bedroom window as if sheer will would lighten the sky. "The moon is full and I so wanted to be able to see the stars."

"It will be perfect, Joanna. You wait and see." Christiana hurried the rest of her toilette. This was Joanna's night and vanity was her sister's alone to command.

"How can it be lovely when the weather is not?" Joanna sounded as perplexed as a man in a milliner's shop.

"The rain will make everyone more relaxed. You will see. They must hurry indoors and there will be a jumble of people in the hall." She took her sister's arm and urged her to the door. "They will all look just a little wet and so no one will worry too much if their dress is a little wrinkled or their hair a little damp. You watch, tonight will be a dream come true."

Apparently mollified, Joanna turned from the window. "One wish has come true. You and Lord Morgan are friends again."

"We are." She nodded and refused to blush. It was obvious they had renewed their friendship. They had spent the better part of the day in each other's company.

"Of course there were plenty of chaperones for the two of you, but he was never far." She paused dramatically then added, "Except for that time when he and Papa went off to the stables."

"Oh, Joanna, please, I assure you there is only going to be one engagement announced tonight."

Her sister actually looked disappointed.

"Jo, that is as it should be. Tonight is your night. Yours and John's. And I promise you the rain will only make it more special."

She was right. As she explained to Lord Morgan later as they stood by the punch bowl, "It helps that everyone knows each other. I think it is so much more convivial than the balls in London."

"Undoubtedly."

"Are you paying any attention at all? You are looking at me, but I think your mind must be someplace else entirely."

"Sprite, I am hanging on your every smile."

She grinned. She could not help it. He was such an engaging flirt. "Well, do you agree with me? Is this not more friendly than any number of balls we attended?"

"I suppose, but we are of a different mind now as well. That might have as much to do with it as anything."

"Oh."

"The only unfortunate consequence of the rain is that there is no garden to wander in."

"I do believe the conservatory is open. And there is always the portrait gallery."

Lord Morgan offered her his arm.

"No."

He looked confused if not disappointed and Christiana hurried to explain.

"We must only wait until Papa announces Joanna's engagement." She nodded toward the small platform that the musicians were playing on. Her father was there, attempting to climb up to make his announcement. But each time he made a move, his wife would pull him back for one more consultation. Finally with an exasperated grimace, Lambert offered to let his wife take his place. She shook her head and moved back with an irritated huff.

"Oh, Mama." Christiana laughed and turned to Lord Morgan. "Do you think I will be that managing?"

"You are her daughter." Morgan appeared to be giving the matter some thought. She wanted to slap his wrist with her fan, but feared that would prove the point. "No, no, my dear, I think that you will learn from your experience and find your own way to rule a household."

The room quieted as her father, finally, was allowed to step up on the riser. He introduced John and Joanna, as if most of the guests had not known at least one of them since childhood. He said all the right things about John's character and Joanna's beauty. They stood together while he pronounced a blessing and then everyone was invited to join in a toast to the happy couple with the champagne the footmen passed around.

Christiana sipped and giggled. "It tickles my nose." And then she sipped again. "This is *sooo* much nicer than brandy."

The musicians began playing again and without a word between them, Morgan and Christiana left the room. Leaving their glasses at the entrance to the conservatory, they walked into the dimly lit jungle of plants.

"We could be lost in here for a week." Morgan could see the path, though most of it was overgrown with some sort of ground cover run amok. "They would have to send a rescue party."

"I think this is what Joanna meant when she said the house had been too long without a woman's touch."

He pulled the branch of a gigantic rubber plant to the side and they found a lovely iron bench near a fountain whose pond was choked with water lilies. The large glass windows were open and the rain added its music to the sound of the fountain.

Christiana sat down. "Was it only yesterday I was counting the days until I never saw you again?"

"Yes, less than twenty-four hours ago I could see you, even talk to you, but the hope of ever kissing you again was nothing more than a desperate wish." He picked up her hand and kissed it and did not let it go.

She put her head on his shoulder and sighed.

"Christiana, there are some things I want to tell you, to make clear."

She raised her head, looking doubtful. "Do I want to hear them?"

"I most sincerely hope so."

"Well, then . . ." she prompted.

"I have never lied to you. The only person I ever lied to was myself." He took her other hand and looked at her with as direct a gaze as his heart would allow. "How could I not see that you entranced me from the first, that mesmerizing dance at Westbourne's? I thought I agreed to our pretend courtship because it suited my ends. What a fool I was. I agreed because it was the only way to be near you.

"And every time you drew me closer I told myself it was the logical progression of friendship." He shook his head, and looked away, words beyond him for a moment. "It was the night of the masquerade that I realized the truth. Odd, what, for the mask to come off at a masquerade?"

He turned to her again. "I am going to tell you now what I realized then." He did not speak right away. He waited as though giving her a chance to stop him. "I love you."

He leaned forward and touched her smile gently with his lips. "I think I must have loved you from that morning we met in the park. You were so embarrassed to be caught riding that impossible nag." He shook his head. "I fell in love with you then and I will love you for as long as I live."

He was finished. And she knew it was her turn. Instead her eyes filled with tears. "The words fail me, Morgan. I'm so sorry, but I am too afraid to say them."

He nodded slowly but she could see his disappointment.

"Everything about you is precious to me, my lord. The way your hair shines in the candlelight, the way your eyes crinkle when you are unsure. The way you pray to every pagan god there is, and the way they come to your aid." She stopped and then laughed lightly. "How silly of me to be afraid of the words. I love you, of course I do."

It was her turn to lean closer and kiss him lightly. Then her smile disappeared. "But I have so recently been wrong. And that mistake led to more heartache than I ever want to experience again. Not only my heartache, but yours as well. I know it is too late to stop myself loving you, nor do I want to. My world is a much happier place with you in it. Saying the words is one thing, but accepting the future they imply . . ." Her voice trailed off and her tears were an eloquent apology.

He stood up and held out his hand to her. She took it, gripped with an unholy fear. Was he going to leave her? "Morgan, what are you going to do?"

He drew her into his arms, his expression filled with reproach. "I am going to wait until you are ready to accept the future." He touched a kiss to her temple and then to her cheek. "But I am going to be an impatient lover, Christiana." The next kiss, full of ardor and longing, proved it. He trailed kisses along her neck, pausing at her ear to whisper, "You must let me know if I grow too demanding."

With a sigh she gave herself up to the feeling of

his lips, his hands, until she thought she would drown in the sensations and die happily. When the kiss ended, she wanted to stand with her eyes closed and remember each blissful moment. When she did open her eyes, she saw he was watching her with an unsmiling intensity that was as arousing as his touch.

"My lord, do you think perhaps we should return to the ballroom?"

"Oh yes, I certainly do. But dancing will seem very tame after this interlude."

They worked their way through the plants, following the overgrown pathway. By the time they were in the hall, Morgan had her laughing at his silly insistence that he had surely saved them from some man-eating plant.

"Are there such things?" she asked between her giggles.

"If there are then they are alive and well in that conservatory. I want you to warn your sister not to go in there alone."

He stopped to talk to a footman on station in the hall. "I think you should put a sign on that door," he said, pointing to the conservatory. "Not everyone will be able to find their way out of there."

The footman nodded in that tolerant way they all learned in the earliest stages of their training.

"My lord, what have you been drinking?" She was almost sure that since dinner he had had nothing more than a few sips of champagne.

"No spirits, my love. I am drunk on the prospect of claiming your affection." He bowed to her.

"Come, let's dance. It is just what we need."

He held her back a moment. "Sprite, it will be our third dance." His raised his eyebrows in a silly imitation of a wicked villain. "Do we dare?"

She nodded as a conspirator would. "My mother is out of the room and we only have the gossips to fear."

"Then we are going to dance. Shall we look for ourselves in the paper tomorrow?"

Christiana laughed and clapped her hands. "It would be perfect, absolutely perfect!"

Morgan nodded and enclosed her hands with his. "We will try, my heart, and at the very least it will be as perfect as love can make it."

About the Author

After thirty years of frequent moves, my husband and I have settled near the Chesapeake Bay in southern Maryland. My lifestyle has changed dramatically. No more suits and cocktail dresses, now each day calls for sweatshirts and beach shoes. We are amazed at how easily we have adapted.

Port Republic is a long way from Regency England, but my wonderful library and supportive network of writer friends has brought the early nineteenth century much closer. I hope to share more of the Braedons' stories with readers soon. I can be reached by e-mail at MaryBlayney@aol.com.